Snakes and Lovers

ANNE LOVETT

Snakes and Lovers

Copyright © 2020 by Anne Lovett.

All rights reserved. Printed in the United States of America. No part of this book may be used or reproduced in any manner whatsoever without written permission except in the case of brief quotations embodied in critical articles or reviews.

Published by Words of Passion, Atlanta, GA 30097.

Editorial: Nanette Littlestone
Cover and Interior Design: Peter Hildebrandt

ISBN: 978-0-9996579-6-6

Library of Congress Control Number: 2020914404

Dedication

For Camille, who insisted.

One

May 2005

I knew it was going to be a bad day when Lorelei took off and left me with the snake. Just not how bad.

It started out as just another day in Paradise—the Paradise Bar in Daytona Beach, spring break just over, summer crowds still up north. A Florida-bright day filtered in on a brisk ocean breeze, mingling with the inside air—tangy and smoky and beery, smudged with a touch of coconut oil.

Hoagie was loafing behind the bar, putting the moves on two girls at the far end, a blonde in little-girl pigtails, a brunette with sparkly toenails. Shorts barely covering their butts, boobs jiggling out of halter tops, they tickled frozen blackberry Margaritas with their tongues. Holton

Carmichael, a man too freakin' handsome to be a bartender, had it easy today.

My customer, the old man in the back booth, signaled to me. I nodded at Hoagie. "Another draft Bud for Mr. Kapolnik."

"What? He never has two."

I smiled. "Maybe it's his birthday."

Hoagie set the foaming glass on my tray. "How about the beach tomorrow? Pick you up about eleven?"

I knew better than to say yes. "I'll meet you there. Eleven's cool."

Just then our entertainer, my good friend Lorelei, came strutting out of the boss's office and stood in the light, the sequins on her T-shirt throwing glitter spots on the walls. She beckoned me over with a gnat-fanning wave, her expression like she had a hot tip on a greyhound.

She was never here in the middle of the day.

I signaled for her to chill and took the beer to Mr. Kapolnik. A regular, he walked here almost every day from his condo.

When I set it on a fresh beer mat, his bloodhound eyes met mine and a sly smile spread under his walrus mustache. "That young man likes you, Daisy." He nodded toward Hoagie.

I shrugged, picking up the empty. "Yes, me and half the female population of Volusia County."

Mr. Kapolnik cocked his head knowingly. "You want someone special."

"I'm through with special," I told him. "It doesn't work for me."

His bushy eyebrows shot up, colliding with his bald and spotty pate. "You're just a young girl! There is time yet!"

"I'm thirty-eight," I said, tucking the tray onto my shoulder and shifting my aching feet, definitely not sparkly like Miss Suckytoes' at the bar. "For me, marriage was a 6.7 on the Richter scale. Ask my two ex-husbands. Better still, don't ask. Do you blame me?"

Mr. Kapolnik sipped at his beer thoughtfully. "Things are blackest, no, right before the sun climbs the sky? My Sofia and I had fifty years before she died, and I almost did not propose to her because I thought she loved my rich cousin."

Fifty years. My own parents had forty so far, and I was hoping for many more. "And now, Mr. Kapolnik? Why did you never remarry?"

"I had my true love," he said, "and yesterday my daughter gave me a parrot. I'm celebrating. Go on, go on." He waved me away. "See what your friend wants. And Daisy? If love calls, you must answer the phone."

I would hang up. Love was like tabloid news—plunk down your money for the sensational story, but once past the flashy headlines, past the mirrors and smoke, you realize you've been had.

"I wish customers didn't take an interest in my love life." I set down the tray on an empty table near Lorelei, the only good friend I'd made since I arrived here to make a new start as a beach bum.

"Oh, that old man is sweet," she said and batted her long spiky black eyelashes, those green eyes wide and innocent. Innocence wasn't Lorelei's strong suit, not with all that black hair piled up high and curled like Cher's, with that cropped sequined shirt and those tight spandex pants, teetering on those Manolos. She was a tiny gal, and she loved those shoes.

She parted curvy Latin lips. "But, *chica*, I want to ask you something. You're my best friend." Each word landed as softly as a lasso.

I knew that tone of voice. "What do you need, Lor?"

"Don't be like that, Daisy. I just need somebody to keep Bogart for the weekend. I'll be back Monday night." She pointed to the fancy flowered rolling backpack at her feet, its top securely fastened.

I took a step back. "Oh no. Oh no. Snakes and I don't get along."

She stuck out a well-glossed lower lip. "My sister is coming on the bus from Tampa to keep my little boy, but she won't have Bogart in the apartment." She gestured at the basket. "Come on, Daisy."

So Sis would babysit, but not snakesit. I couldn't say I blamed her. I took a prudent step back. "No freakin' way."

Lorelei grabbed my hand. "*Please*, Daisy. Don't tell me you're afraid of him."

"Me? Afraid? Of course not." Daisy Harrison, afraid of a snake? Daisy Harrison, who freaked out so bad when Luke McDuffie put a green snake down her shirt when they were thirteen that she didn't speak to him for a month? And she'd really, really liked him? Once upon a time.

"He won't bite."

I took my hand away and waved it. "But he's a *snake*! Doesn't he eat disgusting things like rats?"

"He won't need feeding. He only eats twice a week." She glanced toward the office. "Rasmussen was gonna do it, but he backed out."

"I don't blame him. He probably figured out you're never going to park your shoes under his bed."

She grimaced. "Sshhh, Daisy. I got a good act, but I'm not really that kinda girl." She drew closer. "Come on," she pleaded. "I know you have a heart. Do it for Raj. He worries about Bogie. With you keeping him, Raj can visit and have a reminder of me nearby."

Raj, her little boy. I had a soft spot for the kid, a Mowgli look-alike—big black eyes, silky black hair, caramel-colored skin. Had Lorelei ever mentioned the boy's father? I didn't remember. We didn't get many India Indians here in Paradise.

With my mistrust of getting involved with anybody, I'd wound up babysitting Raj often enough, and now . . .

"So where are you off to, Lorelei?"

She licked her lips. "It's hard to *esplain*. I got a big problem. A man problem. I got to make arrangements." There was a hint of desperation in her voice.

Maybe it was the way she shifted away from me when she'd said it, maybe it was the way she licked her lips, but I felt she wasn't telling me everything. "Are you talking about Vinny? Your old boyfriend? Or is it a new one?"

Her Manolos had been a gift from Vinny. The fancy watch she wore had been a gift from Vinny. The diamond earrings. But there hadn't been any new gifts in a long time. What was going on?

"Oh," she said. "Just a minute. I forgot to tell Rasmussen something."

"Yeah. Uh-huh." I looked over and realized Table Three was dry. "Well, I'm not keeping that snake." I turned and grabbed my tray.

After I'd delivered another set of Bird of Paradise margaritas to Table Three, I saw Rasmussen's hulking form filling the doorway of his office, his cottony head brushing the top of the frame. He crooked a little finger at me, a bad sign. "Get that pack off the floor," he grumbled.

The backpack containing Bogart was right where Lorelei had left it. I walked over. "Sure. Where's Lorelei?"

Rasmussen shrugged. "Dunno. I've got to find somebody to fill in for her Saturday night. You know anybody who can dance with a snake? We got customers who love that. Good tips."

He was looking at me hopefully.

"No, Ras, I don't. The only way you're going to see me in snakeskin is in a pair of fancy shoes."

"You in fancy shoes? Ha!"

I stared down at my Birks while he walked back into his office, then I rolled the backpack to the tiny changing room where the dancers kept their gear. Lorelei wasn't there, nor was she in the restroom. I stowed the snake in a corner. "Take a nap, Bogey," I said.

I looked for Bogey's friend outside, but she was gone.

Yikes. Had she left me holding the pack? I ought to leave the thing here and let Rasmussen call the wildlife people. What else would you do with a five-foot ball python?

I marched over to Rasmussen, who was talking with Hoagie. "Boss, about that snake . . ."

I never got to finish. The door opened and three carloads of sunburned, sweaty, testosterone-high rally fans jostled and elbowed through, whooping and hollering.

"The snake can wait," said Rasmussen.

The thought struck me. Mr. Kapolnik? Maybe he would welcome a nice snake as company for his new parrot. I hurried back over to his table, but the old man had gone, leaving an empty beer glass and a few dollar bills.

I had to face it. I couldn't leave Bogart at the bar. Lorelei knew a softie when she saw one. Finally, my shift was over and I loaded the beast in my purple VW bus, the one I'd insisted on keeping when I left my second husband, the artist-professor with the long gray ponytail and a taste for sophomores as well as my hard-earned money. I stowed

Bogart in the back with the jumper cables, the beach blankets, and the bag of power suits meant for Goodwill, left over from my days in the real world as an art gallery manager.

As I carefully navigated the wide flat boulevards, the jumble of shops and offices, rumbling past fortunetellers and shell shops, seafood palaces and bars, scraps of what Lorelei had told me about Vinny sizzled in my mind like shrimps in oil. All the expensive presents, the long absences. I'd only met him twice, once when he'd come to the bar to watch Lor's act, once when he'd come to pay for the painting he'd commissioned me to do of her and the snake.

Everywhere and nowhere, he'd told me, when I'd asked him where he was from. Darkly handsome, olive complexion, blinding white shirts, tropical suits, eyes that hardly ever stayed in one spot, fingers that liked to snap. Big sparkly diamond on his pinky finger. One day he was here, one day gone.

After he'd left the last time, Lorelei asked me about the apartment for rent downstairs from me at the Sea Spray Villas and moved in a month later. She'd hung the portrait I'd painted of her and Bogart, the one Vinny had paid for, over the apricot plush sofa. I'm not a bad painter, no matter what Ex No. 2 said. Some of my work has actually sold.

I pulled up to the yellow-green block of low-rise apartments. Her little turquoise Mustang was parked by her door.

Opening the back of the van, I hefted the contraption containing Bogart and rolled it through Lorelei's collection of weird and artsy concrete planters to her door. I knocked, rang the bell, and waited, glancing down at the colorful pots of plants with violent tendencies—cactuses with long spines, Venus fly-traps with big green teeth, sundews, pitcher plants.

No answer. I left the backpack in the shade behind the pots. Her car was here, so she must be napping or whatever. I'd check back in a bit.

I clanged up the metal stairs to my apartment and unlocked my door. The hot, stale air hit me with the usual odor of fried plastic and, this time, with a slight musty difference. I turned up the air conditioning, headed to the kitchen for a cool glass of water, and took it to the sea-green secondhand sofa. I sank down, kicked off my shoes, and propped them on the black plastic coffee table. Between my feet and the TV set, I spotted a large plastic tub, the kind you store blankets in. Right in the middle of the floor.

I shut my eyes, and when I opened them it was still there. I went to inspect it and found it was furnished with some kind of sawdust and a water bowl.

With holes punched in it. A portable snake habitat.

I was quite sure I had not, at any time, given Lorelei a key to my apartment.

I'd take the container back later. I dragged it out to the little balcony that faced the pool. Those balconies were really too small for sitting and, anyhow, it was usually too hot. Their main purpose, I figured, was for hanging swimsuits and wet towels, which never actually dried.

By this time my stomach was gnawing on my backbone. How I could be both hungry and nauseated is a mystery to me, but it happens. What did people do before ramen noodles? I put a pot on to boil. The noodles were barely resting comfortably in my belly when the doorbell rang.

Two

The last thing I expected was, well, an expectant mother. Pretty, with a toasty complexion and a sprinkling of moles. Her black curly hair was pulled back at the nape of her neck, and a white muumuu frosted with crocheting draped her expanded figure. Her trembly lips opened to speak.

"Hi," she wavered. "I'm Luz, the sister of Dolores Diaz."

Lorelei. "Daisy Harrison. What can I do for you?"

Just then Raj peeked out from behind her and waggled his fingers at me.

Luz cleared her throat and said firmly, "Dolores said you would take the *serpiente*." She pointed to the snake carrier at her side.

I squeezed my eyes shut and opened them. "Where is she?"

"She has gone on a trip."

"But her car's there."

"She has no money to fix it. She borrowed a car. Please, it would mark the baby." She shook her head. "It is my first baby." Her eyes brimmed with tears and she touched the crucifix at her neck.

I bit my lip. Why didn't Lorelei try to convince her sister? "Come on, girl." I said softly. "That's just superstition."

Luz's face crumpled. "Dolores said you were a kind lady. A nice lady. The very best friend she had."

Now Raj chimed in. "Please, Daisy? Mama's coming back Monday night."

He implored me with those black eyes, as big as those in one of those waif pictures people used to sell by the side of the road. My two days off. Sunday and Monday. Sitting a snake?

I stooped down to Raj's height. "How did the snake box get into my apartment, Raj?"

He shrugged. "I learned from Uncle Vinny about locks."

Uncle Vinny? That explained a lot. A whole lot.

Luz placed her hands together. "I pray for Dolores. That man was bad for her. We never had much, and he gave her so many presents. She lost her way."

Raj gave his aunt a frown, as if he'd heard all this before. He interrupted, "He's been fed this week." And then he gazed at me. "Please, Daisy?

He had me with his eyes, the eyes of a boy who didn't see enough of his mother. I wavered. "As long as I don't have to deal with mice."

"Then you'll do it, you'll take him." Luz's shoulders sagged with relief.

Hey, wait. I hadn't actually agreed. But when I looked from one hopeful face to the other, I couldn't refuse. I let Raj bring the beast in and put him in the habitat. Daisy, I said to myself, how hard could this be?

I took another glance at Luz's tummy. "When are you due?"

She shrugged. "Another month for sure, the doctor says."

"See you Monday," I told them. Lorelei had better not be late.

For sure.

I was all tucked up in bed, the snake in his plastic box on the warm balcony, when the phone rang. I snatched up the handset hoping it might be Lorelei with further explanations or apologies. "Hello?"

"Daisy? Feel like a late date?"

What? "No benefits, Hoagie. I have a date with my pillow. See you tomorrow, chum."

I dropped the phone carelessly back on the cradle and buried my head in the goose down. Tired. I was just tired. Hoagie was good-looking. Great build. Great tan. He wouldn't complicate my life. He should have been perfect for me. Jeez, I was slipping.

When the relentless Florida sun started hammering on the draw drapes I awoke from one of those dumb fantasy dreams about Luke I used to have. It was always the same dream—he and I were lying under covers half-draped over our bare bodies, while the sun was streaming through Venetian blinds. A palm tree waved outside a high arched window in a pale green bedroom, a bedroom I'd never seen, lush with satins and velvets. He was stroking my back, gliding his hand down, caressing, and I had this gorgeous afterglow you get after particularly spectacular fireworks: a feeling of rosy dawn, of happily ever after, no wicked witches or evil stepmothers or double-crossing best friends in sight. Then the real world, the world of snakes and ex-husbands, hit me, and the air leaked out of my pale green, rosy balloon.

The automatic coffee maker was burbling in the kitchen, sending out a Kona smell that tugged me out of the fog. I swung my feet onto the blue shag rug, wrapped my red and yellow butterfly cotton kimono around my long T-shirt, and pattered to the empty kitchen. I opened the balcony door into the humid morning. Bogart was still there, curled in his box like a fat garden hose.

Sunday. Thank God. No work today. I went to the door to get my morning paper and saw Raj down below flipping a Slinky toy in his dusky hands, looking up at my place with those dark eyes. He waggled a wave at me. I ducked back inside before he got the idea to bring up a mouse. Mice should stay over in Orlando.

I huffed the snake box inside. There was no sense in risking heatstroke, and somebody might steal him. I left the A/C on fan for his comfort.

At least my date at the beach with Hoagie would get Luke out of my mind. I threw on my white bikini, red shorts, fake Tevas, and The Scream T-shirt. I jammed my tote with sunscreen, Mona Lisa beach towel, a *People* magazine, and a copy of *Architectural Digest* to give me a little class. I flipped my hair through a visor so the sun would keep it far out of dishwater territory. I got into my purple bus and headed for the sand.

The weather was perfect, with high fleecy clouds. I found a good spot far from the main crowds, a winsome breeze ruffling my hair, and settled happily on my stripey towel to wait for Hoagie.

That dream about Luke had disconcerted me. Not even the buff, muscled guys caught my interest today. I opened my magazine and flipped the pages, pausing at a bedroom that reminded me too well of the dream. I slapped the magazine shut.

"What's up, Daisy? You want to kill somebody?"

Hoagie, grinning, strode toward me, a nylon cooler slung over his shoulder, a towel draped over one arm.

"Sorry," I said. "Something in this magazine bothered me."

He eyed the *Architectural Digest* strangely. "Guess you don't like modern architecture." He plopped the cooler down. With a flourish worthy of a bullfighter, he spread his red and orange towel right next to mine. "After last night, I wasn't sure you'd come."

I turned over on my stomach. "I said I would."

"So what was the problem last night?"

I lifted out some sunscreen and rubbed it on my shoulders. "Maybe I want to be hard to get. Make you want to marry me."

He gave me an *I know you, Daisy* look and let it pass.

I tossed the sunscreen bottle back into the tote and eyed his cooler. "Is that beer? I don't want trouble from the beach patrol."

"No beer. Too many carbs for me." He lowered himself to the towel and yanked his T-shirt over his head, displaying an admirable set of pecs. He already smelled of suntan lotion and, mixed with it, some male undertone that made me scoot a little further to the side.

He shoved a white plastic bottle at me. "Put a little more of this on my back, won't you?"

I took the bottle, wishing I hadn't agreed to the date. I rubbed it into his warm skin, responsive beneath my fingers. I should have been enjoying this.

He sighed contentedly. "Feels good. By the way, your brother Gordon called me this morning looking for you. He couldn't get you."

I sat back on my heels and dropped the lotion bottle in the sand. "Why did he think I was at your place?"

Hoagie shrugged. "He called Rasmussen looking for you. You must have left your phone off the hook. Ras told him to try me. I told him you were home asleep. He said he'd try again."

I flushed. Ras had noticed us flirting and made conclusions. "Hoagie? What could be so urgent that my brother would call people looking for me?" I whisked sand off the lotion bottle wildly.

"Maybe if you quit throwing sand on me I'll tell you."

He gave me a lopsided, practiced, heart-melting smile. It would be so easy to fall into his arms, have a temporary fling, no commitment. What was holding me back? Was it what Mr. Kapolnik said? I folded my arms. "Tell me."

"He'll call you back at six o'clock to explain. He's busy all day." Hoagie sat up and stretched lazily.

Gordon could be downright maddening. "He's always busy. He's a school principal and he sits on the City Council back in Sawyer. He's a church steward. He has 2.3 award-winning children. I wouldn't be him for anything."

"Well, you've got till six, so you might as well stay here on the beach with me. Look here." He opened the cooler, revealing ginger ale and Dove Bars in a bed of ice.

Man, he was good. He knew two things I loved. He extended a Dove Bar in my direction and I took it like a spider monkey grabbing a giant-size banana.

I crunched down on it. Heaven. Hoagie was having too swell a time watching me enjoy the treat, and I got suspicious. "Did my brother tell you anything else?" The Dove Bar was melting, running down my hand, and I licked the gooey chocolate faster.

"I like the way you lick," said Hoagie.

I pointed the bar at him. "You want to lick this off your face? Tell me everything he said. Every word."

"Okay, okay. He said your mother's kicked your father out of the house."

"W*hat?*" The ice cream fell off the stick and landed right between my boobs, freezing cold. Screaming, I ran toward the water.

As I swished handfuls of ocean across my chocolate-streaked bikini top, I felt rather than heard Hoagie's laughter. One thing was certain. The date was off. I was heading home. My folks' marriage was the one sure thing in my life.

Three

My mother didn't answer the phone. She might have been at church or out back in her crafts studio. At least it was Sunday and she couldn't go see a lawyer. Unfortunately, Bobby Radford, one of my classmates who went to Emory Law School, went to her church.

I tried Gordon, but of course he was out, probably at church and Sunday dinner at the Down Home Buffet. What was the problem with my parents? I had to get back home and try to talk some sense into them. They were being irresponsible. They couldn't be irresponsible. That was *my* job.

I got out my suitcase, perused my wardrobe, and threw some dirty clothes into the washer. At least I didn't have much to organize, because I'd become used to living light. The phone began to clamor at precisely six.

I yanked the receiver up. "Gordon, what is it? What's happened to Moo and Pop?" Pop called her Moo, since her name was Muriel, and we kids teased her as Mom-moo, and the Moo stuck.

"Calm down, Daisy. Just get home tomorrow, if possible, and talk some sense into our mother."

What made him think Moo would listen to me? "I can't. I'm sitting a snake. It'll have to be Tuesday."

"You're *what*? Am I the only sane Harrison in existence?"

"You're just the most uptight. Now tell me slowly what's happened."

He took a deep breath. "About three months ago," he said, "Pop rented a studio and cut a CD."

"Didn't the church ladies all buy one?" Moo was proud of Pop's magnificent baritone church-solo voice.

"Worse," Gordon said grimly. "It sold pretty well, just enough for him to get his hopes up. He's decided to follow his bliss and pursue an operatic singing career. He's closed Harrison Realty."

"He's *what*?"

"You heard me. Locked the doors and let Angie go, and you know Angie is one of Moo's students. Dried flower arrangements, I think. There was a big fight and Moo kicked him out. I went ahead and hired Angie at the school for now. We needed a temp secretary for Josephine's maternity leave."

"Gordon. How will they live if he's not selling houses?"

He sighed the sigh of despond. "Well, she's got her craft workshops and her handmade candles and her herbal compounds. A little money but not a lot. She's come up with something else, but that's a whole nother story, Sis. Just get up here soon. See if you can get Moo to take Pop back."

"But, Gordon . . . where is he?"

"On tour, and it ain't Carnegie Hall. Gotta go. Call me when you leave."

My God, my parents couldn't break up! They were the good example I kept failing to live up to.

All right. Lorelei would be back Monday night. I'd hand the snake over, take off early Tuesday morning, and drive all day. I'd get home to middle Georgia, to Sawyer, by late afternoon.

I called Rasmussen and asked for emergency family leave. He wasn't happy. "The Paradise Bar ain't no effing Fortune 500 comp'ny," he grumbled. "I had a hell of a time finding a dancer good as Lorelei for Saturday night."

"I deserve some family leave time, though," I said. "It's a federal law." I bit my lip, not sure of my ground. Federal law was not on my list of reading matter.

"If you wasn't such a good waitress, Daisy, I'd say just take off and I'll see you around. But don't let people tell you Ed Rasmussen is not a reasonable man. Come in tomorrow and then you can have two weeks. Then you get back here, or the job's gone. When the colleges start letting out, we'll have the crowds." He paused. "You could use some time off anyhow," he said. "You ain't got the old moxie like you did when you first came."

What? My skin was nice and tan, my sun-streaked hair got raves, and I still got the leers and the hits. But Ras was right. I wasn't having as much fun as I thought I was. Still, better than being used . . . or having another broken heart.

I pulled the clothes out of the washer and stuffed them in the dryer. I packed short skirts, long gauzy sundresses, sandals and jeans and T-shirts. Who was I trying to impress, anyway? One thing was certain. I was going nowhere near Luke McDuffie. I burned with embarrassment every time I thought of what he'd done to me. It still hurt, after all these years.

In the back of the closet, I found a couple of things that had escaped the Goodwill bag: a little black dress and jacket and a cherry-red silk sweater. I folded the sweater and laid it on top in the suitcase, then smoothed a plastic bag over the black outfit. I wasn't expecting cocktail parties or funerals, but I was going to see my mother, and she'd taught me that anything could happen. Which was a laugh, because life in my hometown was so boring and predictable. Those people had called me a hippie, just because I didn't like boring and predictable.

I picked up the phone to call Moo again, but someone knocked at the door.

Raj was standing there with a dead mouse in a small zipper bag. "I need to feed Bogart now."

I gave him my sternest look. "I thought you said he'd been fed."

"I didn't say when." He had the grace to look sheepish.

Sighing, I opened the door wide. "Please, just go in and get it over with."

He solemnly took his offering over to Bogart's box and dropped it in. I watched from a safe distance, fascinated but repelled. The reptile ignored its dead dinner.

"He likes them live," Raj explained.

"Okay," I told Raj. "You stay here with him and see if he changes his mind." I went on into the bedroom and resumed my packing. In a few minutes I felt I was being watched, and turned from folding a white tank top and stripy bottoms, gift pajamas I'd hardly worn. I liked to sleep in an old T-shirt, or nude. Freer that way.

Raj stood at the door, arms folded like a tiny Arnold Schwarzenegger. "Where are you going?"

"To visit my mother," I said. "Did he eat?"

"Not yet," said Raj.

"Well, I'm not going to leave a dead mouse in the cage overnight. It'll smell."

"What if he gets hungry later?"

I had to put my foot down. "He can wait another day. Take it away, please."

"But . . ."

"NO."

"Okay, okay. Just let me try one more time."

"All right. I'll be in here if you need me."

Nice boy, most of the time, but sometimes he was a handful. What he needed was a father. And as for my mother, she wouldn't like my beachy garb. Maybe she hadn't thrown out the clothes I'd left at home after I'd fled from my ex, Harvey. Probably hideously out of date, but still . . . .

"Bye, Daisy," Raj called from the living room. "I took care of it."

"Thanks, kiddo," I called, relieved.

Packing done, I laid out my barmaid's uniform for the next day and went to the fridge for a nice bowl of Cherry Garcia frozen yogurt. A strange foil-wrapped object in the freezer caught my eye. Curious, I unwrapped it. I screamed and dropped the stiffening mouse on the floor.

I couldn't wait to be rid of this accursed snake. I wanted my mommy. I called her, but she still didn't answer the phone. I left a message saying I was coming, and gingerly picked up the half-wrapped mouse by its foil corners. I folded the foil back around it and put it back in the freezer. Why waste a good dead mouse?

The next day, I slept late because Rasmussen wanted me to work the evening shift. I packed my tote with snacks for the trip and gassed up the old bus, hoping she'd make it back to Sawyer. At last Moo called me back, overjoyed I was coming.

But she deflected all my questions.

"We'll talk about your father when you get here. And Daisy . . ." She took on a severe tone. "You *must* speak to your brother. He's being unbearably stuffy about my new business enterprise."

"What sort of business, Moo?"

"I give people advice," she sniffed.

Was she writing a sort of Dear Abby column for the Sawyer *Buzz*? "Moo, do you have any qualifications?" That is, besides gossiping in the beauty salon as they dissected all the town scandals.

"Best in the world," she said. "Don't you start in on me too."

"Oh, no, no," I assured her. "One problem at a time, please."

"I'll see you tomorrow," she said. "I have a wonderful surprise for you."

Earthquakes are surprises too. I couldn't wait.

Four

As Monday wore on I got a little worried. Lorelei hadn't come back by the time I left for work at a quarter to four.

When I picked up my first order from Hoagie, I asked him if he'd seen her.

"Nope. I'm getting worried," he told me. "I loaned her my Toyota."

"Huh? What are you driving?"

"I've got that black Caddy I inherited from my great-aunt," he said.

"Are your folks rich?" I gave him a look I hoped was quizzical.

He shrugged. "Nope. Just enterprising. My old man hates me. Says I'm lazy. Hey, I like it here. Who knows? Maybe tomorrow I'll find a Rolex with my metal detector."

A couple of girls walked in and sidled up to the bar. He lit up like a phosphorescent eel. "Welcome, ladies!"

I turned away, flushing with embarrassment. Was that the kind of life I really wanted? Share and share alike?

Business turned brisk for a Monday afternoon. Beach weather was perfect, and the cars rolled up and down the tightly packed sands. A foursome of pudgy tourists kept calling for more peanuts; a wild-looking man in a back booth kept calling for mescal, saying he was the Consul. Evening turned into night. The sun bunnies and the beach boys left; the hard drinkers and the lonely souls and the bar hoppers arrived. The mescal man got tequila, because we didn't have any more mescal. He scribbled in a journal while he drank the tequila.

Sometime during the smoky uproar of the evening, I leaned into the phone and called Aunt Luz. Lorelei had not arrived.

The candles I'd lit in the hurricane globes flickered into nubs. The tiny swords for the cherries gave out, and two martini glasses got broken. Rasmussen called a cab for the mescal man, who'd left his journal behind.

Finally, I got home. The lamplight in Lorelei's window might be a good sign, but the blue light coming from my window was a bad one. I hurried up the stairs and slid my key into the lock. When I pushed open my door, my TV was sounding off in the dumdee dum-dum soundtrack of a Batman movie. I froze. I knew I'd left the set off. I peered around the door, ready to run.

Brooding gothic and urban scenes flickered before a small boy curled on my sofa, a fat and happy-looking snake curled in a ball next to him. On the floor lay an empty carton that once held Cherry Garcia frozen yogurt.

This was not good.

I slipped through the door. "Hello, there," I said. "What are you doing here, kiddo? Where's your mother?"

Raj's guilty eyes met mine. He shrank back into the sofa and pulled my old afghan over him and Bogart, trying to hide the snake. "She's not home yet."

"Not home? What about your aunt?"

He shrugged. "Asleep."

My heart accelerated like a NASCAR driver. "Has your mom called or anything?" When he didn't reply right away, I hurried over to my phone, its message light blinking. When the message clicked on, Hoagie's seductive voice wished me good night, and asked me to call if I got lonely.

I slammed the phone down.

"Daisy," said Raj. "Mama did call. She said she was staying a week longer. She asked me to come and tell you. Can I stay here with Bogart?"

My heart raced and my fists clenched. She couldn't tell me herself? She didn't ask my permission! "Young man, please put that slithery thing back in his carrier at once. I'll take him down for you."

His eyes grew wide and troubled. "Tia Luz says she's going to carve him up with a butcher knife and fry him for supper if I bring him home, just like she cuts up the chickens from the store."

What? How could she frighten the child like that? I closed my eyes and counted to twelve. "Raj, she's just trying to scare you, and you should be scared. He shouldn't be out. He might think you're something to eat and wrap himself around you and *squeeze* you." I made a scary face at him. "Bogart can stay here tonight, but I'm going to leave in the morning. I'll just have a good chat with your aunt then. Now go home and slip into bed before she misses you."

Raj gave me a dark look and dragged himself to the door, my afghan still wrapped behind him. "Wait just a minute, young man," I called after him. "Take that frozen mouse with you, and give me back my afghan!" I was glad I didn't have kids.

"He ate it." Raj grinned, dropped my afghan on the floor, and skedaddled out before I could swat him.

To my horror I realized the snake was still curled in a ball on my sofa. If I wanted anywhere to sit, I was going to have to imprison him myself. Should I go get Raj and wake his poor pregnant aunt? *Daisy*, I said to myself, *you can do this*. I slicked on a pair of rubber gloves, opened the box top, approached the beast with the laundry bag from inside his backpack, and found my sofa decorated with snake poop.

If I didn't get out of Florida before the sun was high, I'd have a miserable trip. My bus had a very temperamental jerry-rigged A/C. Dressed in jeans and T-shirt, fortified with two strong cups of coffee, I slapped on the rubber gloves and managed to get Bogart out of the box and into the laundry bag. He'd go downstairs first and then I'd bring the snake habitat.

Luz would just have to deal with it. She wouldn't carve up her sister's livelihood, would she? I tried to tamp down a few guilty pangs.

Just as I tied the bag shut, a siren screamed into the complex and stopped right in front of my building. The living room walls throbbed with a pulsing red light. I rushed to the window. Was there a fire?

A young, burly man in a white polo shirt was hustling, clanging up the stairs toward my place. Before he could knock, I threw the door open. "What's happening?"

The place on the shirt where the polo player should've been was stitched with a blue-green cross and EMS. A yellow-and-white emergency vehicle waited down in the parking lot, red light wheeling. Somebody lay on a stretcher, and another paramedic was opening the rear doors.

"What's happening?" I repeated.

"Ma'am, we've got to get your neighbor to the hospital. She's in labor and there's trouble. She wants to talk to you."

Oh my God. I raced down to Luz, huge under a sheet. She grabbed my hand. "Daisy?" She looked really scared. "Will you look after Raj until he gets on the school bus? Ricky is on the way from Tampa and will pick him up from school."

How could I say no? Especially as Raj, still in pajamas, slipped up behind me and took my other hand.

I deflated like a balloon, breath seeping out. "Sure," I said.

"Okay, let's get going," said the medic. The two slid Luz into the vehicle, closed the doors, and off they sped. Raj looked up at me and said seriously, "Maybe Uncle Ricky will let me stay with you and Bogart."

My mind spinning, I laid a hand on the boy's shoulder. "Raj, don't you see, you can't stay? I've got to leave and go see my own mama. Come on, let's get you ready for school."

I ran up and locked my door. Then Raj reluctantly led me to Lorelei's cluttered apartment, bright with the apricot velvet sofa. The portrait of her I'd painted for Vinny Corvo hung on the wall, along with some small color-splashed paintings that looked amazingly nice. Museum quality, in fact. Paintings that could have graced luxury condos.

I was madly curious, but I didn't have time to look for artist signatures. I helped Raj dress in clean clothes and pack his book bag and check for his lunch card.

"Okay, Sport. What time's the bus?"

"Seven forty-five. But I don't want to go to school. Take me with you to your mama's, Daisy. Aunt Luz and Uncle Ricky, they don't want me. They'll have the baby." He scuffed his toe on the ground. "I wonder if Mama wants me." He paused dramatically. "I wonder if she's ever coming back."

He sounded really pitiful. I bent down to his level and pushed a lock of shiny black hair off his forehead. He was an okay kid, I guess, even if he did pick up bad habits from Lorelei's boyfriends.

"Look, Raj," I said with feeling, "maybe she's got a good reason to stay away right now. Nothing to do with you. Grownups do a lot of silly things before they get their brains in gear, you know? And as much as I'd like to take you with me, I just can't. You ought to be with your family."

He shook his head. "Why can't you stay here? Why do you have to go?" He turned away and ran out of the apartment, leaving the door open. I knew he was going to Bogart.

I called the hospital to see if Luz could reassure Raj. No, they told me, I could not talk to Luz Ramirez. She was scheduled for an emergency C-section.

Oh. Spit.

Outside, the neighborhood children were gathering on the corner to wait for the bus. I picked up Raj's book bag, made sure an apartment key was inside, and walked to the door. A stack of mail on a nearby table caught my eye, mainly because of the foreign-looking letter addressed to Dolores Diaz and Rajeev Diaz.

I picked it up, taking in the unfamiliar stamps, the distinctive upright handwriting. The letter came from *India*. I looked at it again and headed out the door, stopping to lock it.

I found Raj sitting on the grass in the morning sun. "Young man, here's a letter for you and your mom, from India. Did you know about it?"

He reached for it reluctantly and stared at it. "Maybe it's from my father."

"Has he written you before?"

Raj shook his head. "Mama told me he lived in India." He laid it down and started pulling fistfuls of grass and sticking the blades between his sandaled toes.

"Maybe you ought to read it," I said carefully. "It might be important."

"I don't care about my father," said Raj. "I've never seen him."

Don't you want to see him? I thought better of saying it out loud. "Will you give the letter to Luz in case your mama calls?"

"Okay." He got up and stuffed it into his backpack along with the apartment keys.

"All right," I said. "Now get on down there with the other kids." Raj meandered toward the kids standing at the bus stop, and I went upstairs to get my bags.

I bumped my rolling case down to the purple bus and looked back at the kids at the stop. Raj was gazing my way. Why did I feel guilty? Heck, who knew what might happen when Ricky got here? Maybe I'd better just take the dumb snake with me. Maybe I could foist him off on Gordon's boys for the week. I smiled when I thought of Gordon's face when he saw Bogart.

I took the backpack off the frame and slid it onto the front floorboard. I'd need the habitat box too. I huffed back up the stairs one more time, shouldered my handbag, and bumped the box down the stairs. Then I went back and locked the door.

I shoved the habitat in the back of the van and closed and latched the door with a firm click. I noticed with satisfaction that the school bus was loading students, and I got into my colorful vehicle. No more looking back. I turned the key and tapped the gas, sweet-talking the engine into turning over.

As I left the parking lot, a shiny maroon Caddy swooped in, almost sideswiping me. I whipped my head around, meaning to give a dirty look to this senior citizen who should've turned in his or her keys long ago.

Hello? The glimpse I got was of aviator shades, slicked-back black hair, pasty face. Something not quite right about that face. Where had I seen the man? At the Paradise?

The face nagged at me while I drove down the street and away from the sun, now climbing the sky with a vengeance. I had seen that face somewhere. With Lorelei.

Five

When I merged onto the highway, just now thickening with SUVs and Winnebagos, I forgot about the guy. Maybe I shouldn't have. I slid a Travis McGee tape into the boom box I kept inside the van. I bought the tapes second-hand, liking his philosophy of living, nobody to look after but himself. But Travis called himself a knight in tarnished armor, always rescuing somebody. Where did you meet knights? Life today was strictly do-it-yourself in the rescue department.

The miles faded away on that long hot stretch of shimmering highway between groves and pastureland and reptile farms. I was tempted to stop and try to make a deal for snakesitting at one of the reptile places, but it was just possible Bogart might get sold. Then, when Lorelei showed up, where would I be? Heck, I didn't even know if you had to have a license to keep one of these things. *Oh, officer, I'm sorry. Was I speeding? No, but I want to see your snake license.*

The miles peeled away as Travis got himself laid, killed a bad guy or two, managed a narrow escape. Just about the time he confessed to his best bud, Meyer, that he was in love with his gorgeous client, I stopped for gas at a station next to a McDonald's.

I was tired of driving, so I walked over, bought myself a chef's salad, and sat there and ate it in a booth meant for six while watching various little monsters climb and swing. I just didn't have the patience for kids. I thought of Raj back in school with the letter from India and wondered if he'd read it yet.

Then it hit me, a punch in the gut. *Vinny.* That maroon Caddy driver had looked like Vinny minus the tan. So Lorelei hadn't been going to meet Vinny anywhere, if that was Vinny I'd seen. Or had he called, said he was coming, and she was running away?

I visited the ladies' room, washed up, and hit the highway. I crossed into Georgia, passed billboards and strip malls and pine trees and barbecue signs. For some reason I kept smelling French fries and sniffed at my T-shirt. Just being in those places could saturate your clothes with the smell of grease.

I arrived in Sawyer just as the sun was kissing the treetops. I was used to Florida sunsets, and I had forgotten that in Sawyer they could be beautiful too: blazing orange and silver-edged purple, gold clouds banking up behind the black outlines of the oaks and pecans.

I hadn't been to Sawyer since I'd landed in Florida two years ago after my last divorce, shaken, hanging on to my paltry settlement, hoping Harvey wouldn't find me and beg me to take him back. No, I wasn't going to let anybody drain me like that, ever again.

Thank God Pop helped me then, even offering me a job in his office. I disappointed him by opting for a waitress job on the Florida coast and becoming a beach bum. I explained I didn't want any more responsibility, and I sure as heck wasn't coming back to Sawyer.

And then I was there. My childhood home loomed before me before I was ready for it. Seeing the hundred-year-old Victorian with its turret and its whimsical mauve-and-cream paint job, I felt stupidly choked up and weirdly happy.

My "Yellow Submarine" high faded as I noticed the shabbiness. The old house, surrounded on two sides by a verandah topped with fancy gingerbread, looked like a fine lady who'd taken to the streets. The paint was peeling, the shingles were sliding, and the turret was listing like the Tower of Pisa. The front steps, thank God, were solid brick.

I hadn't realized it had fallen into such decay.

The dirt drive circled back of the house and out the side street. I saw an SUV parked by the side entrance and figured it was a craft student or a customer. I parked near the front and walked up the front steps to take a look around. The mortar between the brick steps was crumbling. The old porch swing hung listlessly, its white slats covered with a film of grime. No one had laughed or kissed there in a long time. Maybe not since Luke and I had swung there as kids, twisting, sparring, arm wrestling.

I walked over and gave the swing a push, squeaking the chain. An ivy vine snaked across the porch, and I followed its path up the house and around to a window into the dining room. Inside, the old walnut dining table stood in its usual place. But where were the chairs?

Something was definitely wrong here. I won't say Moo and Pop were obsessively neat and tidy, but this rundown state meant they'd had major distractions. Walking back to the front, I saw the sign.

MADAME ESMERALDA
READINGS

The vaguely Eastern-looking capitals were black shaded with red. I closed my eyes. So Gordon was opposed to Moo's giving people advice? It was too funny. At least it didn't have a palm print on it or one of those meat chart phrenology heads. The front doorknob at least looked polished. I tried it.

The heavy door swung open, and I walked into the wide sunlit hallway, getting my bearings. I glanced up. The ceiling was stained with water spots. Only silence came from the music room to the left, though the red Victorian sofa and the piano, where Pop used to play and sing silly songs for us kids, stood in their usual places. A faint murmur of voices reached me from the back of the house.

"Moo?" I called.

I was answered with a shriek of surprise and then the side door banged shut. Somebody had just left.

My mother hurried up the front hall, flapping her hands. "Daisy! Is it really you?"

I was tempted to say "No!" This couldn't be Daisy Harrison's mother, this woman advancing toward me in a trailing black gown left over from last Halloween, this ersatz gypsy with bangles, beads, and loose, long gray-brown hair tied back by a rose-printed black silk scarf. Her chandelier earrings swung with red stones. She rushed up and hugged me, wrapping me in a cloud of sandalwood and incense. "Daisy, how wonderful to see you."

I nearly choked from surprise as much as emotion. "You, too, Moo."

"How's Florida?" She gave me a big kiss on the cheek and pulled back. It was then that I got a good look at the theatrical lipstick and the eye makeup, as startling as a Chinese opera mask. I rubbed the spot on my cheek; my fingers came away smeared with red.

"You didn't need to come all that way," she was saying, but her eyes were moist.

"I wanted to help, Moo."

"Daisy, I'm managing. Really." She smiled.

"Jeez, Moo." I plucked at her skirt. "What *is* all this?"

"I'm expected to look like a Madame Esmeralda, you know," she said. "My client just left."

"So this is all an act?"

She gave me an exasperated look. "Certainly not. But it's important to give clients what they expect. They wouldn't have faith in me if I dressed in, say, a pastel polyester pantsuit."

I shook my head. "But you never dressed that way anyhow. I want an explanation, Moo. Why didn't you tell me?"

She shrugged and fiddled with her sash. "I thought Gordon might have mentioned it."

"He wasn't very specific, Moo."

My eye caught a reflection, and a fresh breeze blew in. I glanced back to see a small brown Mowgli-face peering from the doorway, a shock of black hair flopping over dark eyes.

"Raj!" I stepped back, stumbled, and almost knocked Moo down.

Moo merely smiled indulgently at Daisy the Spaz and beamed at Raj. "Oh? Who's this?" She held out a beringed hand. "Come here, dear. Don't be afraid." He advanced a few steps into the front hall and stood mute, taking in the weird lady with all the makeup.

She held out her arms invitingly, and he ran to her and hugged her. I looked on, open-mouthed. I guess after Lorelei, my mom looked normal.

Moo released the boy and draped her arm around his shoulder. "Daisy, have you adopted a child from overseas without telling me?"

I was beginning to get my breath back. "Of course not, Moo! He's a stowaway! Raj, how in the devil did you . . ."

"Is that his name? Raj?"

I nodded. "My friend Lorelei's kid. How . . ." The kids. The bus. I smote my forehead.

Raj looked up at Moo. "Good job, huh? I was quiet like a mouse behind your seat, under that beach towel."

I shut my eyes in exasperation. "How did you stay so still? Didn't you get hungry?"

Raj shimmied out from under Moo's arm and settled on the hall rug, hugging his knees. He ignored the first two questions and grinned. "When you stopped at that McDonald's," he said, "I just waited outside until somebody left their food on the table and went to get ketchup or something. Quick as a mouse I grabbed a burger and fries. You had plenty of water in the cooler."

"A regular Oliver Twist in training," I explained to Moo. "He's been blessed with poor examples of fatherhood."

Moo smiled. I could see little wheels turning in her head. "You know, boys can be very useful."

I broke in quickly. "Oh, no, Moo. Not this boy. I'll try to get in touch with his people. They've got a . . . *situation*. We'll put him on the next Greyhound back home."

Raj stuck out his lip. "I don't want to stay with Uncle Ricky and Aunt Luz. I want to be with you and Bogart until my mama comes home."

"Bogart?" said Moo, looking at me intently. "Is this someone new, Daisy? Although I can't see you with a Bogart. Not the Humphrey kind."

Raj turned UNICEF poster boy eyes on Moo. "Bogart's a snake." It was then that I noticed the laundry bag beside him. "He's right here." The backpack obligingly began to bulge and wiggle.

Moo fainted dead away.

I told Raj to mind Bogart while I ran for the smelling salts. I was not surprised to find them in the same spot in the bathroom cupboard as they'd always been. The bottle looked like something you'd find at a flea market, and I had a feeling they'd been there since at least 1967.

I ran to Moo and waved the salts under her nose. After a moment I realized Raj was standing over my shoulder. "How do those salts work?"

"I think the person just wants to get away from the smell," I explained, shrinking back from the pungent fumes. After a moment, Moo came around.

"See, Raj," I said. "Not everyone thinks Bogart is a great pet."

"Oh, you've just got to know him, Madame Esmeralda," said Raj. "I know you'd like him." He looked up at me. "I think he needs to rest now."

"I agree."

Moo sat up. I sprang to my feet and tugged at her arm. She shook me off. "Goodness, Daisy. I'm not helpless," she grumbled. She rose, dusted herself off, and dug in her pocket for a tissue. She blotted gently. "Just call me Miss Essie, Raj. We'll deal with Bogart later."

She fixed her gaze on me. "Darling, just take him away until I can get used to the idea of a snake in the house. Right now I'll take Raj to Gordon's old room. There may be some of his toys in the attic."

My back stiffened when I thought of Gordon. He'd grown up as the responsible one in the family, the favorite, the one who always did everything right while it was Daisy who was in charge of the shmuck-ups.

"Moo," I said, "Raj is not staying."

"Of course he's staying. How long has it been since I've had a boy in the house? Won't we have fun!"

But I was supposed to be the one having fun. At the beach. "Moo, I need to try to get in touch with his uncle. I'll call the hospital."

Moo shot me one of her famous looks. "There's a phone in the kitchen. You must be exhausted, driving all that way. Let me get you a cup of tea, some cookies."

At the word cookies, Raj perked up.

The kitchen's cream-colored walls and blue cabinets hadn't changed, but shutters took the place of the homey calico curtains I remembered, and enough jars of herbs and powders for a Chinese apothecary lined the counters. I glanced out the window to the shady backyard, past Moo's craft shed, to the glider swing under a pecan tree and thought about the night Luke and I had sat there under the moon. He'd given me my first kiss.

While Moo filled the kettle and set out some gingersnaps, I called Information for the number of the hospital. I managed to reach Luz's room, and this time Uncle Ricky answered. He sounded very young and very scared. "You have the boy?"

I explained Raj's stowing away and told him I would buy Raj a bus ticket back to Daytona.

"Luz is very weak," he told me. "And our little boy is premature. It would be a great help if Dolores's boy could stay with you for a little while, until she comes back? I'm worried. She doesn't answer her cell phone. Don't tell the boy this. Can I talk to him now?"

The kettle was steaming and Moo was busy showing Raj her herb collection. I got Lor's cell phone number from Uncle Ricky and handed the phone to Raj.

He assured his uncle he was exactly where he wanted to be. Until, of course, his mama came home. Then he handed the phone back to me.

"Tell him it's okay, I can stay," he pleaded.

I sighed and assured Uncle Ricky it was just fine and that Raj would be well cared for. When I finally hung up, Raj was lifting a stoppered bottle containing some sort of amber liquid. "What's that one for?"

Moo winked broadly. "Making love potions."

I pulled a face at her. "Moo, you wouldn't. You couldn't." I hesitated. "Who would buy such a thing?"

"I can't comment on that," she replied. "Professional discretion."

"Raj, go outside and play ball or something."

"Play ball?" Raj gave me a disdainful look, as though he might be Jesus in the temple, or a trainee Jedi, someone wise who must be about his important business. He gravitated to the counter and picked up another bottle, this time bluish. "Miss Essie, can you cast a spell, like Harry Potter?"

"Well, no, not exactly," said Moo, bustling around, showing him all the colors and labels. "These potions just nudge people in the direction they were going to go anyway. Maybe something was holding them up, such as fear, or misunderstanding, or just plain pigheadedness. Usually it's fear." She raised one eyebrow. "I can tell, Raj, that you're not afraid of much."

He grinned. "Not much."

She cast a narrow glance at me, and I wondered what it meant. I was no scaredy-cat. Was I?

Raj didn't notice. He was eyeing a row of clear bottles holding dark purple, red, and green contents on the top shelf. "What about those?"

"Oh, those," she said. "They're very powerful elixirs. Only to be used in desperate cases."

I wondered how much BS she was feeding him. "Excuse me, Moo. This is all very interesting, I'm sure. But we've got a problem." I explained what Uncle Ricky had told me.

"See, they don't want me," Raj said.

Moo draped one black silky arm around the boy and hugged him to her side. "Of course they do, precious. They just have a lot of problems right now."

He turned the UNICEF poster boy eyes on her. "Then I can stay?"

"Yes, of course you can stay."

"Until his mother comes back," I said.

"And she hasn't called at all?" Moo's brows knitted with concern.

"Just to say she's had some trouble and would be another week. Say, Moo, why don't you ask those spirits if they know when she's coming back?"

Moo gave me one of those death-ray looks she'd given me when I was mooning around because of Luke McDuffie. "Don't be silly, Daisy. We'd need to have a séance to contact her, and she'd have to have passed into the beyond. "

"Never mind," I said.

The tea was ready, and Moo poured two cups for us and gave Raj some pomegranate juice. He drank his right down and went to check on Bogart. I sat at the table with my cup, and after a few minutes, my tight muscles relaxed and a contented calm stole over me.

"Moo, what did you put in this tea?"

"A special blend of herbs and spices," she said, smiling.

"But does it have any . . . active ingredients?"

"That depends on what you mean." She stirred her cup, her eyes twinkling. I decided she wasn't going to tell me, which was probably for the best. I filled her in on my life at the beach, and she just nodded. Finally, she said, "Daisy, why don't you go unpack, have a shower? You must be exhausted after that drive. Raj can help me get dinner on the table."

"But . . ."

The look on her face was sweetly obstinate. She had some plan she was cooking up. I was too tired to worry about it.

Six

Even the familiar blue bedspread was trouble. I tried not to think of the times Luke and I had made out on that bedspread. I concentrated on a ceiling crack snaking from one side to the other. Why hadn't Gordon said or done anything about the house? Was he waiting for Pop to come back? Or was he just too busy with his school to notice?

Restless, I got up and straightened a sagging drapery rod in 40-watt gloom as only one lamp possessed a working bulb. I sighed and went in search of replacements.

Downstairs in the kitchen, Moo was stirring something delicious-smelling on the stove.

"Where are the light bulbs, Moo? And where's Raj? And Bogart?"

She smiled. "That boy had too much pent-up energy to sit here and watch me cook. He tended to the snake, made sure he had fresh water, and then went to play outside." She told me the light bulbs were in the cupboard on the screened porch.

That was where we'd put Bogie's habitat box, laundry bag, and rolling backpack. I walked out, opened the cupboard, and found the bulbs, unable to ignore the porch's peeling paint and rotten boards. I added that to my mental list, right beneath the note that the front porch swing needed oiling and repainting. Everywhere I'd looked since I'd come home, there were candidates for a house makeover. Kitchen tiles curling up. Roof leaking. Ivy in the dining room where nobody dined.

Out in the backyard, Raj was running around having fun, the way he'd never had a chance to do at the Sea Spray. What a life the kid must have had, moving around with Lorelei. How many Vinnys had there been? Maybe she'd been flush with cash one year, broke the next. Did Vinny give her those paintings I saw? Had he stolen them?

A mild breeze drifted across the yard, and I lifted my head long enough to relish it, the feeling of ease it brought, reminding me of long, shining childhood days, bright with sun and possibility.

At the beach I'd sometimes had a feeling, not one I'd had very often. I can only describe it as a feeling of being rich. Not having to do with money, but with the richness of being loved, of having everything I needed, and the illusion that this would go on forever and ever. It was a world filled with flowers and bright green lawns, sunshine, heaping bowls of apples, clean sheets and warm bodies and firelight and plaid blankets, plenty of food, plenty of love, eternally clean, making no messes, needing no washing up afterwards. Bright shifting scenes, washed by rains and tides.

I had that feeling for a fleeting second before the phone rang.

Moo, eyebrows raised, walked out and passed me the handset. "It's a man," she whispered. My belly sank. There wasn't a man I'd welcome a call from right now.

"Hello?" I croaked.

"Hey, baby."

I exhaled a long *whoosh*. "Hoagie? How did you find me?"

I visualized his superior expression. "Simple, grasshopper. I called your brother. His number is permanently engraved on my caller ID."

"So what's up?"

"Have you heard anything more from Lorelei?"

"Me? You mean since she called her sister and said she was going to stay away another week? No."

"Me neither. I'm worried about my Toyota."

"I'm worried about her *kid*. He's here with me."

Hoagie let out a small explosion of surprise. "You've got Raj?"

"Believe me, it was not intentional." I explained what had happened. Then, because I was curious, I asked, "Why'd you let her use your car?"

He hesitated just a moment before he replied with a hint of smile in his voice. "She was very persuasive."

"I'll just bet she was, *chico*. If that's all . . ."

"Hold on, hold on, Daisy. There's something else I want to run by you. I heard you asking Lorelei if that trip had anything to with Vinny, and she stonewalled."

If I'd had foxy ears, they'd have stood straight up. "Hoagie, I think I saw Vinny. When I was leaving."

He gave a chuckle. "You did, sweetheart. He came in looking for her."

That was enough to make me sink to the chair. "I don't suppose he said where he'd been all this time? He's been gone more than a year, right?"

"That guy's tight as a clam." Hoagie snorted. "I even gave him a double tequila on the house, but that didn't loosen him up."

"Hoagie, he was pasty white. Like somebody who'd spent a lot of time indoors. Out of the sun. In state custody, maybe? Think of all that bling Lorelei used to sport."

"Goddamn."

"What?"

"I was mouthing off to him about my pieces of eight, the ones I brought back on that dive I worked. And he knows where I live."

"I think your pieces are safe, Captain. I don't think he's interested in that kind of stuff. You didn't tell him she had your car and was going to bring it back in a week, did you?"

"I'm afraid I did."

"Well, he'll probably lie in wait for her to come back. I'll bet he's camped out in her apartment right now. Maybe we ought to warn her."

"Hey, this is their business."

"What if she knew he was coming and wanted to avoid him? Maybe he's dangerous?"

"Daisy, do not go there. It's not your responsibility."

Ouch. I hated to hear my own sentiments thrown at me like evil baseballs. "Don't you want to see your car alive and well?"

"Hell, yes. And you, Daisy? Are you going to adopt the kid if she doesn't show?"

"Good Lord," I spluttered. "A kid's the last thing I need. She's gotta come back. Hoagie, let me know if you find out anything. Let me know if Vinny comes in again."

"Will do, sweetheart. Hurry back, and we'll have that fun in the sun again."

"Afterwards. After we get this mess cleaned up." I goodbyed and sat back, watching Raj out of the corner of my eye. The pieces were sliding into place. Vinny was a second-story man, he'd taught Raj how to pick locks, and he'd just gotten out of jail. He'd come back for Lorelei, and she wasn't there.

Were their domestic troubles any of my business? Yes, because she'd sucked me in by giving me this snake, and now I had her son. What if she was hiding from Vinny and didn't intend to come back? No, I couldn't accept that. She wouldn't have left Raj behind. No. She loved the kid. I knew that.

I dug out the number Uncle Ricky had given me for Lorelei's cell phone and punched it in. No answer.

"Raj?" I called.

He looked up from poking in the dirt with a stick. "What is it, Daisy?"

"Where did you live before you came to Daytona?"

He shrugged. "We moved around a lot."

"Can you remember the names of the towns?

"Let me see." He dropped the stick and counted on his fingers. "Tampa, Biloxi, Mobile, New Orleans . . ."

"Okay. Okay." So much for that theory. Any of those towns might be the one where she had contacts, was holed up, was being introduced to a high roller—or none. I thought of her shifty-eyed lip licking the day she tricked me into taking Bogart.

Moo called us in for supper, and I was transported back to childhood. She'd made a big pot of my favorite vegetable soup, along with a platter of cornbread. Raj wrinkled his nose at first, but after a taste he was hooked.

Moo chattered on, catching me up on town gossip. I sat back and listened, not wanting to tell her about Lorelei, not wanting to react if she said anything about Luke. I had to concentrate on what I'd come to do, which was to get Moo and Pop back together.

I broached the subject of Pop gently while we were scraping the dishes. She brushed me off with, "I've got a client coming tonight, Daisy. Tomorrow is plenty of time to talk."

"You have clients in the evening?"

"Of course," she said impatiently. "Not everyone wants people to know they consult a . . . a seer."

I snorted. "As if you could hide anything in Sawyer."

She cut her eyes at me before she leaned down to get dishwasher detergent out of the cabinet below the sink. "It's Lally McDuffie."

Moo might as well have punched me in the solar plexus. I tried to make my next question indifferent, but it only came out sounding like the squeak of a half-drowned mouse. "Why?"

"I've explained about confidentiality," said Moo severely, shaking detergent into the dishwasher cup.

She shut the dishwasher with a *whoom*, turned it on, and hung up the dishtowel we'd used on the knives and the soup pot. She gave me a bright smile. "Now. Would you like to see the room where I see my clients?"

"Moo . . ." I pleaded.

"Come on, Daisy." I trudged behind her to our former family den. Raj, who'd been watching the small TV on the kitchen counter, followed us. With a Madame Esmeralda flourish, Moo threw open the door.

Gone was the TV, the recliner, the desk, the bookcase, the stereo equipment. Red damask draperies covered the windows, and a fringed Oriental lamp rested on a four-door credenza on the wall opposite the door. The dining chairs were arranged around a large table covered with a green felt top, which I realized was the old basement rec room el cheapo pool table, under which I had almost lost my virginity. To Luke McDuffie.

Too bad Gordon came thumping down the stairs right when Luke had succeeded in persuading me out of my undies. Or thanks be. I wasn't sure. I'd had to hang around commando until we could make a graceful exit.

Before I could muster up some indignation about the pool table, a creaking sound came from above and then, with a crack, a crash, and a cloud of dust, a chunk of the ceiling landed on the table. Above, a patch of lath loomed, roughly the shape of South Carolina.

With the plaster dust and hunks of the ceiling, the séance room looked like a tornado had swung by on its way to the mobile home park.

"Oh, goodness." Moo waved her hands. "Daisy, we've got to get this cleaned up before Lally gets here."

After Raj and I had hauled all the large chunks out to the porch, we assembled broom, dustpan, mop, and plastic bag, and I sent Raj to fill a bucket with water. "Moo," I said, dragging up a pile of dust, "the house situation is *bad*. How did it get in such a state?" I swiped harder, sending clouds flying toward Moo's dustpan.

Moo sneezed, then gave me a baleful look and a long sigh. "I don't want to go into all that now, not with my client coming. I've got to have a clear head." She dumped the plaster dust in the bag.

"Moo, why did you do it? Why'd you schedule Luke's mother for the very night I'd be coming home? You know I don't want to be reminded of... of *him*. Jeez, what will I say to her? I'd better just go to my room and hide."

"You'll do nothing of the kind, Daisy." She took the mop, wet it, and sponged at the remaining dust. "And besides, you didn't tell me you were coming."

"They never wanted me to marry him. Obviously, Alyssa was more their kind of person."

Moo, leaning on the mop, sighed. "Daisy, there's a lot you don't know."

"There's a lot I don't want to know," I said.

"You've never let us tell you anything about Luke."

"La la la la," I trilled, hands covering my ears.

Moo glared at me, took my hands, and firmly pulled them away from my ears. She looked into my eyes. With her face and forearms covered with plaster dust, she looked like an oracle speaking, a statue come to life. "Daisy," she said, "Alyssa's left him."

I stared at her in shock. "But. But they were the couple on the cover of the Chamber of Commerce brochure.

Standing on the Whiz-Green lawn. With the white picket fence. And two beautiful daughters."

"So you did see that," she said.

"How could I help it!" I wailed. "Those brochures were all over Gordon's house two years ago. Which is one reason I haven't been back."

"We'll discuss this later, Daisy." Moo swiped at her arms. "Now finish this, please. I've got to get cleaned up. If you want to help me and be out of the way, maybe you can make heads or tails of my financial situation. Look in my room, on my desk. The papers are all there."

Fifteen minutes later the doorbell rang. Moo was still combing dust out of her hair, but she hurried to spread a tablecloth over the remaining debris.

"Get the door, Daisy." Moo called. She didn't say please. I had to go, even though I was covered with plaster dust, to meet the lady who had never approved of me.

Seven

I threw open the front door, wondering why Luke's mother would see my mother for advice. I had spent the better part of my adult life trying to avoid it.

Lally McDuffie had developed wrinkles, sags, and papery skin since I'd last seen her, and it shocked me, as though I'd expected her to be preserved in amber, still the elegant woman of the time when Luke and I had been in love.

Still, her striped silk blouse, linen slacks, and bone flats, and her brown-and-gray perfumed salon coiffure were comfortingly familiar. She lifted her gold-rimmed glasses from the chain around her neck and then dropped them. "Daisy?"

I stepped backwards, almost tripping over my own feet. "Well, yes. Hello, Mrs. McDuffie." Heat rushed into my cheeks. Like a drowning woman, scenes flashed before my eyes: the time she had walked in on Luke and me studying in his room, when his hand wasn't where it ought to be; the times I had sat at their dinner table with Mr. McDuffie passing the chicken, asking if I'd like a leg or a breast, Luke smirking at me while his little sister giggled.

"You're just the same."

I picked a bit of plaster out of my hair. "Really?"

Mrs. McDuffie's browny-pink lipstick curved into a warm, amused smile. I shifted from foot to foot as she scrutinized my plaster-dusted cotton jumper and its underlying white T-shirt, my long, dangly earrings of enameled circles and squares I'd bought at an art show. Did she mean I still looked like the bohemian hipster unsuitable for her son? Well, I didn't want him anymore.

"Well," she said mildly, "it's good to see you, dear." She paused for a moment before saying, "I've come to see Esmeralda, you know." Esmeralda. Not Muriel. She held my gaze steady, not saying why. That was understood and not to be mentioned.

I swallowed hard and put on my best formal manners. "Come in, Mrs. McDuffie. I'll see if she's ready."

I led the woman, who, in an alternate universe, would have been my mother-in-law, back to the séance room. So she thought I was just the same? I wanted to tell her that at least once in my life I'd tried to play her game, just to see what it was like.

Once, I'd lived in a big house and had a fancy car. That was my first husband. I should have known, when I began to feel like the doll he liked to dress, that he was secretly gay. Then again, in my second attempt at marriage, I'd had to ditch the Birks to become an art gallery manager, fashionable in my chic suits. One of us had to earn a living.

Now I was back to my old comfortable self, like the jeans-clad girl who'd played Chopsticks with Luke on their grand piano in their music room where portraits of McDuffie and Tremont ancestors stared down from the walls, seeming to follow you with their eyes, daring you to hit a wrong note.

Mrs. McDuffie was kind not to have complained about my playing. My washout as a piano virtuoso was one of Pop's greatest disappointments. My fingers had worked better with a paintbrush. I wondered if Luke still had the painting I'd made of him, rope in hand, at the boat dock at the church retreat, a time when my cup of hearts ran over. I'd worked from a photo, but still. I wonder why I'd let Harvey convince me I wasn't any good. Luke had loved my work.

When we arrived at Moo's consultation room, she wasn't there, but the crystal ball sat on the table in front of her throne-like chair. I gave Mrs. McDuffie a nervous little smile. "Would you like to have a seat?"

"Tell Esmeralda to be prompt, please; I don't like to be out late." She settled in a chair catty-corner to Moo's throne and, fueled by adrenaline and terror, I skittered down the hall and burst into the room where Moo was tying a silk fringed shawl. "She's here. Why'd you do it, Moo?"

She looked at me. "This is a standing appointment, Daisy. And I'll tell you this. There comes a time when you just have to stop running." She checked the mirror to make sure she was free of dust. "If you don't, the monsters will keep chasing you. If you stop and confront them, they will disappear in a puff of smoke."

"What are you talking about?"

"You know quite well." She was on her way out the door. "Please make sure Raj doesn't make a lot of noise."

My freakin' teeth were chattering, but the night was still warm. I found Raj, face scrunched up in concentration, on the kitchen floor beside Bogart's box, stacking one card carefully upon another. The house of cards, almost three stories, collapsed when I lead-footed it into the kitchen.

Raj looked up at me with disgust. "Oh, *shit.*"

I hurried over and knelt to help him with the pickup. "Kiddo, I'm sorry about your cards, but for god's sake please don't use that kind of language here. Not now." I hoped his voice hadn't carried to Moo's consultation room.

He turned those puppy eyes on me. "I know. It's a client. Miss Essie told me. I'm supposed to be practicing card tricks anyhow." He gathered up the cards and began to shuffle them like a Vegas dealer.

"Did Moo teach you that?"

Raj shrugged. "Maybe."

"My mother is going to ruin you worse than Vinny ever did," I moaned. "Don't you want to watch a good, wholesome gangster show on TV? Miss Essie has asked me to help with her bookkeeping, see if I can find some money to repair the house."

"Maybe I can help you," he said matter-of-factly. "I'm good at math. I used to help Mama with her checkbook."

"You did?" I hesitated. "Do you remember any checks that might clue us in to where she's gone?"

He shook his head. "Just rent and stuff."

"I'd better do Moo's bookkeeping myself," I said. "Why don't you come with me and practice your cards there?"

He shrugged and followed me into Moo's bedroom, hands in his pockets. I raised my eyebrows at the Moroccan-style décor, but he said, "Cool!"

I sat at the desk while he settled on the Oriental carpet with his deck of cards. While I laid out stacks of bills, he sprang up to investigate a pile of books. He found one with a snake on the cover, climbed on the bed, and sat yogi-like, turning its pages.

I sorted bills and bank statements, trying not to think about Mrs. McDuffie in conference with Moo. After half an hour of work, I'd come up with a rough idea of Moo's financial situation. On the good side, her seven-year-old black Buick was all paid for. She'd never liked to use credit cards, preferring to pay by cash or check. On the bad side, they'd taken out a second mortgage. Why, I wondered. Everything in the house, including herself, was beginning to wear out and would soon need expensive repairs and replacements.

The doctor bills were telling. Bad feet, varicose veins, aching back. And the Buick had needed a new timing belt along with a water pump and new tires. And Pop was paying at the dentist for his sweet tooth.

And as for income, well, they'd just filed for Social Security, and there was the retirement fund, dribbling away like water from a leaky bucket. I totaled what I could estimate from craft workshops and sales, help from Gordon, and the occasional check from Pop. Heaven knew what she was making with these clients.

Income wasn't going to keep up with outgo.

Suppose they had to sell the house? *My* house? Why, this house was special, sacred to me. It was where all my fantasies had been nurtured. A wonderful place to grow up in. It was too big and funny-looking to appeal to just anyone. What would it become? Real estate office? Bed and breakfast? *Funeral Home?*

I heard a voice in my ear, surely not my conscience. *Daisy, you left here, didn't you? Never wanted to see the place again. You wanted to be free to walk the beach. To be free of memories of Luke.*

I didn't see what my leaving had to do with the present situation. Yet this house was inhabited by all my other memories. They lurked in corners and sat on mantelpieces, coming out when I least expected it, like ghosts.

What kinds of spirits, I wondered, came to Moo's séances? I almost hoped they were real. I didn't want my mother to be a con woman, preying on peoples' longings to talk with their dear departed.

I began another list: Fix house. Get money. Convince Pop to come back and sell real estate. Yes, sure, theoretically I could come back, live here, get a job, help Moo organize, but no way was I going to do that.

I glanced at my watch. Moo's hour with Mrs. McDuffie was not quite up. Oh, God, the way Moo looked was so embarrassing, and I hadn't liked the way Lally McDuffie had looked my ghostly outfit up and down. Doubtless she thought Luke had done the right thing in choosing someone more to their liking. She'd always been polite to me, but I'd always had a feeling she wanted more for Luke. And in marrying Alyssa, he'd done what she wanted.

And Alyssa left? Served him right for being such a chicken not to stand up to them. I guess he and I really weren't right for each other.

I bit my lip and looked back to the corner of the bedroom, where Raj was still flipping the pages from the book. "Do I really come from there?" he asked.

I walked over and saw that he was looking at a book on Indian mythology. "Well, your father probably did." It was then I remembered the letter from India. "Raj, that letter I gave you. Where is it?"

He looked up with a guilty face. "I threw it away."

"Threw it away! Why?"

He looked down.

"Raj, did you open it?" Before he could answer, the front door closed and my mother appeared in the doorway, all smiles, holding three $20 bills. "A very good session." She walked over to the desk and placed the bills in an envelope. "Have you managed to make heads or tails of that pile?"

I'd deal with Raj and the letter later. "Moo, the situation looks pretty bleak. If there were only some way to raise a little more money. You really had no idea how much money you had?"

"So bothersome. Your father did all that."

I sighed. "I may not have been lucky in love, Moo," I said, "but I did learn a few things about taking care of myself. And that means looking after my own money."

"It's just beyond me," she said. "I wonder if I *can* find a spirit guide who knows about such things. Is Alan Greenspan dead or alive, Daisy?"

"Moo," I said. "You don't need an economist. You need . . ."

"A husband," she sighed. "I'll go make some tea."

She was hopeless. Had missed the whole feminist thing. "Look, Moo," I said. "If we don't find any money, and if Pop doesn't come back, you may have to rent or sell this house and move into a condo. And how can you do either one with the house in this shape? It won't bring a good price."

"I can't! I won't rent this house! I can't sell it without your father, and how would I see my clients in a condominium? Those places don't have the right atmosphere at all!" She flipped her shawl around her shoulders and took a deep breath.

A beatific smile appeared on her face. Uh-oh.

"Why don't you go see Luke at the bank, Daisy? Maybe you can talk him into reducing the mortgage payments or something. I'm sure if you explained it to him . . ."

I sniffed. "Me? Why me? I'm sure you haven't seen fit to mention the mortgage to him or his mother! I'm doing nothing of the kind."

Moo pouted for a moment. "Why do we need to fix the house anyhow? It looks more authentic this way."

"Moo," I said, "if the roof falls in on the clients' heads, they won't be back. They might sue. And if the roof leaks, the moisture will rot all your draperies."

She sighed. "They're polyester. The cotton damask ones had mildew and I had to throw them out."

What?

"I'm hungry," said Raj.

"Let's go have some cookies." Moo took the boy by the hand. "And then for you, young man, it's bedtime."

"We can't ignore the problems, Moo." But she and Raj had already decamped to the kitchen. Moo seemed to think that any problems could be solved by enough food. I stood there looking at Moo's antique desk. Good lines. Good wood. It could fetch a pretty penny, but she'd never part with it.

The desk reminded me of some hand-me-downs in the attic, lovingly saved for my wedding. They weren't high-class enough to suit hubby No. 1 and too bourgeois for hubby No. 2. I was not expecting there to be a No. 3.

Eight

Moo and I got into it right after a lovely breakfast the next morning, with the scent of raspberry muffins floating around the sunlit kitchen and Raj busy tending to the snake out on the back porch. He'd informed me that Bogart would need feeding tomorrow.

"Moo," I said. "The house. The second mortgage. We have to talk about it."

She clenched her fists. "I don't want to lose this place! I could just kill Teddy for getting us into this!"

"Talk to me, Moo. Why'd you let him do it?"

Her eyes grew soft. "Have you ever known anyone who could ever stop your father from anything? It was his charm, Daisy. I never could say no to anything he wanted. He just charmed me into it."

"Moo, it's time you stood up for yourself." I thought my parents had a great marriage, but looking back on it, Moo was always the one to give in.

Now she smiled with triumph. "Well, Daisy, I finally got a backbone. When he told me he wanted to go on tour with his cute little accompanist, I told him to go ahead and not come back. And now you and Gordon are upset."

I didn't know what to say to that. She had taken the initiative, but maybe this was the wrong way. "Let Pop come back, Moo. Make him get back to work. You can get out of this. I'll get a better job. I'll send money."

"Will you come back here?"

"Well, no, but . . ."

"Look," said Moo. "With Gordon's help and the checks your father sends and what I earn we're scraping by for now. But we can't make any repairs. And anyhow, he's too stubborn to come back. He won't admit he was wrong, and he's angry at me for making him go. The cute little thing didn't last past the first gig, by the way. I won't ask him. I *won't*."

"Moo, aren't you both being a little silly? The house is in trouble, and you're clinging to your stupid pride?"

"Daisy, you're the last one who ought to be saying something like that."

I knew she was talking about Luke, and it shut me up. But only for a minute. "Moo, you don't have to drag up the past."

"I just never knew what you were trying to prove, Daisy, by shutting him out. By refusing to talk to him."

"After what he did to me?"

"I think you misunderstood that boy."

"I don't want to talk about it, okay? It's gone. Past. Dead. I live somewhere else. I've got a life."

"All right." She smiled wearily and touched my cheek. She was going to drop it, and I was glad.

A few ideas had nudged into my head since the day before. The most promising one concerned all the hand-me-downs that Moo had been saving for me, hoping I'd find Mr. Right.

"Moo, look," I said. "We can sell that old furniture in the attic. With the money, we can start making repairs, even before we get this situation with you and Pop settled."

"Sell your furniture!" Moo gasped. "All those wonderful pieces?"

Some of them were kind of wonderful, yes . . . but I had to be strong. "Moo. I'm not ever going to use them, and they're just a dust farm now."

Moo looked at me curiously. "You might be surprised, Daisy."

I shook my head. "Let's get them appraised. Who knows, maybe some old vase is worth thousands. Remember, I know antiques."

Moo's twisted lips let me know that she hated the idea. "Maybe so, Daisy," she said. "First we need to get some estimates for the repairs."

I was beat. For now.

Nine

And now she wanted me to call one of my old classmates? One who'd hung out with Luke and me in high school? I wasn't keen on calling Earl Hall for an estimate, but I didn't want another lecture from Moo. We might as well know what kind of money we had to raise.

And then she made me a nice cup of tea.

By the time I had him on the phone, I was in a mellow mood. Still, I found it startling to hear a voice I hadn't heard in so long.

"Sure, Daisy," he said, in answer to my question. "Great to hear from you. You coming back here to stay?"

"Not if I can help it, Earl," I said. "I've got sand in my shoes. I just want to see my folks safe and happy, and then I'll be off."

"Shake that sand out," he said. "They'll be happier with you home. People miss you. Why haven't you come to any class reunions?"

Uh-oh. "Do you really have to ask that, Earl?"

He paused for a minute. "Sometimes things don't turn out the way you expect. There are people who would really love to see you, girl."

He might throw the bait, but I wasn't biting. "I appreciate that, Earl, but I hate everybody putting in their two cents' worth."

"It's just because they care about you."

Earl would argue till the cows came home. He loved this town. Thought there was nowhere like it. "Thanks," I said. "Now what about the house?"

"I'll send my brother Jimmy out late this afternoon, okay? I'd come myself, but I'm about to leave for a job site. The town is growing, girl. We have a coffee shop here now."

That was progress. I guess. "I understand. That's fine. Thanks, Earl."

I hung up, embarrassed by the sympathetic tone good old Earl was giving me. Why wouldn't they just forget about Luke and me? Another reason I couldn't come back to Sawyer to live.

How could you stay in a town where your soul mate married your best friend? A friend who was prettier, smarter, and more, um, conventional? A knot under my breastbone was tightening, the same knot that afflicted me every time I thought about my former friends. Alyssa

Tyrell and Luke McDuffie. I realigned my thinking back to the beach, the waves, the soft surf, the sand . . .

Whoo! The tea had really improved my mood. What *did* Moo put in it? I heard the soothing tones of Eastern music coming from her room, so I closed my eyes and let my thoughts drift back to the beach.

"I'm hungry!" Raj burst through the back door.

I decided to be a good daughter and fix lunch. After plundering the fridge, I made chicken salad sandwiches on whole wheat bread for Moo and me and peanut butter and jelly for Raj. I went outside and picked enough flowers to fill a vase on the table.

We were all sitting down at the table before I told her I'd called Earl Hall, who was sending Jimmy over later.

I thought she'd be pleased. Instead, she reached behind her and took a ceramic box from the counter and riffled through it. She took out a card and laid it on the table.

"These fellows stopped by one day and told me they could see I needed some work done. Maybe we ought to get a second estimate. By the way, you did a good job with the flowers. Some of my teaching did rub off, after all."

Suspicious of her praise, I picked up the card.

THE TWO GOODGES

WAYNE AND DWAYNE

FOR ALL YOUR HOME REPAIR NEEDS

"Twin brothers," said Moo.

I sighed. "But Moo, we know Earl. Do you know these Goodges?"

"Never met them before," Moo said. "But those boys seemed awfully eager to get the business."

"I'll bet," I said and laid the card back on the table. Moo gave me a look but said nothing.

"Okay, if I get two estimates, can we go to the attic?"

Moo nodded. "A short rest after lunch, Daisy. It's going to be hard work."

"Why can't I go ahead?"

She flapped her hand at me. "All in good time. Why don't you go through the things in your room?"

"What? Those old clothes? Nobody would want them."

"You're afraid, Daisy." She gave me a superior look.

I had to prove I was not.

Upstairs, I roamed moodily through the dresser drawers and closets. The clothes weren't old enough to be vintage, not new enough to be appealing.

I piled them in a corner chair, destined for the thrift shop at the Methodist church where I'd grown up, where Pop had sung all his solos. Did Moo go to that church anymore? And what did the minister think about her fortunetelling?

A box of keepsakes surfaced in my top dresser drawer, a box that had lain undisturbed since I'd left home. I riffled through earrings without mates, a few seashells, a souvenir bracelet from New York, a stone I'd found on the grounds of

Graceland that Elvis might have trod upon, friends' graduation cards, school pictures, play programs. I unwrapped a ball of tissue and found a dried orchid and ribbon from my senior prom.

Luke had given it to me.

Luke had come home from his freshman year at Westbury University to be my date. Although I'd begged and begged to go to Westbury when I graduated, my screw-up underachiever Daisy grades threw me out of the running. In any case, my father told me, the tuition was too high.

So I worked like hell for a while at Midlands Junior College, certain if I did well I could get into Westbury, certain I could win over my father. Of course, my smart best friend Alyssa, whose father was an alumnus, went to Westbury.

Of course she did. My throat swelled and tears stung my eyes. Just then, Raj came barreling into my room and jumped with a mighty thud on the bed. "Miss Essie says it's time to go to the attic! Come on! Hey, your bed is springy!" He started jumping up and down.

"Stop that!"

"Why are you crying, Daisy? What's in that box?" He leaped off the bed and came to inspect it. "Mama would call it junk."

"That's what it is, Raj," I said. "Junk." I crumpled the dried orchid in my hand, letting the bits fall to the floor.

"Daisy, you're making a mess," Raj said. "Miss Essie's not going to like that."

Moo appeared in my doorway. "Miss Essie's not going to like what?"

I hastily swept up the fragments with my hand, dropping them into the trash basket. I shrugged. "Just some old stuff."

"She was crumbling flowers," said Raj. "One time my mama grabbed a whole bunch of roses out of the water and threw them at the wall. There were petals everywhere, and I had to help pick them up! She said bad words. The thorns stuck her."

Moo raised one eyebrow at me. "Come up to the attic, Daisy, when you get that cleaned up. Let's go, Raj."

I finished sweeping up the fragments with my hand, wondering who could have made Lorelei so mad. Vinny Corvo? I picked up the pad and pen I'd confiscated to inventory the furniture. Ghosts were everywhere here. Little did I know I was going to meet another one.

Ten

Dust lay in an even powder across the attic floor, as if it hadn't been disturbed in a long, long time. But then ghosts didn't leave footprints. Small sharp beams of light angled in from the dormer windows, casting deep shadows. The room smelled of crackled paper and old wood.

Moo pulled the chain of a bare bulb hanging from a cord, and light flooded the space. She pointed to some fairly new cartons. "Your father's CDs," she said, wrinkling her nose.

I noted plastic tubs of folded clothing, piles of cardboard moving boxes, a rocking chair needing a paint job, two folding card tables, three worn Samsonite suitcases, a peeling white iron bedstead, some dead lamps. An old brass chandelier, two footlockers. Ancient tennis rackets.

An electric train. A giant cheap pink stuffed elephant I'd won at a fair.

Against the far wall rested the huge stack of furniture that had belonged to my late Grandmothers Harrison and Jones. All those chests and mirrors and chairs and tables would be mine when I settled down. But that wasn't going to happen.

"I haven't thought about the furniture in a while." Moo glanced back at the cartons of CDs. "All I wanted for myself was Granny Harrison's desk. You know she always loved the unique and the fine."

Raj spotted a box marked TOYS and navigated toward them. He gave us a questioning look. "Go ahead." Moo flapped her hand.

While Raj occupied himself with the toy box, Moo and I lifted the lighter pieces from the furniture stack and arranged them where we could see them clearly.

"This piece is wonderful." Sighing with regret, I ran my fingers over a carved mahogany side chair that just needed a good polishing and some interesting upholstery. A cotton/linen blend, perhaps. Maybe toile?

"Daisy?"

"Sorry, Moo."

"This buffet in the back. I'm told it was very old."

I walked over and eyed the dark, rich, green-brown wood. Oh yes. Jacobean walnut. Couple of thousand bucks for sure. I told Moo, who said nothing.

I whisked off a sheet covering an inlaid round dining table. "That's a great piece," I said, lamenting the loss of it already, tracing the patterns of ash, cherry, and mahogany with my fingers. "It should fetch a good price." I mentally listed shops and auction houses that might be interested. Husband Number One—my interior design client, and the less said about him the better—would have adored it. He wasn't getting anywhere near it.

"Are there any good antique shops in town?" I asked Moo, thinking of freight charges to Atlanta.

"I can ask Lally," said Moo. "She keeps up with all that."

"That's all right, Moo. I can look into it." That roily stomach again. Would she tell her son what was going on? I turned quickly to Grandmother Harrison's old wine velvet camelback sofa. I tugged it out so I could see the back, see if there were any rips or tears.

Behind me, the door to the Jacobean buffet swung open with a loud creak.

Moo looked at me and smiled. "Maybe that's Isolde, letting us know she's here."

"Isolde? You have a pet bat?" I looked up at the rafters.

Moo shook her head and laughed. "The house is haunted," she said. "I didn't know this, of course, until I discovered my abilities."

"A ghost." With a name. Oh dear.

"Yes," Moo went on. "I think she was born in 1883. She's not a very ancient ghost. But you see, that's why I didn't want you to come up here without me. If anything happened, I wanted to be able to explain it. I didn't want to alarm you."

"Moo, I'm not alarmed," I said, despite the fact I was alarmed. Not at the ghost. With my mother. I wondered if Gordon could invite one of his school psychologist friends over sometime for a little tea and conversation. "Look," I said patiently, "we've just moved whatever was keeping the door shut. The lock is probably faulty." I went over to close it and spotted a dull metal lockbox inside. "What's this?"

Moo peered in. "Why, I'd forgotten all about that box. I think it had some cash and old papers in it. Grandpa Harrison gave it to your father a couple of months before he died. Your father took the cash out, of course, and said he would go through the papers later. I think he must have put the box up here and forgotten it."

I tried to open the box, but it was locked. "Do you have the key?"

"I don't know," said Moo. "Teddy could have taken it with him."

"Surely not, if he's forgotten about it." I dusted off the box with an old T-shirt that said SEE ROCK CITY. "Let's take it down and look in it," I said. "There might be something we can use."

Then I closed the door to the buffet. It clicked shut. There was nothing wrong with the lock.

I took out my pad and pen and inventoried all the furniture, describing it as best I could as to date and condition. Raj was busy emptying the contents of the box marked TOYS. He looked up. "Can I take the whole box? Look at all this neat stuff." He held up a jar that was filled with washers, bits of wire, old keys, screws, and nails.

Moo tossed Raj another T-shirt, one saying PINE ROSIN FESTIVAL 1987. "Wipe the dust off first," she said. "I don't know what all's in there but you're welcome to any of it."

Raj pulled out a low, oval wicker basket. "What's this?"

I told him about Freddy, the beagle that had been Gordon's. "He slept there. It used to have a plaid cushion."

"Chewed it to bits," said Moo.

"Could I have the basket?" Raj asked.

Moo shrugged. "Sure."

I was finished with my inventory, a little nostalgic, a little heartsick. This was some great stuff, and I was going to lose it forever. At least Raj was happy.

Moo carried the metal lockbox downstairs, Raj the wicker basket, and I the toy box.

Raj unloaded the box in the kitchen. Besides the jar, there were battery-powered racecars and a rusty yellow dump truck, wooden building blocks and a couple of ray guns, Star Wars action figures, and a box of educational spatial rods, one of Moo's progressive toy experiments that had always baffled me. Mixed in with all of these were trophies and ribbons. Raj laid those carefully back in the box and started lining up the toys.

I went to see if Moo had located the key to the lockbox. She was methodically going through Pop's dresser drawers, even taking all the clothes out. The socks and the underwear and the sweaters were carefully folded. If he was gone for good, why hadn't he taken them?

We did not find the key.

"Let's get a screwdriver or something and pry it open."

"I'm not sure that will work. Look at it, Daisy."

I inspected the lockbox carefully. The asbestos-lined, sturdy steel box was built to keep out fire and flood, as well as relatives with screwdrivers. What we needed were some burglar tools. Or, perhaps, Vinny Corvo.

"Maybe it's a sign," Moo said, frowning. "Maybe we shouldn't open it at all."

"Of course we should," I said. "After all, your ghost opened that door."

"Daisy, I wish you wouldn't be so flippant about Isolde. Hers is a very sad story."

"I'm sure." Seeing Moo's look I sighed. "Okay, tell me."

"She was a young woman in 1904, when her father built this house. She wanted to marry a young man, but her father disapproved of him. She planned to elope with him one night." Here Moo paused, and I waited. She lowered her eyes. "He fell off the ladder to her room and broke his neck."

People did not die for love in modern times, unless their loved one pushed them off a cliff on the honeymoon. "Is that true or just a tale?"

She gave me a withering glance. "I saw the newspaper clipping. It was quite a scandal. They say she still haunts the house waiting for him. She wants us to see what's in the box, Daisy. Maybe she'll provide us with the answer."

I would play along. "Can't you call her up?"

"It doesn't work like that, I keep telling you. She's not on the end of some ectoplasmic cell phone. I'll try to contact her when we have the séance, perhaps. Now, my next client's due in half an hour. How about a cup of tea?"

"Sure."

Raj sat in the corner of the kitchen engrossed in his box of toys. We saw what he'd had in mind for the wicker dog bed. Bogart was curled in it, basking in a sunbeam. But for how long? He'd be out the door and gone, or hiding somewhere in the house. Maybe under my bed! I told Raj to put the beast back in his plastic habitat.

Raj protested that Bogart was digesting his food and shouldn't be moved and promised to move the snake when he woke up. I forbade him to leave the room until the creature was safely enclosed.

Waiting happily for the tea, I saw a beat-up black truck pull into the driveway. Two men got out. As they lumbered toward the house, I felt trouble was coming.

Eleven

"Moo, about these guys..." Moo continued pouring water into her kettle to heat.

"What guys?" She assembled two flowered cups on saucers near the teapot.

"These rodeo cowboys." The men were walking as though they'd just gotten off horses.

Moo finally looked out the window. "Oh, the Goodges. Not that I don't trust Earl, but we do need another estimate. It's the usual thing, you know. Didn't I ask you to call them?"

"Well, um..." I hadn't called them. On purpose.

Moo shrugged. "I knew you wouldn't call, so I did. They said they could come right away."

I'll bet. They saw the combination of a sagging porch and a lady who gives psychic readings as an easy mark.

We walked out to meet them. With broad smiles, Dwayne and Wayne shook our hands. They were stockily built, not too tall, and one wore a red shirt and one a blue. They walked all around the house. Wayne, the one in the blue shirt, poked his keys into the wood, chipping off little bits, saying "You've got serious problems." His brother, Wayne, echoed "serious problems."

Moo picked up her skirts in one hand and we serious-problemed our way around the house, looking at the roof and the front porch and the steps, the dollar signs in Wayne and Dwayne's eyes getting bigger and bigger, and then we got to the kitchen. "Oh, wow," said Wayne. He dropped to his knees and dug his treacherous knife into Moo's homely old vinyl tiles. He pried the tile right up.

Moo winced when she saw it, wringing her hands. "Is it bad?"

Wayne assumed the expression of a kindly doctor telling you that you have an STD, but not the fatal kind.

"Looks like the subfloor is rotting," he said. "We'll have to replace the whole thing. She couldn't cost more than two or three thousand."

Moo turned to me, a study in panic. "Daisy. Don't go back to Florida. You can't leave me here with rotten floors."

I narrowed my eyes like Greta Garbo. "Moo, don't you see . . ."

Just then my glance fell on Bogart, curled up in the dog bed Raj had found in the attic. That boy had not followed my instructions. The basket lay underneath the bay window, just outside of a patch of sunlight behind the big potted fern.

Just as Dwayne and Wayne were telling me how they would go underneath the house and see if we needed to shore up the floor joists, Bogart heaved his bulk over the side of the basket and crawled out, looking for the shifting sunbeam.

The motion caught everyone's eye. The two guys looked at him. Bogart raised his head and flicked his tongue. I made a leap and grabbed him by the middle. "Raj!" I yelled.

He came running, looking sheepish, and ran back for the laundry bag. We hustled the snake inside. "Ma'am," said Dwayne, "my beeper's going off." He quickly consulted it. "I've got to go to the truck." He tipped his hat. "Excuse me, ma'am." Wayne followed him out.

They stayed out there an awfully long time.

Raj took Bogart to the plastic box, and I decided I'd better go out and see about the twins. They told me they had to leave. They'd been called to an emergency job over in Pine Lake Hills, and they'd be in touch.

"Well," said Moo.

For the first time since he'd come into my care I thanked Providence for Bogart.

"And they didn't even get to look at that ceiling in the séance room," Moo huffed. "That's a priority."

"I could use that cup of tea," I told Moo.

"What do you think could have gotten into those boys?"

I shrugged. "Maybe they saw a ghost."

She clicked the kettle on.

Moo fixed some of the herbal brew she called Happy Flowers. This tea also tasted remarkably good, and I hoped she hadn't put anything illegal in it. Just like Moo to do something like that without even knowing she was breaking the law.

We talked about the lockbox, about how to get into it, and about poor Isolde, who never married, pining for her lost lover in this very house. I hoped Moo didn't think I was pining for my lost lover.

Moo glanced around the kitchen. "Now where did that boy get off to? I was going to ask him if he wanted some juice."

"Raj?" I called.

Just as I was getting worried, he showed up, bearing the lockbox. Unlocked.

Twelve

Moo looked at Raj, amazed. "Did you hear anything, child? Did anyone speak to you and tell you what to do?"

He shook his head.

I frowned at Moo. "He's not psychic. He's been on good terms with a burglar, remember? Thank you very much, Raj."

"You're welcome," he said shyly. "The key was in my jar." He scampered back to his treasure box. He took out the racecars, poking at their empty innards.

"I'll have to find some batteries," said Moo.

While she was looking in the kitchen drawer, I lifted the papers from the box and laid them carefully on the table. They included promissory notes for debts that had long been paid, as well as various other financial papers. A sheaf of fancy-looking folded sheets caught my eye and I flattened them to find stock certificates, dated from 1936 to 1952.

"Moo," I said. "Look at this."

She edged over to inspect the certificates, running her fingers across the green- and orange- and maroon-edged crackling pages. "Do you think they're worth anything? They're awfully old. And I've never heard of those companies. Grape-Co Bottling? The Haloid Company? Eckelburg Optical Products? The Trans Georgia Rail Road?"

I thumbed through the certificates. "Worthless, I imagine. Some of the engraving's pretty. Look at this train!" I held up the railroad certificate. "I've seen people frame them. Most of those companies must have gone out of business long ago. Maybe we could get a few dollars for them from collectors."

"Well, surely we could find out."

"I'm not sure how to go about researching them. That would take time, a computer, phone calls, and there's so much else to do."

Moo's eyes lit up. She looked positively diabolical. "We'll go to the bank. Luke will know. I want you to talk to him, anyhow, Daisy, about that second mortgage."

"I thought we already had this discussion."

Moo went on as if I hadn't spoken. "He'll know where to find out about these certificates. And I've already been late with the last two mortgage payments."

I could feel a noose tightening around my neck. "Luke McDuffie? How could you expect me to talk to him, Moo!"

She sniffed. "Lally's my client, and there are a few things you ought to know about Luke, Daisy."

"I don't want to know them. He betrayed me, Moo."

Moo looked at me steadily. "Yes, Daisy. But you weren't entirely blameless. You did give him back his engagement ring, as I recall, before he took up with Alyssa."

"No, he started dating her behind my back and *then* I gave him back his . . . it wasn't an engagement ring. It was a fraternity pin. They're not the same thing."

"Engaged to be engaged. Yes."

"Don't remind me, Moo. It was double treachery. She was my best friend!"

"Daisy. You need to forgive and forget. Why—"

"No, Moo. Not another word. Don't speak of him. I'll call Gordon. Maybe he knows some other banker. Surely."

"Gordon uses him too, dear. After all, his father has always been my banker, and now that he's retired, of course I go to young Luke."

I couldn't stand any more. I walked outside, letting the lumpy screen door slam behind me, and took deep, suffocating breaths of the muggy outside air. When I had calmed a little I sat in the swing set and twisted from one side to the other as I'd done as a child, my mind in a muddle. Well, she could take those papers to Luke McDuffie if she wanted to. But there was no way she was going to drag me with her.

Thirteen

At two-thirty on the Buick's dashboard clock I turned Moo's Buick into the parking lot of a spiffing new bank, one I'd never seen before. Luke's bank.

At the entrance, I let Moo out, hair twisted up and secured with a glittering clasp, a wispy rose-printed shawl about her shoulders. She gathered up her black macramé bag with the stock certificates inside. "I still think you should come with me, Daisy."

To please her I'd traded my dusty jumper and Birks for a clean pair of jeans, the cherry-colored scoop neck top, and sneakers, but there was no way I was going in there. "Raj and I will wait here."

She knitted her brows. "It's awfully hot out here, dear." I shrugged and she got out, trailing clouds of sandalwood, and hobbled into the bank favoring the right ankle she said she'd turned on the attic stairs and, therefore, was unable to drive herself.

The parking lot was surrounded by spindly trees that might shade a Harley. The afternoon hour was ripe with heat, but the sun had dipped past its zenith, and the minimal shade would at least be a help.

I drove over and parked under the leafiest of the saplings. Outside, humidity was rocketing up from the Gulf, wilting and flattening everything in its path like a giant ray gun in an old Mystery Science Theatre film.

The A/C wheezed, dribbling forth lukewarm air. I fiddled with the controls with no success. Another thing on the Repair list.

"I'm hot," Raj whined.

I tried to ignore the beads of sweat trickling down my neck. "Let's be patient. She'll be back soon."

"You said I could see the bank," said Raj.

"There it is, ta-da. The bank."

"I want to go inside where it's cool."

I cut off the car and swung the door open wide. "Maybe there's a breeze outside."

Not a breeze was stirring, and I had no hat. The sun hammered on my bare head. Still, hats looked dorky on me unless they sat exactly right, and I'd never figured out how to get them exactly right. The sweat was plastering the cherry silk top to my body, threatening damp half-moons under the arms. I hadn't thought about Sawyer's climate in mid-May.

The white pedestal columns and black marble front of the McDuffie State Bank looked inviting. Cool. Raj took my hand and tugged. "Come on."

I felt silly being tugged by a child. An elderly lady who'd just driven up watched us with amusement. Maybe we could just go stand in the vestibule until Moo finished transacting her business.

I followed Raj in. There was no vestibule. Teller cages lined the back wall of the huge room. Moo was obviously in one of the small offices to the right, and I wasn't going there.

Four comfortable club chairs, banker gray, reposed in the middle of the cavernous space. I sat in one, my back to the offices. I scanned the tellers and customers. No one I remembered.

"Where do they keep the money?" asked Raj, bouncing up and down on the chair beside mine.

"In a big safe called a vault," I said.

"How much do you suppose they've got?"

"Billions and billions." I mimicked Carl Sagan talking about astronomical numbers. "Really, Raj, I don't know."

"Can I go ask that lady?" He pointed to an office where a woman in a dark print dress was tapping on a computer.

"No, you may not."

"I'm bored."

Raj bounced up and down again. Then he spotted a table with a coffee jug and plate. "Hey! Free cookies!"

"Go have some. Please." What was taking Moo so long? Surely it didn't take this long for, um, *him* to tell Moo those certificates were worthless. My heart began to thump in my ears. Raj reappeared, cookies in both fists, and offered me one. I couldn't even think of food, and shook my head No. He proceeded to munch them and fidget, scattering crumbs, watching people in the teller lines.

I settled into the cushions and picked up a financial magazine. The first article I turned to offered "Investing in Your Thirties: Strategies for Singles." After reading a whole page, I had no idea what it had said. My mind was with Moo, what was happening with those stocks, *what she was saying to Luke.*

I started over again. *Later will be too late!* the article screamed. *Start Now! Investments should be balanced!*

I inspected a diagram laid out like a food pyramid. Instead of Fats and Sweets at the top there were Collectibles: stamps, coins, antiques, paintings, with the same kind of warning. Use Sparingly. Well, sure. Anything that's fun is not good for you. Hoagie's pieces of eight, I supposed, would be classed in the Use Sparingly section, assuming he hadn't used them already.

The next level was Securities. Equal to Starches, I supposed. I was concentrating so hard trying to make the food categories and investment categories match that I didn't hear the footsteps approach my chair.

"You're welcome to take the magazine, Daisy."

That voice. A flush spread across my freckles, and I looked up slowly, just in case it might not be Luke McDuffie, but his evil twin, Fluke, whom they'd hid in the attic all these years. I squeezed my eyes shut. Oh God, please let him look old and paunchy.

I slowly rose out of my chair and turned. And there he was facing me, older, the same Luke, but *different*. Yep, six feet, slender, broad shoulders, handsome face just enough quirky not to be boring. But his brown hair was combed neatly, and he wore a pinstripe suit. Wingtips. Killer tie. Definitely not my type.

"We keep them for the customers to take," he said, smiling.

"What?" I said stupidly.

He smiled. "The magazines." He took my copy from me and turned it over. "See?" On the back was stamped *Complimentary Copy*. He gave it back to me and shrugged. "Hardly anybody takes them."

What an inane conversation. In the mirrored wall I saw my face, still red. "I'll take it," I heard myself saying, and stuffed it in my hobo bag, not wishing to seem ungracious.

He saw me looking at myself in the mirror, which was even more embarrassing. "You haven't changed a bit, Daisy." The moment hung like a ball on the edge of a table.

"Thank you," I mumbled. He sure had changed. He hadn't been Mr. Preppy in college. He'd been an individual. He'd had Birks too. I said, "What about those stocks we found?"

"Certainly interesting documents."

"Does that mean worthless?" Horrid Harvey liked to say my paintings were "interesting."

"I'm not sure yet. I asked your mother to leave them with me. I have a network I can use, and there are companies that will research stocks for a fee. But I know your mother needs to save money, and I told her I'd do what I could about the mortgage."

"Oh Luke. You don't have to do that research. If I get hold of a computer and a library, I can—"

"I want to help," he said. "That's better for us, you know. If they're worth money, she'll have an easier time repaying the loan. And the library might not have the books you need. I have the resources."

I sighed. "Yes, we owe your bank money. If I could only get Pop to come back."

"Where is he?"

"I don't know exactly. Moo says she doesn't know, either. I have a hunch he's playing in seedy nightclubs."

"Maybe I can help you find him."

"You'll do no such thing." My hands went to my hips in defiance. "It isn't your problem."

"Oh, but it is," he said.

"Don't do me any favors, Luke." I gazed out the front window.

"I'll do it for your mother. She's helped my mother more than you can imagine."

I stared at him. "You're kidding." A shadow crossed his face and he looked distinctly uncomfortable. "Ah . . . I'll tell you about that sometime."

No, you won't, I thought. I couldn't believe I was standing here having an ordinary conversation with the man who had betrayed me. *So Alyssa left you*, I wanted to say. *Good. Now you know how it feels.*

No, I was better than that. I *had* to be better than that. After all, my mother told fortunes and I was babysitting a snake for a woman who was off hiding from a man who'd just got out of jail. Maybe. Not to mention my daily work was serving beer to lonely old men who kept parrots while giving advice to the lovelorn.

I looked around. "What have you done with my mother?"

"Here she comes," Luke said. "She went to the teller to cash a check." I knew she'd done it on purpose to give Luke a chance to talk to me. She had the cash Luke's mother had paid her in an envelope on her desk.

Raj picked that moment to rejoin me, his face a mask of cookie crumbs. Before Luke could ask, I said, "This is Raj. I'm watching him for a friend of mine. And he seems to have been into your cookies in a big way." I dug in my pocket for a tissue, but Luke whipped out a handkerchief and handed it to Raj.

Moo rejoined us. "I'm so glad you two had a chance to visit. Thanks for all your help, Luke."

"No problem, Miss Essie. I'll give it a try. They may not be worth anything, but they may be worth a great deal. You never can tell. And I've told Daisy there are other ways I can help."

Now he was calling her Miss Essie too! With a pasted-on smile and a handshake I took my leave of Luke, the fiend. Why was Moo going to all this trouble to throw Luke and me together? He wasn't my kind of man anymore. Pillar of the community, the very kind of man the Chamber of Commerce puts in its brochures. Forgiveness? Was that what she was after? Sorry, that well was empty.

We walked out to the car. I looked straight at her and said, "Don't say a word. I'm *glad* I didn't marry him." We got in.

"I'm sorry you feel that way, dear," she said, as I pulled out into the street. "He's often asked about you."

"Yeah, well, you told me about Alyssa. What happened there? I always thought they had the perfect marriage."

"There's been talk," she said carefully. "Watch that telephone pole, Daisy." I riveted my eyes on the road. Moo continued, "He doesn't talk about it. It's just as stupid as what your father did."

"Maybe she couldn't stand him anymore," I said meanly.

"Well, I really shouldn't say this, but there was talk she was seeing someone else. Some man she met at Hilton

Head." She lowered her voice, ardently looking out the window at the street she'd seen one billion times before.

"I don't care," I shot back. "My feelings for him are dead. Murdered. Killed. And you can't resurrect the dead."

"Don't be so sure about that," said Moo. "You can communicate with the dead."

"You can't really talk to ghosts, Moo," I said.

She folded her hands in her lap and looked at me seriously. "It isn't a matter of talking to ghosts. It's a matter of adjusting your spiritual stance to let yourself be receptive to the energies out there. Just like you need to adjust your heart to be receptive to changes. You'll see," she said. "I'm expecting you at the séance tomorrow night. My regulars will all be there and you can meet them. And, since Lally doesn't like to come to group sessions, I've invited Luke."

I groaned. "Good Lord, Moo. Give it up. I don't want to see him. Surely he won't come."

"He said he wouldn't miss it."

"Can I come too?" Raj piped from the back seat.

"I'm going to hope and pray your mama calls me soon," I said. "With any kind of luck we'll be on our way back to Florida to see her."

"Oh, no, you can't go yet," said Moo. "I need you, Daisy. Things are already so much clearer since you've come home. I'm hoping I can persuade you to stay."

Did she know what she was saying? "Moo, I won't even discuss it unless you and Pop work things out."

"Then if we do, you mean you'll come back?"

"No! That isn't what I meant at all!

"Then what did you mean?"

Fortunately, we were back home. I pulled around to the back and parked in the garage that had once been a carriage house.

While I was still trying to collect my thoughts, Moo opened her door. "I just remembered, I've got to make a phone call," she said. She hurried down the herb-lined walkway to the house.

To whom? I wasn't about to ask.

Fourteen

Seeing Luke at the bank had one big effect. I had to solve my problems fast.

There was just this small problem of a boy in my care. Maybe if I looked on the Internet for a mention of Lorelei, I could come up with a clue as to where she was. Also my father. Something just might turn up.

I hadn't taken my laptop out of the case since we'd arrived in Sawyer, because there'd been too much to do. I went up to my room, unpacked the machine, and looked around for a grounded plug. Victorian houses are not known for their up-to-date wiring. Another thing to add to the list of Things to Do: *Rewire House*.

And how much would *that* cost?

The nearest grounded plug, I found, was in the kitchen. I placed the laptop on the kitchen table and looked for a phone line. The cord was too short to reach.

I wrote on the Things to Do list: *Phone Cords.*

Moo interrupted me to tell me she had a craft class, and the ladies would be arriving in the next fifteen minutes. To avoid freaking out the ladies in case she invited them in for tea, I managed to drag Bogart's box into the séance room.

I'd barely sat back down to my list when another pickup truck arrived.

This time it was Jimmy. Jimmy, who I'd last seen when he was a bratty kid.

He'd grown up to be a tall, lean, no-longer-bratty dude, who sported a well-worn Caterpillar cap and said he'd just come back from a tour of duty in Kuwait. He got out his tape measure and went around the house, not digging into anything, not saying much, while from the outdoor studio came chatter and the occasional giggle.

Raj was up in Gordon's old room, absorbed with the new toys, so I didn't worry about him while Jimmy and I looked at the roof, the porch, the siding. Jimmy seemed to think a little patching would do the trick, nothing dreadful at all. When we got to the kitchen to look at the worn-out floor tiles, he brightened. "I know the perfect flooring for here." He took out his tape and I held one end while he measured and scribbled in his notebook.

"You don't think the subfloor needs redoing?"

He notched up where Dwayne, or Wayne, had dug. "Nah. Somebody tell you it did?"

"Well, yes."

He snorted and walked over to the spot where the empty dog basket lay. He nudged it out of the way and measured the window. "Where's your dog?" he said. "I love dogs. I've got an Australian shepherd. Greatest dog in the world."

I shrugged and chose my words carefully. "I shut him away. He makes people nervous."

"Oh, he wouldn't bother me," Jimmy said. "I have a way with dogs."

I smiled, to show I understood. "He's kind of . . . unpredictable."

Jimmy wrote more numbers in his notebook. "This kitchen will really brighten up with a new floor. A dog just needs obedience school. You ever tried it?"

"No," I answered truthfully.

Raj came into the kitchen then.

"Hey there, young fella," said Jimmy. "I'm Jimmy."

Raj eyed Jimmy suspiciously. "I'm Raj." Jimmy looked at me for some explanation but I wasn't inclined to give any. Let them wonder if I had, or did have, a subcontinental husband.

"Where's Bogart?" Raj wanted to know.

"In the séance room," I said. I assumed by now everyone in town knew about the séances.

Jimmy didn't bat an eye. "You keep him shut up like that," said the contractor, "and he'll get fat and lazy."

"He only looks fat after he's eaten," Raj replied casually, "and then it's more like lumpy."

Jimmy cut his eyes at me. "Just what kind of a dog do you have?"

Raj spoke up. "It's a—"

I clapped my hands over Raj's mouth. "Whole lot of trouble." I looked at Raj severely. "We want Jimmy here to be able to do his job." I said these last words deliberately.

"I'm going to see Bogart," said Raj. "I don't want him to get fat and lazy."

"Let's walk out on the back porch, Jimmy," I said.

"That dog isn't vicious, is he?" asked Jimmy. "You could get sued."

"Oh, he's not vicious," I said. "Just unusual. And he'll probably be gone before we start the work here. He belongs to Raj, who's staying with us while his mother's away. Now, can you come by tomorrow with those flooring samples and the written estimate?"

"Sure thing," said Jimmy.

Raj called from the séance room. "You forgot about the ceiling that fell down."

Oh. I took a deep breath. "Come on."

Bless the boy's heart. By the time we got there, he'd covered the plastic box with one of Moo's shawls. Jimmy didn't seem to notice but just stared up at the plaster-speckled diagonal ceiling laths. "Yep," he said. "Not a problem. I'll add that to the estimate."

That done, I walked with him back to his truck, talking about the town and how it seemed to be prospering. He shoved his cap back and scratched his head. "Seems there was something I was supposed to tell you. Oh yeah. Earl and me saw Luke McDuffie in Ma Hopkins' Café about lunchtime. He said to be sure and do a good job for you."

Dang.

After Jimmy and the ladies had left, Moo had half an hour before one of her clients arrived. She put the kettle on to brew more of that delicious tea. "Daisy, I'd like for you to pick out the new floor."

I flopped in the kitchen chair, all wrung out. "Moo, you aren't trying to lure me back home by letting me get really involved here, are you?"

She put on her injured face. "Certainly not. I am not a manipulative woman, Daisy. You go over with Jimmy what needs to be done. I've got to focus my energy on the séance Friday night."

"In any case, I've got to get in touch with people about the antiques," I said. I'd make a few calls to some of the connections from my ill-fated first career. "We don't have any numbers yet, and I'm not sure what repairs you can afford."

She sighed. "As long as I don't have to worry about it right now, dear. I need to keep my mind clear for the séance. Too many chattering thoughts, what the yogis call monkey mind, interfere with the proper communication with the spirit world."

The kettle was shrieking. Moo poured the boiling water into an elephant teapot, his trunk the spout, and looked out the window. Raj had gone out to the backyard and was wandering around, picking up rocks to look for grubs. Bogart liked them.

Moo turned toward me with the most alarming look on her face. I knew that look well, that light-bulb-over-the-head look. It was the look that, in childhood, had resulted in Gordon and me dressed up like reindeer, antlers and all, for our family Christmas card. Neither of us would agree to the red nose. Pop and Moo, of course, were Mr. and Mrs. Claus.

Moo's craziness, her talent, had been under wraps. She'd never been able to express herself with Pop around. After all, you can't have more than one star in any family. Somebody's got to be the gaffer, the caterer, and the key grip.

"Moo, what are you up to?"

"Imagine!" she said. "That child! Suppose I make him a little costume, with a turban, pantaloons, and all that? Wouldn't it add to the atmosphere of the séance?"

"Moo," I groaned. "I won't let you do it."

"And why not?"

"It's not respectful of his ethnicity," I said. "It's exploitation."

"Heavens, Daisy, I think it's very respectful. Look how he was reading that book on India. Why don't I just ask Raj what he thinks?"

She deftly poured the tea, handed me my cup, and went out into the yard. I took my cup to the window and watched the two of them talking. Raj looked skeptical. At first.

The two of them came in looking conspiratorial. Moo went to the freezer and handed him a goodie, which she'd bought especially for him, and said nothing while we finished our tea and he ate his chocolate-covered ice cream bar.

"So what about it, young man?"

"I don't know, Miss Essie," he said. "It sounds weird."

"Let's look in the book about India," she said. She left the room.

"Has your mama ever told you about India?" I asked.

He shook his head.

"But yet she gave you an Indian name," I said.

"She said she named me after my father." He scooted back. He looked as though he was ready to run.

"Raj," I said softly. "What else did she tell you about him?"

"You asked me that before."

"Maybe this time you'll tell me."

He looked down at the floor and walked over to the spot where Wayne, or Dwayne, had dug. He poked his finger into it. Finally he said, "She said he came from far away and was very important in his country and that he had to stay there." Raj looked out into the distance. "I don't care about him." He glared at me, then, a hard look in his eyes. "And I'm *not* going to India!"

"Who said anything about going to India?"

"He did! My father!"

"But I thought you'd never met him."

Raj's eyes grew angry. "That letter. He wrote a letter to Mama and me. I read it."

"The one you threw away," I said slowly. "What did it say?"

"I forgot."

"Come on, Raj, tell me! What is this about going to India?"

He turned away and stared out the window.

Moo came back into the room bearing the lavishly illustrated book. "Look, dear." She turned the colorful pages. Raj gazed at the picture of the Taj Mahal in the encyclopedia, at a rider on an elephant, at all the people who looked a lot like him. He looked at the historical figure of a maharajah in full regalia. He looked at the picture of a snake charmer with basket and cobra and stuck out his bottom lip. Then his expression became sly. Mischief danced in his eyes.

"I'll dress up if I can hold Bogart. Do you suppose he would come out of the basket like that? Do you have one of those things?" He pointed at the flute.

"Oh, no," said Moo, fluttering her hands to her face. "I'll lose my clients, every one. People here are more afraid of snakes than they need to be."

"And maybe it only works with cobras," I pointed out. "Bogart is a python."

"But we could try," Raj insisted.

Moo gazed over at the cage. "Here, in the Bible Belt, it's hard enough for a spiritualist. Why, the Baptist preacher looks at me funny when I see him in the hardware store. If I brought in a snake, my Lord, what would people think?"

"It says in the book," said Raj, pointing, "the snake is the symbol of life."

"In Hinduism?" I said.

"I'm sure I wouldn't know," said Moo. "Religion is so hard to keep straight. Who dunks, who kneels, who sprinkles. Women in hats, men in hats. Thank God for Methodists."

"Mama and Tia Luz are always fighting about religion," said Raj. "Luz says Mama is going to purgatory forever. Mama says no, she is going to be reincarnated like my father. This makes Luz furious."

"Your mama has become Hindu? Does she go to any temple?" asked Moo, with interest.

"On Sunday she sleeps all day," said Raj.

"I think we'd better leave religion alone," I said. "The child is confused enough as it is."

"Well, please don't bring the snake, Raj, that's all I ask," said Moo. "Now, may I go ahead and make your costume and let you be the prince you really are?"

"Cool." His face held an innocent smile.

I suspected he still had the letter. Somehow, I was going to find out what it said.

Fifteen

I still had time to get to the electronics store before it closed. By the time I got back with my phone cord, Moo's latest client had left, thank goodness. I plugged in the laptop, and like a woman in the desert confronted with an oasis, drank deep of the well of Information. I cruised through my email, deleting all suggestive messages from Hoagie. No message, of course, from Lorelei.

The news from Daytona was the usual stuff.

I did a search for LORELEI SNAKE DANCER and found nothing except some salacious sites. I tried her real name, Dolores Diaz, and found that there were quite a few ladies who bore that name. The obituaries, thankfully, did not seem to apply to my missing person, and I kept searching. I was about to give up when one of those funny little news-of-the-weird squibs popped up.

NEW ORLEANS WOMAN ARRESTED FOR DESECRATING CEMETERY PROPERTY, INJURED IN DARING ESCAPE

> Dolores Diaz, 32, would give no explanation to police as to why she was smashing cemetery urns with a hammer in Metairie Cemetery. As the officers tried to take her into custody, she broke free and ran but tripped and struck her head on a cemetery vault. She was hospitalized. No further information at this time.

Something about cemetery urns nagged at me, but I couldn't remember what it was.

I shut the computer and put in a call to Luz. I found that the baby would be in the hospital another week, and Luz was staying at Lorelei's apartment until the tiny boy was released. Ricky had gone back to Tampa and his job, and her mother-in-law, Pilar, had come to stay.

"Have you heard anything from your sister?" I asked. "You sure she didn't say anything about going to New Orleans?"

Luz sighed. "No, just that she was going out of town. I had her cell phone number, of course." She hesitated. "But she did live there once. That's where she met Vinny, that horrible man."

"Holy spit," I said. Why had no one mentioned this? "Have you called her?"

"Yes. Many times. The phone just rings and rings."

I told her about the news from New Orleans. She gave a strangled gasp. I had the feeling there was something she wasn't telling me.

"Let me have the number," I said. "I'll try too. If she's under arrest, they've taken the phone away from her. Maybe checking it to see who calls her. Tell me, why on earth would she be smashing cemetery urns?"

Once again, that hesitation. Then, in a small voice, she said, "She always loved pottery."

Pottery. Now the thing at the back of my mind that had nagged me came into focus. The pots on her patio with the plants that ate things. Pots of every shape and color. Plants were often planted in cemetery urns. "May I have that cell number?"

Luz told me. I scribbled LORELEI in big letters and the number on the pad by the telephone. "It doesn't make sense," Luz was saying. "They say she was smashing them? Maybe she wanted to copy them, but why smash them?"

"What? Copy them, you say?"

"Yes." She spoke on in that small, hesitant voice. "It was her hobby. She liked to make the cement pots and statues in her little backyard, when she lived in New Orleans."

I was speechless for a moment. "What else can you tell me?"

Luz cleared her throat. "Dolores and I were not always on speaking terms, especially after our poor mama got a bad sickness. Mama was always worrying about her." Luz, the good child, talked on and on, of how she had cared for her mother, and Lorelei did little or nothing, always hanging around with that horrible Vinny.

"Luz—"

Gone was the hesitation. Her voice grew heated. "I told her to dump him, he was no good for her, but she showed me all the pretty things he gave her. Diamonds, emeralds."

"Luz—"

"I think he steals them from the condos."

That confirmed my suspicions. "Look, Luz. Have you seen him hanging around there?"

"What? Around this apartment?"

"I think he's looking for her. Watching for her to come back home."

Luz said something in rapid-fire Spanish to her mother-in-law and then got back to me. "He'd better not show his face here."

"Be careful, Luz. He might be dangerous."

"I'm not scared of him, two-bit burglar. But, Daisy, you won't mind taking care of Raj a while longer, would you? I just can't have him here, 'specially if Vinny is hanging around . . ." She sounded close to tears.

I told Luz that Raj was safe with us—for the time being. I would try to get in touch with Lorelei. Or if that wasn't possible, surely somewhere, on some piece of paper in some New Orleans bureaucratic office, Miss Dolores Diaz would have a next-of-kin listed and they'd call her sister.

I saw it now, the way the pieces fit.

I wanted to tell Moo about this, but she'd laid out cans of tomatoes and sauce and jars of bay leaves and basil and a package of ground beef for her special pasta sauce. I knew better than to disturb the cook.

I took a walk after a delicious bowl of Moo's spaghetti to get my thoughts together. I walked all the way down to Luke's bank and back again, certain that he'd be home with his kids. I wondered if he was a good father. How could any woman go off and leave her kids?

Not that I had any experience.

Injured and facing arrest, Lorelei was going to need a lawyer. She hadn't called me. She hadn't called Hoagie. She hadn't even called Luz to check on Raj. Therefore, I concluded, she was either too badly injured or she didn't want anyone to know she'd been arrested. Maybe she had connections there in New Orleans from the time she'd lived there. Maybe she knew a lawyer or two.

Listen, I told myself. This lady is scrappy. She'll do all right. I just wish I believed it.

Sixteen

I spent a troubled night, tossing and turning, tangling myself in the sheets, and finally dropped off in the wee hours. Bright sunshine, which was trying hard to escape from behind the blinds, smacked my face a split second before I heard the knocking on the back door.

"Moo?" I called. I shoved myself out of bed, pulled on some sweats, made for the window in the back bedroom, and peered down. There, standing on the back porch steps, was Earl Hall himself. Standing right beside him was none other than Luke McDuffie.

I narrowed my eyes. Earl, well, he was all right. But how dare that faithless banker come here!

The window was hard to raise—the paint was flaking off but I bumped and joggled the sash wide enough to lean out. "What are you guys doing there this time of morning?"

Earl laughed. "Honey, we're not a member of the leisure class."

Excuse me? I looked over at the clock. It read nine thirty. I glanced at myself in the mirror. Baggy eyes, messy hair that needed washing, rumpled sweats.

"We need to talk to you," said Luke. "There's news."

Oh. Spit. My heart sank to my bare feet. "Be down in a sec."

I splashed water on my face and combed my hair and put on a smear of lipstick. Heck, my sweats were more or less clean. And those guys had their nerve, coming over without calling. But then again it was nine thirty. And this was Sawyer, where people did things like that.

I slid my feet into flip-flops and pattered down to the kitchen. I heard Raj somewhere in the house, and Bogart was snoozing in his plastic habitat on the back porch. No worries. I threw open the back door. "Come in," I said.

They greeted me and stepped into the kitchen, inspecting me like I was merchandise in the flea market. I didn't care. I wasn't trying to attract either one.

"Where's that mysterious dog Jimmy told me about?" Earl said.

"I didn't want to spook Jimmy," I explained. "We kept Bogart shut up."

"Jimmy's pretty hard to spook," said Earl. "And Bogart's a name for a hound."

"Hound's on the porch," I said and pointed back toward the plastic box.

I have to hand it to those boys. Luke got this expression on his face, like uh-huh, I see, and Earl put his hand to his chin. Neither moved, as though Bogart might be a rattler poised to strike. "Big 'un, ain't he?" said Earl carefully.

"Daisy," Luke accused, "you were always scared of snakes. Remember when I put the green snake down your shirt when we were twelve?"

"Yeah," said Earl, grinning. "At the church picnic. Wow, did she scream!"

"I'd forgotten," I said coolly, wishing my face wouldn't give me away. I wasn't going to let them get my goat, although the memory tugged at me painfully. And I was thirteen, not twelve. I forced myself to smile. "I still don't like snakes. I'm just keeping this for a friend."

"Is that like keeping pot for a friend?" asked Earl.

"It's a long story," I said firmly. "Now what did you two show up here for? Luke, aren't you supposed to be banking or something?"

He shrugged. "It helps to be the boss. I wanted to tell you the news in person. One or two of those stocks might be worth quite a bit of money. But we'll need to get them authenticated and get your father back here. He'll need to sign in order to sell them, of course, since they were his after all. And there might be tax considerations, so he'll need to talk to his CPA. I saw Earl at the bank just as I was leaving and told him to come on here with me. You'll probably be wanting to go ahead with the renovations."

Earl was grinning. "How'd you like to update the bathrooms? Add a room or two?"

I cocked my head. "How much money, Luke?"

"I don't want to raise your hopes too much. Let's make sure they're authentic. But if they pan out, it'll be enough to do the renovations and then some."

I nodded. I wasn't willing to cheer just yet.

"I can get started next week, Daisy," said Earl.

"We don't have the money yet, Earl."

"I'll take a chance," he said, rubbing his hands together. I wondered what Luke had told Earl.

An awkward silence fell. No one knew what to say. It was clear Luke wanted to talk to me, but not with Earl standing there, and Earl had no intention of leaving. He looked around the kitchen like it was candy store and he was a kid with a fistful of nickels. "How old is that stove?" he asked. "Those cabinets..."

"I'm sure you guys have to get to work," I interrupted. I gestured to the computer on the kitchen table. "I've got things to do myself."

"Well, sure," said Luke. "Do you know where your dad is?"

"He sure was something on that commercial for Lucky Buck's Used Cars," said Earl, grinning.

I tossed my head. "He's been kind of busy with better gigs," I said. "Any day now he'll be performing at Carnegie Hall."

Earl's cell phone rang, beedle-de-be. He flipped it open and talked into it while Luke and I warily watched each other. "Jimmy can't handle it? They want to talk to me? Yeah, I'll be right there. " Earl snapped the phone shut and shrugged. "Never ending. See you guys later." He loped out the back door, down the back steps.

Luke gave me a searching look. "Well, I guess I'd better not keep you." He was angling, I thought, for me to ask him to stay for coffee. But like another household ghost, Raj materialized between us. How long had he been listening? "Good morning, Daisy. Hi, Mr. Luke. I'm hungry."

If Luke wanted to talk to me alone, Moo's Grand Central Station wasn't the answer.

"Well, thanks for the great news, Luke," I said. "It was good of you to come in person." What else was there to say between us? I could have said I had heard the news about Alyssa; I could have said I was sorry. But I wasn't sorry, was I? He deserved it. So there.

He frowned a little, as though he could have been reading my mind. "See you, Daisy."

He strode gracefully down the back steps and out to his car, a big navy blue Beemer. I watched him go, this quirkily handsome man in his well-cut tropical-weight suit, his TV anchorman hair. Not my type at all. But what was my type? Hoagie, the beach bum? The artist-professor? My first husband? The less said about that particular dude, the better.

Moo bounded up the back steps and into the kitchen. "Did I see Luke's car leaving here? Did I see Earl's truck go by?"

I told her the good news from Luke, and she clapped her hands like a child. "Oh, wonderful!" Then she gave me that practical look. "Let's not count our chickens, just yet, but, my, my. That takes one load off my shoulders." Then she bit her lip. "There is the problem of your father."

"Take him back, Moo."

"I don't want to," she said stubbornly. "I've found it rather nice here being on my own." She brightened a little. "Maybe your father can straighten out all this stock business and then move into a little condo out by the mall. Then he can go on and do his singing. I don't think he's going to give that up."

I smote my forehead. "Moo!" I said. "You two need each other! And where would he put the piano in a condo?"

"Who says I need him?" She left the piano question unanswered and glanced at Raj. "We need to get this boy some breakfast, and my next client is due in fifteen minutes."

"What would you like for breakfast?" I asked him.

"I can fix it," he said. He walked over to the counter and took a round of pita from the bag lying there. He covered it liberally with butter and jam, then put the electric kettle on for tea, seemingly at home in the kitchen. Nine years old. I realized with a sinking feeling that he must have been taking care of himself for a long time. I'd never noticed it when I babysat with him, for he'd always been reading, watching TV, or playing video games.

I took out two tea mugs and looked at Moo questioningly. "Just tea," she said. "I had breakfast early."

I placed a regular Lipton's teabag in each mug. I needed a change from Moo's joy brew. "You do a pretty good business. Are your customers happy?"

She spread her hands like the Bird Girl. "They leave here more aware. So many people go through life missing half of it, because they just aren't aware. They miss the beauty, they miss the pain. They walk along with blinders on, going straight ahead, not seeing what doesn't fit into their prefabricated boxes. How shallow such a life is, Daisy! Beauty is all around us, easing our days, compensating for our sorrows, making life worth living. It's too bad that some people choose to live within four gray walls."

I poured the boiling water into the cups. Moo was saying, "Awareness. Energies in the air. The essences of people. Not the masks they put on, not the little lies they tell themselves. It comes out in the auras, Daisy."

While I was trying to take this in, the doorbell rang.

"Oh, pish." Moo sighed. "There's Florence. Early."

"Want me to get it?"

Moo's eyebrows shot toward the ceiling. "Certainly not. Go put on some decent clothes. What will people think?"

I was still wearing the baggy sweats I'd pulled on earlier. "Moo, I cultivate the natural look."

"Natural does not mean sloppy."

That was the Moo I remembered. I went upstairs to dress.

Now on my list of responsibilities:

Look after snake.

Look after Raj.

Look after Moo.

Look after house.

Get Lorelei out of trouble and/or hospital.

Find Pop.

And dress stylishly.

Impossible.

I didn't know where to begin. And if I didn't get Lorelei out of the hospital and trouble, then what was I going to do with this boy? And if I didn't get back in two weeks my job was gone and I only had a couple of paintings left to sell. I changed into jeans and an old pink T-shirt with palm trees on it.

I found that Moo had given my tea to her client. I made another cup and ate some toast and some fruit salad I found in the fridge.

The house fell into a hush. Soft murmurs filtered from the séance room, the snake lay curled in his habitat, and Raj, breakfast finished, occupied himself with the toy box. I sipped the rest of my tea and thought about finding Pop. The Internet search engine had found a few mentions of clubs in which he'd been playing in the Florida panhandle and south Alabama, but no more information.

Maybe that ghost in the attic would tell me something, huh? I ought to go up and look at the furniture again, dust it, polish it, get it ready for the buyers. I'd already found an antique dealer in town who was willing to come over and look at the whole kit and caboodle, whenever I was ready.

Raj agreed to join me after he finished his electronic game, and I went back up to the attic with dust cloths and plastic bags.

I unstacked as much as I could and spread the pieces out. And then I stood quietly under the eaves in the dusty room and waited for Isolde to manifest herself.

"Isolde?" I whispered, feeling foolish. I waited, straining my ears, and heard only the twittering of birds in the branches outside.

A soft cloth in my hand, I worked lemon oil into the Jacobean sideboard, glancing from time to time at the intricately carved roses that graced the Victorian sofa. Maybe one day I would have it, after all. If the stocks were worth money, perhaps we wouldn't have to sell it. Perhaps . . . oh, who was I kidding? This stuff would never fit into a Florida beach bum life.

Funny how things seem more valuable when you're on the brink of losing them. I polished and brushed and almost didn't hear Raj calling to me from the foot of the attic stairs, asking if he could play games a little longer.

I replied that I needed him to come up and help me sort boxes. He grudgingly agreed, and we attacked boxes with reckless abandon, archaeologists unearthing strata of 20th century civilization. I even found a few of Gordon's clothes that would fit Raj. Luckily jeans are jeans, and so what if Gord's old T-shirts were totally uncool. *Sawyer Chess Club*, for example. The boy happily piled them up, and I sent him to carry them to the washer so I could get the attic smell out.

After he'd gone, I spotted a cardboard box without a label, the flaps folded together in a crisscross pattern. I pulled the flaps apart and looked into a part of the past I'd wanted to bury. College memorabilia. Term papers, party favors, that kind of stuff. That wasn't who I was any more. I tossed it all into the black trash bag. Then I took out a fat spiral-bound history notebook. Underneath lay a packet of letters tied with a blue ribbon.

Letters Luke and I had written each other.

Luke and I had missed each other so much that fall when he'd gone off to college, leaving me in high school. Unlike most of our classmates, we knew we'd found The One. So I was boho, so he wasn't quite. He just wanted to be different from his uptight parents. We'd found common cause in our idealism. Our plans were to marry right after college and go into the Peace Corps. After that stint, Luke would enter law school, planning to combat injustice, and I'd teach art and paint. He didn't want to go into the bank with his father. He'd leave that to his brother, the economics major.

I fingered the letters and set them aside. I couldn't throw them away, couldn't open them. Each choice would have been a dagger in my heart. I lifted out a brown manila envelope instead, opened it, and pulled out a sheaf of letters from other friends. With trembling fingers, I picked a letter from Alyssa out of the pile.

Sure, I'll keep an eye on Luke for you, Daisy. You be sure and keep an eye on Brad for me. Of course, I don't think I'm serious about him, but I want to make sure I have a date for the big New Year's Eve dance back at the club in Sawyer. I haven't met anybody nearly as cute as him here.

I ripped the letter to shreds and let the pieces drift to the floor, tears blinding my eyes. That Christmas Luke had given me his fraternity pin.

It was at the New Year's dance that Alyssa had snagged him to dance with her, again and again. Why hadn't I paid attention? I hated those dances anyhow, refusing to dress up in chiffon that itched and girdles that smooshed me in. Moo was okay with my vintage red velvet, but Alyssa eyed me with a superior air, wearing a demure blue satin gown and sparkly earrings. Best friends weren't supposed to have superior airs. Stargazer me didn't see the warning signs.

I kicked the box to one side.

Raj hadn't come back from taking the clothes downstairs. Wrung out and slathered with dust, I'd run out of things to do. I meandered down and washed my arms and face and applied some lipstick to please Moo. I found her in the kitchen.

"Ah, there you are, Daisy." My mother was busy with a length of fabric, draping and tucking on Raj. More fabric lay on the kitchen table, along with sequins and spangles.

"I see you're going ahead with this silly project," I said.

"It's not silly," announced Raj, now thoroughly on board.

"Moo," I said, "I've been waiting all morning to ask you this. Do you have any idea if Pop is near the Gulf Coast now? Surely he's called you, something?"

"All I know is, he just sent me a check from Biloxi. He may still be there, he may not. You know how gigs go."

"Actually, I don't. Don't you have a way to reach him?"

She shrugged. "I cancelled his cell phone. One less bill to pay. He can find a phone if he wants to talk to me."

"I think you're both being very stubborn."

"I'm not going to ask him back, Daisy. He knows my conditions. When he's making enough to support me and the house both, he can come back."

It looked fairly hopeless.

Seventeen

How could I find Pop? If I didn't get him back here, I'd never get away from my mother's guilt trips and scheming. I needed to return to my relatively safe beach and sort of safe non-boyfriend.

The problem was, there wasn't a database anywhere of clubs that hired elderly crooners. I checked a few venues I found in Biloxi, but I came up empty. Moo said the check he'd sent her had been a personal check from the presumed club owner. Pop's CD, *A Blissful Heart*, was still listed on Amazon and a couple of other places. Like, um, eBay. He didn't have a website. A couple of old real estate listings that still carried his name slapped me in the face.

I concluded Pop wasn't a headliner anywhere but an opening act, a piano player, a vocalist mentioned in small type, an aging Josh Groban baritone belting out Italian arias, crooning Tony Bennett songs to well-seasoned Romeos and vintage chicks out on Match.com dates.

Moo was no help at all. In fact, to my consternation, she informed me that the séance she'd planned was happening this very evening at eight o'clock. I once again pleaded for her to uninvite Luke, or at least call off the séance. Moo, concentrating on the cutting and pinning of Raj's costume, was having none of it.

"Of course I won't. Lally knows he's coming. I can't uninvite the others and ruin my business. And the spirits? Perhaps they're expecting to be summoned. Now why don't you go and dust the séance room? Vacuum the carpets to make sure there's no sneaky plaster dust we overlooked. And what about Bogart? Make sure he's happy. Does he need feeding or something? And what do you feed him, anyway?"

"Um," I said.

"He doesn't need feeding much, Miss Essie," Raj volunteered. "Once or twice a week is fine. He had a mouse before we left."

"Mouse."

"Yes, Miss Essie."

Moo knit her brows, considered the problem a moment, and then brightened. "Well, we can solve two problems, it seems. There are mice under the house, Daisy. There are some traps out in the garden shed. Humane traps, of course. I just haven't been able to bring myself to set them.

Of course, if I knew the mice were going to a good cause . . ."

"Moo, I respectfully point out that the mouse is doomed anyhow. Very few die of old age. Some critter's going to have it for lunch."

She waved her hand. "Nature is nature; we humans don't have to be cruel."

I found the traps where she'd said, made my way under the house, and set them, halfway hoping they wouldn't work. But the big guy had to eat. Did anyone ever try him on hamburger meat?

Raj, while we were tidying the séance room, told me Bogart preferred meat that was undead, though it was best to kill the prey so it wouldn't fight back. To avoid hearing more details about snake feeding, I glanced up from rubbing the credenza with Pledge and casually mentioned the letter from India.

"You didn't really throw it away, did you?" I asked. "Not the letter from your father."

He squirted some Windex on Moo's crystal ball and rubbed it clean, then tried to see his reflection in it. He shrugged. "How does this look? Is it shiny enough?"

"It's fine. You're doing a good job. Did your mama ever write to him, your father? I mean, in the past."

"I don't know. Have you heard from her yet?" He looked around for something else to squirt, and I didn't like the way he was looking at me.

"No, Raj," I told him. "Your aunt Luz has promised to call the minute she hears from her." I didn't want to tell him she was in the hospital, not yet.

Raj set the cloth and bottle down on the table and looked down. "Mama told me . . . she told me we might be moving again. I hope she didn't go without me," he finally blurted.

"Oh, no," I said. "No, she would never do that. She loves you very much." I felt that was true, but right now her going anywhere wasn't an option.

"What are you thinking about, Daisy? You look so serious."

I plugged in the Hoover. "I'm thinking about the séance tonight. Please make sure that Bogart's put away beforehand. You may *not* drape him over your shoulders. There's no point in freaking out the guests."

He scuffed his toe. "I still don't see why . . ."

"Yes, you do, you stubborn boy," I said. "Is your outfit ready? Are you sure you want to wear it?"

"Yes! Let me go ask Miss Essie!"

He scampered on out, leaving the Windex and cloths on the former billiard table, cleverly concealed with a plywood top and a long maroon velveteen cloth that Moo had trimmed with cream-colored fringe. I powered up and Hoovered away, hoping I wasn't sucking up any necessary ectoplasm.

In a few minutes Raj was back at the door, suitably arrayed. I had to admit he looked every inch a maharajah.

"Now put away your cleaning supplies, your royal highness," I said.

In reply he stuck his tongue out at me. I pretended to swat him. We were both laughing hysterically when Moo showed up.

"I'm glad you're both so positive about this," she beamed. "We're going to have a great time tonight."

Eighteen

No pay, no séance. Ten minutes before eight o'clock, Moo stationed me at the door to collect the money. Sixty dollars seemed a little steep, but I thought about the falling plaster.

A girl of about twenty with red-rimmed eyes, who wore tight jeans and midriff top, her pale, pale hair cut in the chewed-off mode, was the first to hand me her money. She didn't introduce herself but pressed three twenty-dollar bills into my hand.

Colonel Anderson, a tall, bald widower with an iron-gray mustache, strode up the walk on the other end of a dog leash, snapped three crisp twenties out of his billfold, and handed them over. "I remember you, Daisy," he said. "Not like your brother, were you?" He handed me the leash of a huge German shepherd smelling mightily of canine, who rolled his eyes and pricked up his ears at me.

"What am I supposed to do with this dog?" I knew Moo wouldn't allow animals in the séance room.

"Just tie Rufus to a post," said the colonel. "He's trained to wait."

The colonel walked off. I flailed around looking for a post and finally tied Rufus, thankfully older than he looked on first viewing, to a porch railing, praying it wasn't rotten. Rufus half relaxed and put his nose between his paws, keeping a lookout.

An ancient Cadillac pulled up with Mrs. Ida Jane Pike, a lady I couldn't ever remember being young. She pulled a cane out of the back and hobbled down the walk in Minnie-Mouse-looking shoes.

She paid with numerous five-dollar bills.

Five minutes later Jonah and Penelope Quill, who owned the town's only bookstore, The Quill Pen, came hurrying down the sidewalk. My gosh, the town skeptics had arrived. Everyone knew Jonah had been a heathen until Penelope dragged him to the Episcopal Church to spite her old mother, a Primitive Baptist who'd been against the marriage. Jonah handed me a check for $120.

It was almost eight o'clock. Had Moo really asked Luke? He hadn't said anything about coming when he'd stopped by earlier. I left the door to see if Moo meant to go ahead without him.

Raj, now in jeweled turban—I recognized one of Moo's old brooches—to go with his pantaloons and vest, looked like a character from the Arabian Nights. He stood, arms folded, a serious smile on his face, beside Moo's ornately carved throne with its maroon plush seat.

The female clients were murmuring their appreciation and admiration. I had to hand it to my mother. It was a grand piece of showmanship.

"Madame," I said, as I'd been instructed to refer to Moo in the presence of clients, "is everyone here? Shall I be seated?"

"No, Miss Aggie's always late," said Moo. She didn't say anything about Luke. I wasn't going to ask, that was for sure.

I returned to the front door just in time to see Miss Aggie, the lady who'd tried to teach me piano, hurry up the walk, Einstein-electric hair flying in all directions. That hadn't changed. She shrieked when she saw me and enveloped me in a bear hug. "What are you doing with your music, girl?"

"Miss Aggie," I replied, with as straight a face as I could muster, "I work in the entertainment field."

A broad smile spread across Miss Aggie's face, and she pinched my cheeks between piano-hardened fingers. "I always knew you could do it."

Huh. I seemed to recall hand-wringing and advice to take up archaeology instead. Oddly enough, Miss Aggie hadn't kicked me out. Maybe Pop had paid her extra to keep me on. He firmly felt that teaching me might strain the father-daughter relationship. He was wise.

After Miss Aggie had flown back to the séance room, arms swinging, I counted the money. If Moo could increase the clientele to a séance every week, and maybe have a promotion to draw in more customers (how much did an ad in the Sawyer *Buzz* cost?), maybe she could really make some money.

Hey, wait. I was supposed to be talking her out of this foolishness.

I closed the front door, haunted only by the person who had not come.

I was glad he hadn't showed up. Wasn't I?

I edged into the séance room and took my place at the table next to Miss Aggie, who smiled and patted my hand. The one empty seat was on her other side.

Raj, in his turban, presided beside Moo on a kitchen stool, holding her crystal ball in his hands, capturing all eyes. In the background, sitar music wafted from the stereo, not unlike the kind that Lorelei used to dance to. But what was that sneaky little smile playing across Raj's face? Then it disappeared, replaced by a haughty expression.

Moo, her long, unbound gray hair secured with a cerise scarf, her long black dress draped with a purple shawl embroidered with brilliant orange flowers, beamed at the assembled group. Amid layers of necklaces she fingered a huge moonstone.

"It's time to begin," she said, "but I feel a disturbance in the atmosphere." She slowly took the ball from Raj and fitted it into the wooden stand in front of her.

Just then the doorbell rang.

"Ah. That was it," she said. "One of our number was in transit." She rose from her seat and glided gracefully toward the door. She returned with Luke McDuffie in tow.

Miss Aggie absolutely bubbled when she saw him and moved to the empty chair to give him a space next to me.

"Oh, Miss Aggie, you didn't have to move," I murmured and bit my lip. That was what I hated about small towns. The whole dingdong population of the town knew that Luke and I had been high school sweethearts. They probably all knew that we were both now unattached.

"We meet again." Luke winked at me.

"So we do," I said coolly, my serious expression suitable to the proceedings at hand. As far as I knew the spirits were not famous for a sense of humor.

"You don't believe in all this, do you?" he murmured.

I straightened in my chair. "If you don't, then why did you come?"

"Your mother asked me. And I wanted to see you."

Moo, excuse me, Madame, said, "Silence, please." She clapped her hands.

The room quieted and dimmed, except for the single lit candle behind Madame Esmeralda's crystal ball.

"Neat trick," whispered Luke. "But no mystery."

"Silence, please," said Moo again, looking directly at Luke. "The psychic energies cannot be received where there is doubt."

She sat very straight, her hands folded, eyes closed, until the room became completely still. I could hear the dripping of the faucet in the kitchen and the ticking of the old grandfather clock in the hall. And Luke's breathing beside me. I felt heat radiating from his body. I smelled his after-shave, which hit me in the solar plexus of memory. I closed my eyes and tried regular breathing. In to a count of four, out to a count of four . . .

Moo placed her hands on the crystal ball and gazed into its depths. Then she began a sort of mystical chant. What with the regular breathing and the chanting, I felt hypnotized, lulled, and as the mood in the room liquefied, I relaxed. I forgot that Luke was there beside me.

Sound, warmth, flickering candles. I was feeling sleepy, very sleepy. And then a sound broke through the fuzziness, a bumping, perhaps, from the credenza behind me. More of Moo's tricks. The spirits were on the move.

I opened my eyes and glanced at Moo. Her eyes were still closed, her hands on the ball. Raj, on his kitchen stool, broke his superior look just for a moment as he glanced at the credenza, and then he whipped his eyes straight ahead. Was she having the boy help her hoodwink the customers? I felt a flush spreading up to my cheeks. Luke would rag me after this was over. When would she start talking to the spirits, or psychic energies, or whatever name they went by?

I glanced across the table at the shadowy faces. Some stared straight ahead, some had eyes closed, some looked apprehensive, expectant. All were still and quiet.

I glanced back behind me, trying to pinpoint the sound. The credenza door was ajar. I was tempted to close it but couldn't without leaning back behind Luke and drawing attention to myself, or perhaps ruining Moo's trick. I bit my lip.

Moo opened her eyes. The single candle in the middle of the former pool table flickered, drawing shapes out of the crystal ball, casting watery shimmering patterns on the ceiling.

"Now, *everyone* close your eyes," Madame told us assembled souls. She waited for the rest of us to comply and then said, in a voice I had never heard before, "Seekers, what questions do you have?"

The first came from Brandi, the young woman in jeans, who began to sob, and through the sobs asked her question: "Have you seen Heath? Does he have any message for me?"

Moo hummed and murmured, "Heath has just recently arrived on this plane, and his astral body is not yet strong enough to send messages. He is still feeling his way through undifferentiated matter. But he longs for you. I can feel that."

The girl sat back, relaxed, tears dried. Luke leaned toward me and murmured, "Wreck on the interstate. Going a hundred."

The group sat in silence. "Another question?" Moo asked gently.

"Do you have a message from my dear mother?" This came from Miss Aggie, whose mother had died a month or so before at the age of ninety-nine, thus cheating Miss Aggie out of having a hundredth birthday party for her.

Madame hesitated a full minute, humming, while the clock ticked, the faucet dripped, and faint scraping noises came from behind me. Then Madame said, "Eunice says you must follow your heart."

"What? She never said that while she was alive," quavered Miss Aggie.

Moo passed her hand over the ball, peered into its depths. She sat silent, listening, as though someone were speaking to her. "Eunice says that she has gained in understanding since she lost her physical body. She says that she never should have opposed your marrying Otis Doolittle all those years ago, and now that he is widowed, you must tell him yes."

Miss Aggie burst into tears. "Thank you, Madame." She sniffed and wiped her eyes. "Though it might give him a heart attack when I tell him."

Luke mumbled something under his breath, and I kicked him. "I'm not talking to *you*," he whispered to me.

"Quiet!" Madame said. I strained to see her in the flickering candlelight. Her shadowed face was a study in concentration. "I see . . . blobs of whiteness . . . no clear picture . . . interference . . . someone is trying to come through . . . someone is trying to enter this plane . . . not successful."

The room quieted down to ponder the interference. At that moment I heard another round of the thumping, then a rustling. People began to murmur.

"The spirits are restless," said Moo, back in her own voice. I was aware of something moving very near my chair. I stealthily slipped my hand down the side of the chair. I grabbed something alive. Luke's ankle.

"Why, Daisy," he whispered. "I didn't know you cared."

"I'm looking for a snake." I tried to keep my voice low.

"She hissed," Luke said.

"Silence," said Madame.

"Did she say *snake*?" Ida Jane Pike shriek-whispered.

"Raj?" I murmured. "Where is Bogart?" He would not meet my eyes but concentrated on the candle.

Chairs scraped uneasily. "Is Bogart a spirit?" Penelope Quill wanted to know. "Are we talking to Humphrey?"

"Spit!!" Luke's knee jerked up and banged the table. "Ow! That thing crawled across my foot." He pushed his chair back, revealing a serpentine form trying to escape. "What's that damn snake doing here?"

The women, every one of them, screamed.

Colonel Anderson leaped up, flipped the light switch, and rushed around the table toward us. Mrs. Ida Jane Pike fainted, and Jonah Quill grabbed a piece of paper and began to fan her brow. Col. Anderson whipped out a handgun and pointed it at Bogart.

"No!" Raj and I cried simultaneously. He left his perch and ran to the snake, covering it with his small body. "Don't shoot!"

I must say, Madame was magnificent. She stood and extended her arms. "Peace," she intoned. "Peace. A momentary interruption. A mere serpent, not dangerous. It is the sign of Nag, the symbol of fertility. Daisy and Luke, please leave the séance room and take the serpent with you."

My face flamed. Did she realize what she'd *said*? Take the symbol of fertility with us?

"Let me take him out," Raj said stubbornly.

"I'll do it," said Luke. "Raj, get up."

Raj unfolded himself from the snake and stood. Luke, surprising the bejeezus out of me, picked up the snake like a pro. Limping, he carried it out. I followed him, hearing Moo admonish the Colonel for bringing a weapon into the séance room.

I found the box on the back porch and deposited Bogart. "Poor baby," I said.

Luke looked at me skeptically. "Poor baby? You might show a little concern for me as well as that snake."

"Are you okay?" I said. "Did he bite you?"

"I'm not bitten, Daisy, but I think I've dislocated my knee."

I looked at him. He did seem to be in some pain, and my heart softened a bit. "I'm sorry, Luke," I said. "Let me see your knee. Maybe we should put some ice on it."

"That's all right," he said, straightening.

"Don't play the wounded hero. Please sit down and let me look at your injury." I pointed to a kitchen chair.

Luke grinned. "Yes, ma'am." He'd come in slim jeans, impossible to roll up that far. "Shall I take them off right here?"

"That's not necessary," I said stiffly. "I'll just put ice on top." I filled a plastic bag with ice cubes and wrapped a flowered linen dishtowel around it.

"Now prop your leg on that other chair."

He smiled wickedly. "Yes, ma'am."

I tucked a cushion under the propped leg, conscious of the heat of his skin.

As I bent to place the ice-filled towel on his knee, he took my wrist and gently pulled me to him and, too mesmerized to pull away, I let him kiss me. Long and hard. And hungry.

I pulled back, tingling all over. My body, letting me down at a time like this! It wasn't supposed to *respond*.

Luke gazed at my T-shirt, too thin to hide the pertness underneath. He smiled. "Daisy, Daisy," he said. "That was *our* pool table, wasn't it? Doesn't that bring back memories?"

"Not especially," I said, angry at myself. "Most of the games I played there were pretty boring."

"Daisy..."

"I don't want to think about it, Luke."

"After all these years, do you still hate me?"

"I should, Luke. You betrayed me. There were times when I'd have wished Bogart had been a cobra and sunk his fangs deep. But no, I don't hate you."

"There's some little part of you that still remembers," he said softly. "For a few seconds there you kissed me back."

"Stupid of me. And rude of you to grab me."

"I'm sorry. Truly."

For a moment no one said anything and then I had to say it, had to ask him the question I hadn't ever wanted to ask him, because I was sure he had no answer that I would like. "Why did you marry Alyssa, Luke?"

"It's a long story." He looked down. "I wanted to explain, but you wouldn't let me." Then he looked into my face, and his eyes were serious. "Come out and have a beer with me. Let's talk. It's been *nineteen years.*"

Why should I? Just so he could explain how much he had loved her? I didn't want to hear it. "I think you'd better go."

He took the ice bag off his knee and handed it to me. "I don't think my knee's dislocated or anything. It's really nothing."

I had heard that thwack, and it sounded painful. "Do you think you ought to have it X-rayed?"

He shook his head and picked up his leather jacket off the chair. "If it still hurts tomorrow, maybe." He got up and put on his jacket. "I just wish you'd sit down and listen to me for once, Daisy."

"Why? So you can justify yourself? No thanks."

He gave me a troubled look, then turned slowly and walked away, out of the kitchen, down the hall, on the way out of my house, on the way out of my life. For the second time.

I stood by the kitchen chair, the bag of ice dripping freezing cold drops on my foot, and listened to the uneven tread, the limping sound of Luke's Nikes on Moo's wide wooden hall. The door latch clicked softly.

The telephone on the counter, flanked by its message pad, its cup of pens and pencils, stared at me, silent and unringing. No call from Lorelei's sister. No call from Hoagie.

I could stay here and wait for the phone to kick-start the process to deliver me back to the beach, or I could go back into the séance room.

I didn't want to do either. Suddenly, I wanted to know the truth, even if it was painful. I wanted to get to the bottom of what had happened. I was ready to let him tell me things I didn't want to hear.

I ran out the door and caught Luke just as he was getting into his navy blue Beemer.

Smiling, he opened the door for me.

Nineteen

Luke headed out to the highway, out past the Burger Shop, past the strip mall by the river. I watched the soft, warm night glide past me, carrying all the familiar landmarks I knew so well. So familiar, yet now so strange. To my eyes they were the same, but to my heart the magic they'd promised as a child, when every creek or bridge or stand of trees against the skyline held mystery, had vanished.

Luke, laid-back, piloted the car half-smiling. Why not? He was in his territory, a territory not mine any longer. He talked about Earl Hall, how he was making a success of his father's construction business. Earl's super coolness in school had made adults peg him for the life of a slacker. They'd been wrong.

"Earl thinks you're quite a looker, Daisy," Luke said.

"As opposed to high school, you mean? When I was the class hippie in the days of preppy, when everybody had little polo players on their lavender Polo shirts?"

"I always thought you were beautiful," said Luke.

"Luke. Stop it."

"Stop what? I'm only speaking the truth."

I fell quiet for another couple of miles down the dark familiar highway, feeling the strangeness of being here with him, and yet so natural, as though the years had never passed. It was the naturalness that bothered me. Luke turned into a roadhouse out on the highway, one built of dark timbers, glowing blue and red with neon signs. It hadn't been there those years ago when Luke had loved me. Maybe I'd never noticed.

"It's not the country club," he said, "but it'll do."

I had to laugh. "Luke, I'm a long way from country club dances. I hustle drinks for a living and the rest of the time I hang out on the beach. And you? The model citizen? I guess you play a lot of golf."

There in the neon glow he looked at me. "Less than you might imagine. Maybe we're not as different as you think."

He walked around and opened my door. He took my hand to help me out. It seemed nice, somehow. Old-fashioned in a way I'd had forgotten about. Cared for. Respected.

My ex-husband, Harvey the professor-artist, had not opened doors. He'd called himself a feminist, and said he was all for equality. It took a while for me to understand what equality in a marriage meant to him—it didn't mean the end of men doing men's work and women doing women's work. It meant the woman doing it all.

We walked through the door into smoke and darkness, conversational hum, and barbecue tang. Luke guided me to a knotty pine booth near the back, not far from the old-fashioned Wurlitzer juke box. Its pink and green bubbles looked almost out of place among the wooden walls, the Western gear, and the red imitation leather upholstery.

A waitress whose name tag read Misty, her lank yellow hair caught up in a ponytail, took our order for beer. I could tell she was new by the way she stared at the order, brows scrunched, lips pursed, as though she was memorizing it. I smiled at her in solidarity and thought of Mr. Kapolnik.

When two tall glasses sat foaming in front of us, Luke took a swallow. "So are you happy, beach bunny?"

Was I happy? I didn't know.

I let the silence hang there while some lyin' cheatin' music slipped comfortably out of the jukebox and across the floor. I fingered the side of the frosted glass, tracing a snakelike pattern up and down. I twisted the trace line back upon itself, making seaworthy knots. Was I happy?

I managed a wry smile. "Well, Luke, do you mean am I happy now, in this place with you, or was I happy before I wound up looking after a little boy, a snake, and a mother who communes with the spirits? I didn't have money, but then I didn't have any responsibilities, either. Isn't that what's meant by nirvana?"

Luke gave me a sideways glance. "That doesn't sound like the Daisy I used to know."

I cocked my head sideways. "Maybe she wised up. And what happened to the Luke I knew? The idealist? The one who was going to the Peace Corps, then law school, then into politics to change the world?"

He shifted uncomfortably and clasped his hands together on the table in front of him. He studied me, maybe looking for some sign I'd understand.

"Okay. That first year at Westbury, it was hard being away from you, but I got a lot of studying done. The second year, Alyssa came. Since she was your best friend, I hung out with her some, introduced her to some of my friends."

I closed my eyes, remembering. "Yes. I told her to keep an eye on you."

He looked down and fiddled with his paper napkin. "She started seeing a buddy of mine, a pre-med, but he told me he thought she was dating somebody else too and he lost interest in competing. I forgot all about that for a few months, and then out of nowhere she called me.

"She was having trouble with philosophy class and she asked me to help her study since I'd done well in it. You know how hard she's always worked. She's never been satisfied with less than a 4.0."

"How well I know. An overachiever, always. I was helping her in high school and she made valedictorian."

He chuckled. "You were always such a rebel, Daisy. You could have had that 4.0 if you'd wanted."

"Nobody would've noticed. The golden child position was already taken by Gordon."

Misty came by and asked if we wanted refills. We did. She gave us a little glance when she walked off, as though she couldn't quite figure us out.

Luke shook his head. "Lissy confessed one night how guilty she felt because she'd fallen in love with me. She seemed all shook up about it. I hugged her and told her I understood, and . . . well . . . it got out of hand."

I put my head in my hands. "I don't want to hear any more. Let me guess. It went on. You didn't tell me. And then shotgun, right? What a cliché, Luke."

"No, Daisy. No. I was careful."

"Worse, then?"

"Much worse."

"That's all I can stomach right now."

"Let's dance," he said.

Faith Hill's voice soared from the jukebox speakers. The first time I'd heard that theme from *Pearl Harbor* at work I'd gotten all choked up. Now it was just background music, the soundtrack to this little tragedy.

We danced slowly around the room. Nostalgia washed over me in waves, though I tried hard to hold it back. How could I, when our hearts beat so close together, when the scent of him was the same, that scent with its hint of piracy, of ships and spices from Samarkand, of ancient wood? He kissed my cheek.

"Luke, don't." I felt eyes on us from every corner of the room, that small-town feeling of being watched.

"Daisy," he said, "I've never forgotten you."

I raised my eyes to his and wished I hadn't. That kiss had kindled a spark inside me that now threatened to fan into flame. I couldn't let that happen. "Luke," I said, swishing a damp strand of hair from my cheek, "we'd better finish our beer and go."

"I'm not getting any place, am I?"

We went back to our booth and sipped in silence.

Luke spent a few minutes doodling on a napkin with his pen. Finally, he looked up and said, "What about you? What's happened to you all these years?"

How could I tell him how I'd taken my art degree and my broken heart to the city, asking it to heal my wounds? Instead, I said I'd worked for a decorator for a while. Got my license. Did up a couple of big houses. Married the man in one of them and had a well-upholstered life for about a year or so, before I found out that he was AC/DC. Shane was fun to be with, but that kind of life didn't work for me. He might have told me first, you know?

Went back to school thinking I might try graphic art to earn a living. Met a professor, divorced, a good bit older. Married him on the rebound, hoping to undo my mistake. Worked in a gallery, trying to promote his artwork. After all, he was the established artist and couldn't be bothered with the mundane details of life. Found out his roaming ways.

No children, of course. He already had three children from his other two wives and didn't want any more. I stuck this marriage out nearly five years, hating to admit I'd made another mistake. I saved a little money, planning my escape, and then I was footloose again. I knew however long I perched, I had to keep moving, traveling with very little baggage.

I looked at Luke and didn't like the way he was looking at me, frowning and smiling, like he was trying to understand. I didn't want him to feel sorry for me, and I didn't like his attitude. I just said, "In conclusion, I made a few mistakes. I was happy at the beach until all this happened."

Luke reached across the table and picked up my hand. He began to count my fingers the way he used to do. "That just doesn't sound like you, Daisy. I remember when we were going to change the world together. We talked about making it into a good place for our kids. Buying the world a Coke. What's happened to you? What happened to your ideals? You've just been drifting."

I had forgotten about that me. I kind of missed her. And the Luke that used to be.

"Your way doesn't seem to have worked, either, Luke. How funny. You've changed into someone I'm not sure I like."

"Daisy, don't be bitter. You were always kind. That's part of why I loved you."

I wasn't kind anymore? I softened my voice. "I see bitterness in you, Luke, but you're trying hard to hide it underneath that cool exterior."

We were quiet for a long time after that, listening to the jukebox, to the songs of love and loneliness, of empty nights at the end of long hard roads. I felt at a loss for words, not wanting to say what was on my mind.

Finally Luke called for the check, and when the waitress set it in front of us, I could read the look on her face. It said: *That customer looks disappointed. The evening's not gone well for him. I hope he remembers to leave a tip.*

As we got up to leave, I noticed the napkin Luke had doodled on. It was a schoolboy's heart, with LUKE + DAISY written inside. An arrow pierced it. My hand went out to pick it up and then dropped by my side. When he wasn't looking, I slipped the napkin into my pocket. Just so nobody else would see it.

We pulled up in front of the house in silence. All the windows were dark except the ones of Moo's bedroom. I gathered up my bag. "Everybody's gone," I said.

Luke turned off the car and turned to me. "Daisy, I never stopped loving you."

"Now you tell me? You think you can start everything up again, just like that? Do you think we're the same people, those people that were so much in love and going to do great things? Look at you. A stuffed shirt. Look at me. A burned-out beach bum. What on earth could we possibly have in common?"

"More than you can see right now," he said.

"Luke, I'm never going to come back to Sawyer to live, and you're never going to leave. You're nineteen years too late!" I threw open my door, leaped out of the car, and ran into the house.

Twenty

"Moo!" I called. I wanted my mommy. Moo was sitting up in bed reading, wearing a red silk dressing gown embroidered with dragons. Her hair was done up in rag curlers.

She put the book, an Agatha Christie, face down on the comforter when I came into her room. "Nothing like a good murder to make you sleep well," she said. "Of course, it must be in the past." She patted the bed for me to sit, and I plopped down with a sigh.

Before I could dump my woes, Moo said, "It's nice that you've been out with Luke, Daisy. That young man is not happy. He never has been. And just think, Alyssa going off and leaving him with those girls! He had to hire a nanny . . ."

I shook my head. "All I've been hearing from Gordon is that he and Alyssa were the model couple."

"Gordon can't see auras, dear, and I can."

"Why didn't you tell me?"

"I didn't want to stir up trouble. You were always with some new husband, anyhow. You've had two, more than your fair share."

I stared at her. "Moo, what a notion."

She shrugged. "I wasn't surprised that Luke came tonight, though I knew he'd be too much of a skeptic to get much out of the séance. He doesn't approve of Lally's consulting me, you know. I hope you'll see him again."

"I have no intention of seeing Luke again, Moo. It was just a crazy impulse that made me go with him." After a minute I said, "Why does Mrs. McDuffie come to see you?"

"Well, I shouldn't tell you this, Daisy. You're not to mention it to anyone except Luke, who knows it. She's positive she lived before, and she's trying to communicate with her predecessor."

"Does she know who she is?"

"She feels she worked in some sort of circus."

"What?" The thought of the proper Mrs. McDuffie as a circus . . . what? Fortune-teller? Aerialist?

"Have you found this . . . circus performer?"

"No, but I know we will, eventually."

"Moo, that's crazy."

"A lot of life is crazy, Daisy. But it's good crazy, rather than bad crazy. Don't be so quick to judge."

"Mrs. McDuffie in the circus? Maybe that was the secret desire she had to squelch to please the world she had to live in. Moo, you know very well you're somewhat of a psychologist. You're telling people what they want to hear."

Moo gave me a wounded look. "Daisy, surely you wouldn't think that of me. I never know what the spirits are going to say."

This conversation could reach no good conclusion. I sighed. "Where's Raj?"

"Gone to bed, of course. I told him he had been very naughty, and all he did was giggle. But you can't stay mad at that child."

"He needs his mama," I said. "I've just got to find her. I hope she hasn't . . ." I thought of the spirit trying to come through, right before Bogart interrupted the connection.

I looked over at Moo's dresser and there was a picture of my father before he went bananas. He was a jovial man, my father, wavy white hair framing his hearty handsome face, a striking, operatic face, in contrast with my mother, who had always been the unnoticeable one. Until now.

"Moo," I said, "come on. Why can't you use your powers, if you have them, to find Pop? Or at least have one of those spirits to tell him to call us?"

"Oh, Daisy." She wouldn't look at me.

I looked over and saw his CD, *A Blissful Heart*, on the dresser, next to her Bose CD radio. I picked it up and read the list of songs. The hymns and opera pieces, I'd expected, but a Josh Groban hit was here, along with two of Michael Crawford's. "He does Michael Crawford?"

"Yes," she said. "Your father is very good, after all, despite his lack of common sense. A fabulous voice. Raj was in here listening to him earlier. He sang along with *Memories* and asked oh so many questions."

Moo's face was aglow. She still loved Pop and wouldn't admit it.

Twenty-one

The phone downstairs kept ringing and ringing, jolting me out of a dream.

I lay still, getting my bearings. Luke had been in that dream. He was driving me on a dry, dusty road out west. We'd stopped because Indian pottery was blocking the road and we couldn't get our car through unless we moved all those pots—pots glazed with blue and pots of plain terracotta, jugs with handles, cement urns like Lorelei made to hold her bug-eating plants.

What did it mean, the pottery? The vision evaporated before I could grasp it. I heard Moo downstairs, answering the phone, talking to someone.

Her voice floated up the stairs. "Daisy, it's for you." I groped around for my old Mickey Mouse phone before I remembered that I'd taken it with me when I moved from home. I couldn't find it when I left Shane. He'd probably given it to one of his new loves.

I slid out of bed and pulled on the white wrapper. "Coming," I yelled, not bothering to search for my flip-flops.

I peeked into Raj's room on my way down. The boy lay on his back, one arm flung across the pillow. What was I going to do with him? And that snake? I still couldn't get used to that thing. I did not want a snake. I had never wanted a snake.

The voice on the phone sounded crackly and far away. "Daisy? It's Lorelei." I didn't like the weak way she sounded. Gone was the old bravado, the old confidence. Her words came slowly.

"How are you?" I asked, my annoyance gone. "Are you still in the hospital in New Orleans?"

"How . . . did you . . . know?"

"I saw a news piece on the Internet. Were you really smashing cemetery urns?"

"Daisy . . . no time to esplain . . . I woke from coma . . . they say my head needs surgery if I don't get better. They told me . . . I can see my boy one last time . . . in case I don't make it."

Not make it? A cold shiver pierced me from head to foot.

"What can I do, Lorelei?"

"Bring him here, Daisy. Bring him . . . please."

Let this cup pass from me. Some echo of my days in church. And Luz and Ricky could not be called upon, not at this stage. It was up to me.

"Can I call you back?"

"Soon. Call soon. Please, Daisy."

I had no choice. I told her I would call her as soon as I worked things out.

I hung up the phone just as Raj wandered sleepily into the kitchen looking for breakfast. "Did Mama call?" he asked. "Can I talk to her?"

"She didn't want to wake you," I said, my heart thumping way out of tune. "She had to go."

I hunkered down to the floor and looked in his eyes. "She loves you very much," I said, my heart in my throat. "We'll talk to her soon."

Moo and I had to discuss a few things, and I finally had to shoo Raj outside to play, telling him I'd let him know when it was time to talk to his mother. I didn't want him to overhear. I told Moo what I had in mind. She put her hands on her hips like a fishwife in a stage production and gave me, well, a fish eye. "You want to take that boy *where*?"

"New Orleans, Moo. That's where his mother is. She wants to see him before she goes into surgery." I told her about the cemetery urns and the escape from custody.

Soom we were sitting at the kitchen table drinking some of that delicious tea she brewed. I was feeling mellower about the whole thing. A trip to New Orleans would get me out of Luke's radar range. What I was going to do with Raj after that was something hazy in the distance.

"I won't have it," Moo grumbled. "She's not thinking of the child's best interest. Will there be a policeman there? Will Raj know his mother's a thief?"

"But she wants her son, Moo. She might die."

Moo tapped her fingers on the table and got a faraway look. "It might be better if he just thought she died in an accident instead of finding out she's a criminal."

"Moo, you're reverting to being a small-town mom. Where's Madame Esmeralda?"

"Where's the beach bum?" she countered.

Against her words, her face was the picture of grandmotherly concern. Still, she wasn't exactly being altruistic in wanting to keep Raj here a while longer. The phone had been ringing off the hook with people wanting to come to her next séance. They'd heard about the darling boy in the turban helping her, the one with the snake. It all seemed so terribly exotic.

And of course there were Luke and me to fire up the gossip mill among the crowd sitting around the bar at the Bisons Club. When you live in a small town like Sawyer, you have to take what excitement you can get.

The phone rang again. I grabbed for it, hoping it wasn't the NOPD or the hospital.

"Daisy?

"Hello, Luke." I tried to sound blasé, but my heart bumped in my chest like some poltergeist in the attic.

Luke sounded as tickled as if he'd put another garter snake down my top. "I've got some wonderful news, Daisy, and I'd like to take you and your mother, and Raj, of course, out to lunch to celebrate."

"What is it? What's the news?"

"One certificate I told you about—it's good. In fact, great."

"Which one?"

"I'd like to wait and tell you at lunch."

"Luke, I'm not sure . . ."

Moo had just begun to mix up something in a big tan earthenware bowl. "Is he inviting us to lunch? Tell him yes."

What? "How did you know, Moo?"

She shrugged. "I'm psychic. Now tell him yes."

I met Moo's eyes, pleading No, but she was having none of it. She wrested the phone from me with a flour-encrusted hand. "Hello, Luke. What time do you want us to meet you? Ma Hopkins' at 12:30? Fine."

"Why Ma Hopkins'?" I wailed when she'd hung up. "Half of Sawyer will be there!" My choice would've been one of the trendier places out on the highway, with a food bar and tourists and traveling salesmen I didn't know.

"What do we have to hide from, Daisy?"

I sighed and went over to look in the bowl, full of some tan glop that had little dark things in it. It had a wonderful smell. "Cookies?" I looked at her in disbelief. "You haven't made cookies in years!"

"I haven't had any little boys to eat them," she said. "Now run up and change, dear. "Look nice for that poor boy."

That poor boy? *Luke McDuffie?*

When the four of us—me in jeans, sneakers, and the cherry silk top; Raj in Gordon's old Sawyer High Band T-shirt; Luke in proper banker suit; and Moo in a trailing black dress and fringed rose-printed shawl—walked into the café, customers paused their forks. Their ears alerted like a room full of bird dogs. I felt I was in the middle of a surreal painting, something by René Magritte, in which I was surrounded by faces speaking with no words coming out, and the caption below read *This Is Not a Café*.

Somehow I greeted the people who spoke to me and ignored the sly glances of those who didn't as well as the knowing looks passed from person to person, any one of whom could have been my cousin many times removed.

Ma Hopkins' Café was neither trendy nor quaint. The basic lunchroom decor—chrome-legged chairs, yellow Formica tables, menus with plastic covers, heavy white divided plates—persisted no matter what party was in power. The people lunching there all knew Moo, and they all knew me, and of course they all knew Luke. And one or two, I swear, greeted Raj by name.

"Hop" Hopkins himself, in white apron, greeted us, motioned us to an empty table, and handed us menus.

"The country fried steak is on special today, Luke," he said, and winked.

Luke used to like country fried steak a long time ago. With mashed potatoes. With peas he'd scoop up and spoon into the center of the potato mound. I wished I didn't know that.

It didn't take long to make a decision. I ordered a vegetable plate and cornbread, as did Moo. Raj wanted a hamburger. "Should he have beef?" Moo asked.

"He hasn't been raised Hindu," I said.

"It doesn't seem right though," she said.

"Well," I said, "I see Mr. Goldberg over there eating the ham du jour. And I don't recall our having fish every Friday."

"We're Methodist," she said.

"But somewhere back there our ancestors weren't."

"We were Methodists when John Wesley was Episcopalian," said Moo haughtily.

"Church of England," I muttered.

"Country fried steak plate," said Luke. Hop had been standing there with his green pad poised the whole time, looking bemused.

He scribbled and went away, and in a few minutes his cousin Emma Jean, red-haired and pleasingly plump, brought our iced teas. Luke raised his glass. "To success. Are you ready for this?"

We all raised our glasses. "To success," Moo said, a giddy smile lighting her face.

Luke took a swallow of his tea and cleared his throat.

"Come on, come on, tell us," I grumbled. "I don't see why you couldn't have just told us on the phone."

"Well, it's like this," he said. "You know that one share of Haloid stock? The one you laughed about? The one where you asked if they made haloes?"

"I remember," I said, warmth creeping into my cheeks. I'd been so certain that was just another one of my grandpa's crazy investments.

"That company became Haloid Xerox in 1954," he said. "After a time they dropped the Haloid. Your shares are now worth over a million dollars."

"Sakes alive," said Moo.

I swallowed. "I guess we can tell Earl to go ahead and fix the house."

"Not yet," Luke said. "The stocks now belong to your father. We have to find him and convince him to sell."

"Does anyone have power of attorney?" I said desperately.

"Not me," said Moo.

"Not me," said Luke. "Gordon?"

"I don't think Pop ever thought about power of attorney," I blurted, hoping it wasn't Gordon who'd have to sign. "It just wouldn't be like him. He thinks he's invincible."

"I'd say omnipotent," Moo added, but a tug-of-war seemed to be playing out behind her eyes.

It came to me then. I leaned forward and said softly, "You know where he is, Moo, don't you? Why won't you tell us?"

She held her head high and shrugged, unrepentant. "I told him my conditions and, so far, he hasn't lived up to them."

"What conditions?" It was hard to keep from shouting at her.

She ignored me. "I've enjoyed being alone. He's so demanding, you know, such a prima donna. Or should that be primo don? And as far as singing here, I couldn't bear his making those used car commercials again. And I like learning to do for myself, you know? It's quite empowering."

Stubborn, stubborn, stubborn. "Can't you just tell him things have to change?" I asked.

"Those are my conditions," said Moo. "No commercials. No touring. Able to support us. He hasn't listened."

"Mrs. Harrison, I'll bet he'll listen to you now. I have a hunch he's finding out that life on the road isn't what he expected."

I stared at Luke, furious. He had no right to horn in on this family argument. But Moo was nodding!

"Look, people," I said, to break up the love fest between Luke and Moo. "I don't want to throw a shoe in the punch bowl, but . . ." I noticed that Raj was taking in every word, and I didn't want him to hear the real reason. Not yet.

"But what?" Luke said.

"But I just noticed that Raj has dirty hands. Look here," I said, addressing the boy. "You'll need to wash up before the food gets here."

He frowned and pouted. "I don't know where the restroom is."

Luke volunteered to walk him halfway, and in a minute he was back. "Okay, what do you need to tell us?"

I lowered my voice. "I heard from Lorelei. She has to have surgery in New Orleans. She's afraid and lonely and wants to see Raj in case she doesn't make it. I think she may be exaggerating, but what if she's not?"

Luke considered this. "What if it's all a trick?"

"She sounded pretty bad off," I replied. "And I think I ought to take him."

"And then what are you going to do?"

"I haven't gotten that far," I said. "You know me. I play life by ear. But I have to be back in Daytona in a week or so."

"Says who?" Moo raised an eyebrow.

"My boss. Otherwise my job's gone."

"I think your job ought to be finding your father," Luke said. "Otherwise, your mother can't afford to repair her house."

But the job in Paradise? My independence? My plan for a life of no responsibility?

"Why can't Gordon find Pop?" I pointed my fork at Moo. "I dare you to tell me he's too busy."

Nobody said anything for a long minute. Then Moo smiled. "You're so resourceful, Daisy, I know you can do it much faster."

My fork clattered to the mat.

Raj arrived back at the table with clean hands, settling into his chair just as Emma Jean arrived with the plates, pickled peppers, and Durkee's dressing. The food smelled perfect, and my mouth watered. I asked for another fork and got it.

Luke's plate held steak and gravy in one compartment, mashed potatoes and buttery peppered peas in the two others. Slaw came on the side. Mine and Moo's were heaped with squash casserole, turnip greens, black-eyed peas, and sliced tomatoes. Raj grinned and grabbed one of the crunchy thick-cut fries that crowded his juicy hamburger.

He took a big bite, swallowed it, washed it down with lemonade, and then turned to me.

"What were you talking about without me?"

"What do you mean?" I took a measured sip of tea, hoping I looked calm.

He dipped a French fry in a puddle of ketchup and ate it. "Mama always sent me out of the room when she didn't want me to hear her fighting with Vinny."

I could have said "nothing," but he'd have seen through it, and we needed to let him know about his mother. Maybe not just yet. I licked my lips and hoped I was saying the right thing. "Your mama wants to see you, and she wants me to bring you to New Orleans."

"Right now?" he asked.

I nodded. Luke lifted a square of cornbread, buttered it, and leaned toward me confidentially. "I just don't think you should go to New Orleans by yourself," he said. "I ought to go with you."

"What!" I screeched, the squash on my fork falling into my lap. I flailed at it with a paper napkin as heads at nearby tables turned.

Moo glanced sideways at me, paused with a forkful of peas and gave us a smile like a creamy-whiskered cat. "Why, that's a wonderful plan. Now I won't be so worried about you out on the highway in that awful old bus."

"Of course," said Luke. "I'll drive you in my car."

Ooh, that was tempting. "That won't work," I said. "We'd have to come back to get my bus. I'd rather go straight to Florida, because I'll have to take Raj back to his aunt and uncle. And I do have a job waiting."

"I'll buy you a new car, Daisy," Moo said eagerly. "We're going to be rich."

"We don't have the money yet," I reminded her.

"But you and that child in New Orleans alone! It's full of all sorts of partying people! You need a man along!"

"Moo, I can handle myself. I've met all sorts of partying people in my job."

"But your friend wound up . . ." Luke began.

"Hush," I said fiercely, glancing at Raj. "We'll discuss this later. Anyhow, I want to go back to Daytona afterwards."

He didn't hesitate. "I'll drive you in the . . . what is it? VW bus? Then I'll fly back."

That sounded like a wonderful plan to everyone but me. Emma Jean was pouring more tea, ears at the ready.

I waited until she had stepped away. "Sorry, Luke. No way."

Moo leaned forward, her chandelier earrings dangling. "Daisy, your stubbornness has slipped over your eyes. I'm telling you, you need a man along. You may find yourself in some seedy neighborhood. You just don't know."

"Moo, I'm not going to any seedy neighborhoods." Or into cemeteries to smash urns. Still, I was a little uneasy. My conclusions about the urns pointed toward Vinny Corvo, who was obviously out of prison. And I thought I'd seen Vinny outside my apartment. But I wasn't going to tell Moo this.

"There's another friend from Daytona who'll be there. A guy." I didn't look at Luke and crossed my fingers behind my back. I was hoping Hoagie would be there when we arrived, but I wasn't sure our paths would cross.

"Who?" Moo and Luke chorused.

"Hoagie works at the Paradise Bar, where I wait tables and Lorelei dances. He foolishly lent Lorelei his car, and he's on the way to collect it." I quit talking then, because it occurred to me that if Vinny managed to find out Hoagie was going to Lorelei, he would follow him.

"I'm going with you," Luke announced. He nodded at Moo. "And didn't you tell me Mr. Harrison sent you a check from Biloxi? We'll have to go through Biloxi anyhow, so I can call around and see if he's there. That's bank business, you know. The loan's in danger of being delinquent."

I was defeated and I knew it. But I wasn't going to take it lying down.

"We'll discuss this later," I said, "when half the town isn't listening."

Luke cocked one maddening eyebrow. "Guess who's coming in?"

I looked up, aghast to see my brother Gordon blustering into Ma Hopkins' in his khakis and blue blazer and school principal tie. He made his way over to our table and grabbed a chair from one of the other tables, wedging himself in beside Moo.

Hop came over. "What can I get for you, Gord? Tired of school hash?"

"For your information, we serve very tasty meals," Gordon said. " But a glass of sweet tea would be great. Sugar is so verboten these days. Mother, what's going on? I've heard you found some stock certificates in the attic."

I turned, wide-eyed, to Luke. "Did you call him?"

"I swear I didn't," he said, spreading his hands. "The walls have ears."

"Do you have Dad's power of attorney?" I said quickly.

"Of course not," he said. "Our father may be nuts, but he's not incapacitated."

We filled in Gordon the best we could while he swigged tea like he'd been trekking the Sahara. He mopped his brow. "Well. That takes a load off my mind, Mother, and I'm sure it does you too." He drained the glass. "Ah. That was so good." He looked around. "So restful in here. You can actually hear yourselves talk." Just then his cell phone rang. He flipped it open.

"Yes? What? What? They did *what*? Who left them in the lab unsupervised? *Evacuation*? I'll be right there."

He rose abruptly. "Got to go." He patted me on the shoulder. "I'm glad you're seeing it clear to come home and do your duty. Great to see you, Luke. We'll have to get together sometime for a drink. Sayonara." He gave Moo a kiss and then threaded his way back through the tables gracefully, swivel-hipping like a football player. Like a principal negotiating a corridor full of students.

We finished our meal talking about the weather. Emma Jean arrived, took our plates, and placed the dessert of the day, a hunk of whipped-cream-topped oozy cherry pie, in front of Moo.

Moo picked up her spoon. "One more thing, Daisy."

"What?" I snuck a look at Emma Jean to see if she was listening, but her experienced face was impassive as she set pie in front of Luke and Raj.

Moo pointed the spoon at me. "The snake goes with you."

Emma Jean hardly missed a beat. "Mrs. Harrison, you sure have an interesting life." She placed the last slice of cherry pie in front of me.

Twenty-two

How many men could arrange business matters so that they could take off and go to New Orleans the very next morning? Luke could, and did. Even had the nanny to look after his girls. This did not encourage me to like the situation more.

As I loaded the bags in the bus in the early morning mist and kissed Moo goodbye, I wished she would take that gleeful smirk off her face. Nothing was going to happen between Luke and me on this trip. We were going to accomplish our missions and then he was going to return to Sawyer and raise his two daughters and then I was going to return to Daytona. I wasn't sure what would happen with Raj. Or Bogart now in his plastic box in the back of the van.

I hadn't told the boy yet about Lorelei's being in the hospital. I had tried a couple of times after breakfast, but seeing how excited he was about the trip, I couldn't get the words out. I hoped she'd be better by the time we arrived. I hoped she was exaggerating.

Driving over to Luke's house, I considered having a relationship with Hoagie, after all. Better the devil you know that the devil you don't. It's safer, anyhow, to go out with Mr. Wrong. If you know it's doomed from the start, you won't get hurt when the relationship goes sour, the way they always do.

I told myself I'd treat Luke just like an old friend and forget we'd ever shared secrets or kisses or teenage fumbles.

Raj and I pulled into Luke's driveway, Bogart in his plastic box in the back of the van. I'd timed our arrival to happen after the nanny had left to take the girls to school and run morning errands, so as to avoid any awkward introductions.

Raj bounced out of the car and stared. Luke's house was Americana on steroids—big white boxy clapboard, green shutters, green lawn; not a bit original. Not like the Luke I had known.

Two huge magnolias on the front lawn were sending out a perfume that went straight to my core, sending shivers up my neck. Big, massed *Indica* azaleas in the foundation plantings would be breathtaking next spring, and I was sorry I'd missed them. I just knew they'd be a rich magenta to play off the white.

We meandered up the brick walkway to the front door. Luke opened it for us before I could ring the bell. "Home sweet home." I wished he didn't look so damn good this morning. Impeccably dressed, as usual, in khakis and button-down shirt. "You don't have to be a banker this morning, dude," I said.

He lifted his eyebrows. "You look nice, Daisy." I was acutely conscious of my choice of clothing—jeans and Birks and a clingy shirt tied at the navel. Moo had given me such grief about the roomy hand-dyed jumper I'd planned to wear that I'd given in.

Raj, without waiting to be asked, darted before me into the entrance hall. "Wow!" His glance darted right and left, up and down.

"Come on in," Luke urged me.

I shifted from one foot to the other, unwilling to step inside, to smell the Luke-ness of the house, see the Alyssa-inspired home decor. "Are you ready?" I asked.

"I think Raj wants to take a look at the house. I'd like it if you'd come along." He gave me one of those maddening, knowing smiles, as though we shared a secret. Of course, if you look at it one way, we did, but then again, we didn't. Not as far as I was concerned.

"We really need to get on the road before it gets too hot." I was really afraid the nanny would come back and I'd have to endure being looked over and judged. But Luke was taking my arm and gently guiding me into the living room, gleaming with yellow walls, white trim, and silk draperies puddling on the floor. Hung above the white damask sofa were impressionistic portraits of the two girls in white dresses, blue satin sashes in big bows. At least they didn't have snowflakes on their noses and eyelashes.

Across from the sofa, the white marble fireplace mantel was topped with Grecian style urns and faux greenery. Faux greenery!

My artistic sense jiggled out of its lengthy torpor, and I began to mentally rearrange the room. I'd take out that tight-assed sofa and put in one plush and comfy, in rose velvet, perhaps, with fringed cushions, and I would loosen up the room, make it less touch-me-not. Greige walls. A painting over there—I knew just the artist—and Luke could come in and relax. It needed some casual clutter. I stopped myself short. Luke was not my decorating client, nor my antique-shop customer.

He was not my anything, except my past.

I was far from the decorating world. I was going back to the beach and serve drinks, let myself go with the flow. No responsibilities.

Luke led us back through the kitchen, breakfast dishes and cereal boxes still on the table, and then through the red, white, and blue family room, still scattered with the remains of the morning—a forgotten sweater, a notebook, white blips of popcorn on the Berber carpet. Then we came to Luke's book-lined, paneled study. "I spend a lot of time here," he said. Raj walked in and spun the floor globe. He stopped with his finger on India, then shrugged, stuck his hands in his pockets, and looked at the prints of biplanes on the walls.

I stood in the doorway and scanned the bookshelves, itching to walk over and take a good look at the spines. Did Luke still read mysteries and crime novels and books on politics, or was he strictly business now? All banking and management? Or did he read at all? I didn't take the step inside. I didn't want to know.

I admired the retro desk, the wooden blinds, the framed diplomas. But really, those window treatments! Nobody used pelmets anymore. So out-of-date. And why didn't he have a comfortable chair by the window? Raj said, "Come on, Daisy." I turned back to the hall and Luke was looking at me strangely.

"Nice room," I said quickly.

"You like it?"

"It looks like you," I said. "Except I think it's missing a good chair by the window for reading."

"Oh, I picked out the desk, but I let the decorator do the rest," he said. "It didn't seem worth fighting Alyssa over."

She wouldn't let him have say-so over his own office? I kept quiet. Not my business.

"Well," said Luke, showing us back to the entrance hall where we'd come in. "Those are the main rooms. Out back's a laundry room, food pantry, mud room, garden room. Unused these days." I admired a nice bombé chest topped with a marble lamp. Letters were piled on the chest. An envelope on top was addressed to Mrs. Lucas McDuffie, Jr.

Luke saw me looking at it and met my eye.

"Alyssa's been gone how long?" I asked.

"A year."

"And what's the situation?" I willed myself to stop gazing at the letter.

Luke crossed his arms. "Do you care?"

"Just curious as to whether I'm going to Louisiana with a married man."

"But just as friends, of course."

"Of course, but still."

"The divorce was finalized last month."

"I see."

Raj, who'd been running a few steps up and down the graceful curving stairway, hands on the banister, interrupted. "Mr. Luke, what's up here?"

"I'm sure we don't need to see the bedrooms," I said.

"Sure we can," said Luke, and Raj, his eyes wide, scampered up and out of sight.

I shrugged and gave Luke an exasperated look. "I guess he's never been in a house like this before. The best you can say about Moo's house is that it's shabby chic. This is so . . . elegant." In fact, it could have used a lot less elegance and a little more comfort.

"It's all right," Luke said. "Let's go on up. I'm not house-proud. I thought I was neat, but Alyssa couldn't stand for anyone to see a cushion out of place. She just told the decorator she wanted something that looked expensive." He held out a palm. "After you, my dear."

"You know, we really should be getting on the road."

"I hope your air conditioner works," said Luke.

I scampered a few steps ahead. "Not all the time. It's aftermarket."

"Daisy, you're being ridiculous. We should go in my car. It's comfortable, air-conditioned, and full of gas."

"I know I'm being ridiculous, Luke. Logically, you're right. But you've already reserved your plane ticket, haven't you? And I want to go on to Daytona. Just say I'm stubborn."

"I'll say you're stubborn."

We were standing in front of the master bedroom door. The first thing I saw was a king-size bed covered with a pale cream satin spread holding masses of ruffled pillows and, horror of horrors, a frilly doll. A portrait of beautiful Alyssa, shoulder-length auburn hair tucked under in a pageboy, gazed down, her smile faint, her expression bland.

"Nice striped slipper chairs," I said.

"What the heck are slipper chairs?" Luke said.

"Those armless chairs over by the louvered doors."

"Those doors are for an empty walk-in closet that once was filled with Alyssa's wardrobe. I never go in here." Luke walked a few steps down the hall. I followed him, wondering about that doll. Dolls with teeth always give me the willies. Why hadn't Alyssa taken the freaky thing with her, if she'd taken all her clothes? Why hadn't Luke gotten rid of it?

Luke stopped at a smaller room. "This is mine. It was once a guest room." I looked in at the heavy mahogany sleigh bed, the plaid comforter and draperies, the forest green chenille throw, the bordered jute rug over the hardwood floor. Yes, a room for visiting gentlemen where hunters on horses leaped across walls. A corner shelf held books with leather bindings. His top-of-the line Powerbook rested on a small, exquisite writing desk.

"Raj is definitely not here."

"Oh, I know where he's gone," Luke said, smiling at me. "We'll go there, but first I thought you might want to see the girls' rooms."

Hayley's room was done in blue and yellow and lavender flowered chintz, Amelia's in peach and green with rose accents. Their beds were still unmade, soft pastel sheets thrown back. I noted the accents of woven textiles and antique toys and wicker. The rooms told me *nada* about their interests.

"In here," said Luke.

I walked into a big playroom transformed into a media room. Each girl had her own computer and game equipment. They shared a TV and project table. Shelves held baskets and boxes of old toys. A Schwinn Airdyne stood in one corner, in view of the TV. He shrugged. "Alyssa used it for about a month. The girls get on it every now and then, but they're so active anyhow, soccer and softball . . ." he trailed off.

The nanny had an apartment over the garage, he told me.

"What's the nanny like?" I asked, thinking of Jane Eyre, of Mr. Rochester.

He shrugged. "Her name is Vanessa. She's a student at the community college, wants to be a nurse, loves hip-hop, and has a boyfriend who plays football for Georgia Southern."

She didn't sound like a love-starved governess. Anyhow, Luke was a serious jazz buff, as I recalled. He was as disappointed as Pop over my failure to become an accomplished musician. "Do you still play the guitar?" I asked.

He gave me a look I couldn't read, partly disgusted, partly sad. "I haven't picked it up for years."

"Luke, that's a shame. You loved playing."

"Well, I've had other things to occupy my time," he said a little bitterly. "Before all this ... domestic trouble started, I was trying to organize a pops orchestra here in town, and your mother and father were helping me. We tried, but it fell through. Maybe someday."

So that was the reason Moo knew so much about Luke. Just then Raj popped up from behind an enormous exercise ball. He rolled over on it and flipped to his feet. Then, face alight with excitement, he scooted to one of the computers and booted it up. I didn't know he knew how.

"Raj," I admonished. "For heaven's sake, ask permission. We have to be going, anyhow. Remember? We're going on a trip."

He ignored me and turned to the man beside me. "Can't I play with the computer, Mr. Luke? Can't we stay here a little longer? Look at all this neat stuff!" He pointed to a pile of computer games on a shelf.

I spoke a little more sharply than I intended. "Raj, don't you want to see your mother?"

"Oh. Sure."

"Bogart's getting impatient out in the car."

Raj fixed me with a withering look. "He's a *snake*."

You couldn't con this kid. He burst out, "I wish I lived here. I would never be bored." He jumped up from the computer and ran his hand down the shelves full of books and games. My heart went out to him, then, wondering what kind of education he would get with Lorelei, assuming she survived. I wondered about that letter again, about his father. I intended to ask him again. Or maybe get Luke to ask him. There'd be time on the trip.

"What's wrong?" said Luke.

"Nothing," I said.

"Daisy, I could always tell when you were troubled about something."

I glanced at Raj and murmured, "I'll tell you later. Are there any old tapes here that we could play in the van? It doesn't have any sound system, but I have a boom box. Raj needs something. I don't know the first thing about entertaining a child on a long trip."

He looked at me wryly. "I have a little experience with that." He plucked an old backpack out of a closet and filled it with cassettes and handheld games from the shelves. He handed it to Raj. "Come on, big guy. Let's go."

The boy slung the backpack over his shoulder and trudged down after us, complaining the whole way how unfair we were, how unfair his mother got hurt, how unfair life was.

Out of the mouths of babes.

I wish I had a picture of Luke's face when he got a good look at my purple bus. "Good God," he said, when he saw the mobile sideshow. "We're going to Louisiana in that? It looks downright dangerous."

"Not your basic Bankermobile," I said. "It's not so bad once you get used to the smell of burning hemp that's sunk into the upholstery."

"I was right," he said. "We're going in my car." He touched the sea creatures and mystical octopuses, the bright and shining stars and clouds, the snakes and ladders. "Where did all this come from?"

"My ex-husband painted it. That's where I got this vehicle, in the divorce. They're symbols," I said. "It was a game. Snakes and Ladders."

"Oh, I get it. The girls had Chutes and Ladders," he said.

"Yes. The original game was a morality game. If you landed on Faith or Generosity, for example, you got to go up the ladder, and if you landed on Debt or Drunkenness you slid back down on the snake's back."

"Life is kind of like that," said Luke.

"That's the idea," I said. "It was supposed to teach Hindu kids how to reach nirvana."

He smiled. "And is it reachable?"

"Nirvana," I retorted, "is slippery, ethereal, and never lasts. Why look for it?"

"When did you get cynical, Daisy?"

"I was fine in Daytona."

Raj had already climbed into the back seat and buckled his seat belt. He stuck his head out the window. "If you're going to keep talking, can I go back inside and play computer games?"

"We're going, all right," I said, reaching for the driver's door.

"I'm driving," said Luke, putting his hand over mine.

"It's my van," I said.

"I'm the man, and I'm driving."

"What is this sudden machismo?" I said. "I drove to Sawyer from Daytona."

"Nevertheless," said Luke, "I'm driving to New Orleans." He lifted the keys from my hands. "It will provide a good example for Raj, who needs a positive male presence in his life."

"Good Lord," I said. "I didn't know you guys watched Oprah at the bank."

Luke shrugged. "I read a couple of books on kids after Alyssa left."

He walked around to open the door for me, surprising me once again. I looked at him. "Luke," I said, "why do you really want to come with us? I know it's not to chase down my dad for a bad debt."

He looked me squarely in the eyes. "I want to do something for you, Daisy. You've got a lot on your shoulders right now, and I can help. I can do this."

I shook my head. "You don't owe me anything, Luke."

"I want to open the door for you. Let's just leave it at that."

I let him. How did he have the power to melt my resolve, after all these years? I decided to armor myself with silence. No communication except the business at hand. I unfolded the map and said, "Well, have you planned the route too?"

"I'll leave that to you," he said.

I glanced back. Raj was busy with one of the handheld games. "Getting out of Georgia is the trick," I said. "After we get to I-85 near Alabama it's smooth sailing. Here's how I would do it . . . ."

I didn't like his proposal to go by roads less traveled, no matter how picturesque, until he got used to the bus and was convinced it would make it to New Orleans. But I stayed quiet to keep the peace. At least the radio picked up a jazz station, the one thing we could agree on. For now.

I tried to manage a weak smile. Pretty soon he'd be convinced and we'd be on I-85 with miles of pleasant monotony.

Or so I thought.

Twenty-three

We rolled along, passing small towns and long flat stretches of farmland, and I felt as if I was going back in time, to places I thought no longer existed, wrapped up as I'd been in that beach world, so hip and yet so hippie. Tension curtained the space between Luke and me. What on earth had I been thinking of, letting him drive us to New Orleans?

After miles of jazz and silence Raj looked up. "That music is boring," he said. He scrabbled in the bag among the tapes and handed one to me. "Can we play this?"

I looked at it. "The Irish Rovers? I remember them from when I was a kid."

He grinned happily and I fed it into the boom box. "Mrs. Crandall's Boarding House" filled the car. I happened to know some of the lyrics came from an old English folk song.

When the dog died we had sausages,
When the cat died, catnip tea.
When the landlord died, I left there . . .
Spareribs were too much for me.

Soon Raj was beating time with his hands, and Luke was singing along, and I laughed and joined in. It was silly and the sun was shining and Raj was bouncing on the seat. "This is my best day ever!" he said.

I wondered how many good days he would have in the future. I looked over at Luke. He was smiling. "Pretty good, fella," he agreed.

The highway unspooled while the sun climbed the sky and the Irish Rovers poured out of the tape player, and I entered an alternative world where Luke and Raj and I were some happy family on the way to Disney World for a little fun. Whoa. What was wrong with this picture? The kid was borrowed, the man was treacherous.

Still, we sang, we laughed, while the landscape rolled. We passed tidy farms, cattle in vast fenced fields, massive live oak trees, quaint country stores, and occasional white-columned mansions tucked among magnolias on a small-town corner. Too bad that in between were construction sites, junked cars, ramshackle shacks, billboards, and litter.

Kind of like life.

The last nice thing about that trip was lunch. In a red-painted barnwood building with sawdust on the floor, we found barbecue pork sandwiches and Brunswick stew and creamy slaw, accompanied by huge paper cups of sweet tea with an advertisement for a funeral parlor on the side. We left the barbecue place, crossed the sandy ground to our bus in good spirits, and I felt pleasantly sleepy after all that food. After we got on the road, gray-tinged clouds banked in the west, blocking out the sun. A gloomy mugginess settled in.

The ancient boom box chose to eat the Irish Rovers tape on its second trip through. We rode along in silence, the gloom, the sweltering heat. The air conditioner, though doing its best, was no match for the humid afternoon, and my shirt clung to my back like I'd just surfaced from a hot tub.

Luke, his hands on the wheel, looked unflappable, his khakis still creased, his plaid shirt unsoppy. "You look so cool," I said.

He smiled. "That's what Daisy said to Gatsby, you know, and Nick knew that she was telling him she loved him. *You always look so cool.*"

"You don't always look so cool, Luke McDuffie," I said, heat rising to my face, making it hotter than it already was. "And your name's not Gatsby."

"But yours is Daisy," he said. "I can be a bootlegger if you want me to."

I laughed at the absurdity of Luke as a bootlegger. "We speed on, boats against the current."

I don't know what Luke would have said next, for at that moment an ominous clanking noise came from beneath the bus and then a loud whining from the engine.

"Damn!" said Luke. He pulled over to the broad sandy shoulder and coasted to a stop.

"What is it?" I asked.

"Tranny's gone." To his eternal credit, he did not say *I told you so*.

Please, Jesus, I murmured. To Luke I said, "How can we get it fixed?"

"I recommend no fix," he said briskly. "It's time to give this heavenly wagon a trip to car Nirvana. I'll see if I can find a place to rent an SUV."

"I've got to fix it," I said, alarmed. "I can't afford a new vehicle."

Luke tapped me on the shoulder. "Madame Esmeralda, as I recall, offered to buy you a brand new set of wheels."

I opened my hands in protest. "We're all so ready to spend money we haven't got yet. In any case, I can't take that from her. Why—"

"Still the same old independent Daisy? Not willing to ask for help? Even when Miss Essie would love to buy you something you need? When selling that stock will replace your father's midlife crisis money and repay the loan with plenty left over?"

I shook my head. "This car is mine. It's my past history wrapped up here."

Luke said evenly, "Somehow this is not about a car, is it, Daisy? Where did you get this van?"

I choked out, "It belonged to Harvey, actually."

"You mean your ex-husband? Keeping this relic of an unhappy relationship, clinging to it?"

I found myself shredding a Kleenex. "It's unique, and . . . I love it, and . . ." I stopped. Did I really love it? Or was it my revenge, thinking I had gotten Harvey's old van away from him, the one that held such nostalgia for him? He'd probably been "camping" with those other women in it. He'd been left with the Taurus. Maybe this was Harvey's last laugh.

We were out in the middle of nowhere. Farms stretched around us for miles. In the distance, on a rise, stood a farmhouse surrounded by oak trees.

Luke nodded in that direction. "I'll hike up there," he said. "If we'd been in my Beemer, I'd have had road service. Maybe the farmer can tell us who to call. You stay here with Raj."

I nodded curtly. Luke alighted from the van, rolled up his sleeves, and set off toward the house's dirt driveway. Even with the windows down, the suffocating odor of the heat-liberated plastic fumes and herb smoke rose from the van's upholstery.

"Can we get out?" Raj piped up from the back.

"Sure. Sorry about the argument."

He shrugged. "Mama and Vinny argued all the time."

I didn't want to ask for particulars. Tiny specks in the vast landscape, we stood in the muggy heat among the waving weeds at roadside, industrious bumblebees tugging at the spindly plants. We watched Luke disappear behind a rise. Occasionally a Cadillac or some other upscale car passed.

Raj squatted down, studying an ant bed. "Watch it, those might be fire ants," I warned.

"They're not," he said. He crumbled bits of cracker to watch them carry the pieces away. He looked up. "I'm thirsty."

"I'll get some cool water." I remembered the ice chest Moo had made us bring, over my protests that we'd never be far from a Quik Stop of some description.

I opened the tailgate and drew out two bottles of water. Bogart appeared to be dozing in his box. Raj's duffle bag lay beside the cooler. I glanced back. Raj was still playing with the ants, arranging obstacles in their way to see how they would get around them. I slid open the bag's zipper.

I knew Moo had helped him pack his bag with the new clothes she'd bought for him, as well as the old clothes of Gordon's I'd found. She hadn't packed the costume she'd made. Was she expecting us to come back? Ha.

I riffled among the clothes. Nothing unexpected. Then I spied an inside zipper pocket. I slid my hand in and felt the crackle of paper. I pulled out the supposedly thrown-away letter from India. Fumbling, I unfolded the sheet and read a letter on World Health Organization stationery from Dr.

Rajeev Patel to Ms. Dolores Diaz. He was coming to America for a conference and wanted to visit his son. Perhaps they could even arrange a visit to India for the boy someday. There were a few words to Raj.

So Lorelei didn't know he was coming? This was awful. This might be Raj's only chance to meet his father. I wondered how Lorelei the dancer and Dr. Rajeev Patel had gotten together and what had happened between them, well, besides the obvious. I looked out into the distance, into the field.

"Daisy! They're here!"

I wheeled around and almost bumped into Raj behind me. "You've been reading my letter!" he howled. "I hate you!"

Sobbing fiercely, he snatched the letter from my hand. "I'm not going to India!"

Luke closed the door of a shiny new red pickup truck and came over. "Hey, hey, what's going on?"

"She was snooping in my bag," cried Raj. "She read my letter."

My cheeks, I'm sure, were an unflattering shade of pink. "Oh, Raj. I'm sorry. I did it for your mother," I said. She would need to know.

"Hey," said Luke. "We can discuss that later. Woody here called us a tow truck. It'll be here soon." I looked up, and a grizzle-jawed elderly man, all wire and sinew, tipped his cowboy hat.

"I'd try to fix it myself," the man said, "but I don't have no parts for that thing."

I shrugged. "Thank you anyway. We were really in a pickle."

The farmer slid his eyes at Raj. "Lots of people adopting them forrin chil'ren." He ran a disapproving hand over the fanciful figures on the side of the car.

"He's American," I said. "As American as you or me."

Luke frowned at me. A culture war with our rescuer might be inadvisable.

The farmer harrumphed. "Myrlie thought you might be hungry." He went back to the truck and came back with a Chinet plate of sliced chocolate layer cake. I took it, blushing, and Luke thanked the farmer for all his help. Shaking hands, Luke told him we'd be all right, and, sliding easily into small-town mode, asked him about his crops, how they'd fared with the recent rains. He walked with the farmer back to his truck, smoothing over my bluntness.

Raj scuffed his feet in the dirt. "When are we going to see Mama?"

"I'll call her when we get to New Orleans, and then we'll go to see her when it's the right time."

"Why can't we go as soon as we get there?"

It was time to tell him. I sat with him in the weeds on the side of the road and told him that his mother was in the hospital, that she had been hurt.

"She's going to get well, right?"

"We hope so. Seeing you will make her happy."

"Okay."

He leaped up and went back to the bus to check on Bogart. Luke appeared at my side. "Tow truck's on the way."

In the late afternoon we were standing in a shade tree mechanic's shop next to his house. "You couldn't have picked a better place to break down," the grinning, black-bearded young man, B.J., told us.

"Why?" Luke didn't look cool at all now, but dirty and sweaty, thumbs in his pockets.

The young man gestured. In the field opposite his shop, an automobile graveyard stretched on for what seemed miles, car upon car upon car. "I think I can find a tranny for this thing. Not sure how new it would be."

From Luke's dark look, I could tell he'd hoped I'd leave the bus to its doom, but what other choice did we have than to fix it? I supposed he could've managed to rent a car in the nearby town or pull some mumbo-jumbo and have a limo pick us up.

I didn't want to have to be that grateful.

We spent a dreadful night in two adjoining rooms in a motor court that had obviously been built in 1934. I huddled in my bed, Raj sleeping in a twin bed next to mine, listening to sounds of wild passion, of drunken heaving, of rebel yells, of twangy music pulsing right through the stained walls, while trying to ignore the sounds of scuffling bug legs.

By the next afternoon, when we'd collected the van from B.J. the mechanic, Luke and I were barely speaking.

We hit the highway at last, and the monotony set in. I dozed a little, and when I woke up the land was getting flatter. I didn't know what to say to Luke. I fiddled with the radio and stared out the window and hoped the snake was faring all right. At least the windows were down and the air was fresh. And now we plowed on relentlessly, getting sweatier and smellier as the land got flatter, the fishing signs more numerous, the greenery more dotted with scrub and water-loving plants, trees more draped with Spanish moss.

"I think it's important that we get on to New Orleans," said Luke. "We won't stop in Biloxi. We've already lost a day. We've got our computers and our phones. I'll search for your dad from a comfortable room, and if I find him, we'll backtrack."

Seized with a yearning to see my father, I pouted. "But what if we miss him by a day?"

"Daisy, that's an asinine thing to say."

"How dare you call me asinine."

"I didn't say you were asinine. You're just not thinking."

"You always did like to do the thinking."

"I thought that's how you liked it."

I stared out the window and let the scenery slide on by, making no demands on me. I just knew we'd be passing within shouting distance of my father and traveling right on. I sank into muddy misery.

The highway signs for Biloxi slid past. In about three hours we'd be in New Orleans, if the good Lord was willing and the bus didn't break down again. I leaned back in the seat and closed my eyes. The next thing I knew Raj was shaking me. "Wake up, Daisy!"

On the causeway at sunset, orange light glinted off boats on the lake, and the smell of mudflats crept into the van. A smile played across Luke's lips when I stretched and yawned. "Nice nap?"

"I feel sticky everywhere." I tried to discreetly flap my elbows and shake my thighs loose, plastered to my jeans. I found that Luke had unpacked two cool water bottles for us. I seized one gratefully and took a deep swallow.

"Where do you suppose we can find an affordable place to stay?" I asked Luke, swiping my mouth with a tissue.

"Not to worry," said Luke. "My treat."

I sat up straight in my seat, almost dropping the water. "Luke, it was bad enough with you paying last night. I only agreed because I was too tired to argue. I'm not letting you pay for my hotel room again!"

He whipped the old van smartly around a slow-moving clunker plastered with bumper stickers GREENPEACE and YOU CAN'T HUG WITH NUCLEAR ARMS and WHY BE NORMAL (upside down). I glanced over and the bearded driver gave us a thumbs-up. Luke was saying, "Of course I'm paying, Daisy. I want us to be comfortable."

"I can be comfortable in a nice clean, quiet, budget motel in a safe location."

"You don't know this city, do you?"

"Well, no, but . . ."

"I've made business trips here."

"Luke McDuffie, I've been on my own in more strange cities than you can imagine. And if you think I'm going to make myself obligated to you any further, you're very much mistaken."

He didn't slow down, not a bit, when I said, "Look, there's just the kind of place I was talking about. A Budget 6."

"Nope." The miles rolled along, and we entered the city limits. He left the main highway and I found us heading into the French Quarter and a little beyond. He finally pulled the bus, clanking and shimmying, up at Le Perroquet Bleu, a bed and breakfast place which looked as though it might be listed on the National Register of Charming Places. Luke switched the machine off. It sighed gratefully.

I gazed up at the sky blue mansion with its balconies and columns and graceful vines spilling over the balcony sides, at hibiscus and bougainvillea in rococo pots. Polished, stately, *expensive*. Definitely not my kind of place.

I lifted my chin. "We can't stay here."

Luke turned to me with an exasperated, amused smile. "I always stay here. They know me. And besides, I've made reservations."

The porter, who resembled Louis Armstrong (I wondered if he had been hired for that reason) approached, frowning at our mode of transportation. He looked as though he was planning to tell us to move along. Then he got a good look at Luke. "Why Mr. McDuffie! What you doing in this vehicle?"

Luke shrugged. "I'm bringing this hunk of the past to town for a friend."

"Better look out, you got friends like that," said the porter, smiling, hauling open the doors for us.

"I know, Jean-Claude, believe me," said Luke.

The desk clerk, a polite young man with café-au-lait skin and wire-rimmed glasses, greeted us. "Welcome to Le Perroquet Bleu." He frowned and checked his computer. "The junior suite is not available."

What? The suite for couples with a kid? My overheated cheeks turned even warmer. Luke said briskly, "No, I reserved two separate rooms. McDuffie. Frédéric knows me."

The frown turned into a charming smile. "Ah yes, I believe he told me to be looking for you. He'll be in later. By the way, I'm Louis, his nephew. My sister Daphne and I are working here now." Louis consulted his computer again and looked over his glasses. "The connecting rooms."

Oh, really? "Raj will stay with me," I said.

"I stayed with you last night," said Raj. "I want to stay with Luke."

"Sounds like a winner," said Luke. He mock-punched Raj. "Us guys have to stick together, don't we?"

We signed in. "You realize," I murmured to Luke, "this means you get the snake too."

"The snake!"

"Ssh, not so loud."

Louis was regarding us suspiciously. And there were no elevators. We'd stashed Bogart in the rolling backpack, and I didn't want any porter handling him. If he suspected anything, we might get tossed out before we checked in. "Luke, would you take the backpack?" I asked in my sweetest voice.

Raj smiled encouragingly at his new hero as Luke shouldered the fancy flowered pack, grumbling.

Heading for the stairs, I noticed the French chandelier throwing sparkles across the ceiling. At the polished banister and the appealing parlor with a Persian carpet and French sofas.

Nice place. Connecting rooms. Well, they had locks on the doors, surely.

Twenty-four

I forgot about locks when I saw my bedroom.

Pale pink walls, navy flowered comforter, heavy draperies to keep in the air-conditioning. A French door that led out onto a balcony. An Italian chandelier. While Luke tipped Jean-Claude, Raj went immediately to the French doors, opened them and walked out, letting in muggy air. At my objection, he reluctantly came back inside and went to explore Luke's room.

"Luke, I can't let you pay for all this." I had put my foot down about paying for the bus repair, and it had taken a sizable chunk out of my bank account.

He gave me a sideways glance. "Daisy. I want to."

His hand encircled my waist, he drew me close, and, with a shiver, it all came rushing back to me, the night in June we'd almost made love underneath my favorite magnolia tree.

He'd brought me back from a date one night and parked his car at the curb, the starless black night surrounding us, the moon high overhead. Walking me to my door, he stopped and kissed me, filling me with stars and honey. I took his hand and led him under the magnolia as we'd done as little kids, and we laughed softly and sat inside a glossy green curtain on the crackly leaves, breathing in the heady perfume of the blossoms. We lay on the leaves and explored one another's bodies, playing tentative notes on a piano that turned into warm heavy chords, so lovely that we didn't hear my dad come out onto the porch.

"Kids?" he called. "Where are you?" Panting, laughing, sheepish, we scrambled up and out, trailing tough brown leaves.

Pop was not amused. "Be careful," he said. Bless him, he never mentioned it to Moo.

And now we were together, however briefly, so many years later. I turned away from him. Careful. "Don't. Please don't. We came here to see Lorelei, and the sooner we get this over with, the better."

Luke dropped his hand to his side. "I'd hoped we could stay a couple of days, and you'd let me show you the city."

"Oh? Is this the honeymoon you did me out of when you married Alyssa? Now you're going to give it back to me, make it up, and the slate will be clean, the books will be balanced? I don't think so."

"You're not being reasonable."

I didn't see that reason had anything to do with it. "Maybe all I need is a little rest, Luke. Okay?"

"Maybe you do." He nodded and left.

I shut the interconnecting door, walked to the queen-size bed with its four shining barley twist posts, and dug in my jacket pocket for the information Lorelei had given me. I spread the paper out on the side table and punched in the cell phone number. I gave it ten rings. Had they taken her cell phone again? I called the hospital and confirmed that she was a patient. I absorbed the rules for ICU visitation. The sooner we got there, the better, they told us. They advised us to come tomorrow morning.

I placed the phone back on the cradle. What now? I walked over to the French doors and stepped out. Hugging myself, I looked out at the colorful street life, at a singer on a corner playing a guitar and singing plaintive ballads.

The connecting door opened and Raj came in, Luke behind him. Before me, the sun was just about gone, the sky in that blue hour, that deep purple color, with banks of lighter purple clouds in painterly swirls.

"I'm hungry," said Raj.

It had been a long time since the barbecue sandwiches. "She's not answering the phone, and at the hospital they think we ought to come tomorrow morning," I said dully.

"We've had a long drive," Luke said. "Why don't we freshen up and have dinner? I know a good café nearby."

Raj said, "Can we go to McDonald's?"

"Not this time," I said.

Luke patted Raj on the shoulder. "Ever have crawfish? Mudbugs, they call them here."

"Mudbugs? Eeeww."

Luke laughed. "Ever had lobster?"

Raj made a face. "Vinny brought some once. They crawled around on the table, waving their *pinchers*. Then Mama threw them into a big boiling pot. It was *cruel*." He thought a minute. "What about tacos?"

"Don't ever go to the stockyards," said Luke.

Raj crossed his arms. "What are you talking about?"

"Never mind. I can see you're just as tired as we are. Come on, fella." Luke patted his shoulder. "A shower for you, to keep you awake long enough for supper. I'm sure they have a burger here, or a grilled cheese. God knows I need one. A shower, that is, not a grilled cheese."

Luke and Raj retreated into their man cave. I closed the door, started to lock it, and then left it unlatched. Luke wouldn't come barging in without knocking, and Raj might need me for something. Of course, if Raj had been with me, I could have locked the door. Was this a plan on Luke's part?

All I wanted at this point was a hot bath. I needed to get myself, as Moo would put it, "centered." I filled the tub, using the heavenly lily-of-the-valley bubble bath nestled in the goody basket on the side of the tub. Soaking was pure bliss.

I sank deeper into the water, enjoying the feel of bubbles on my wet, slick, naked body. I heard the shower stop in the next room and Raj call out that he was done. A few minutes later, the shower started again, and this time I was keenly aware that on the other side of the wall was a naked, wet, slick, man. It hit me then, like a punch in the gut—a rush of yearning. My breath quickened and a rush of warmth invaded me where it mattered.

I had never seen Luke naked. Our teenage explorations had all been in the dark. I may have been boho, but I wouldn't have gone all the way with him, not in high school. I'd felt the eyes of Mama and Daddy on my back every time I went out, and I wouldn't have wanted to give Gordon any more reasons to feel superior.

Alyssa had no such scruples. Her mama was hell-bent on her being the most popular girl in school and let her do most anything. That was only one reason I wanted her as my friend. The other was that Alyssa was dangerous. And dangerous meant exciting.

I couldn't forget the time she'd been sleeping over at my place on a school night because we were working on a history project, building a model of the Parthenon out of papier-mâché and cardboard and wooden dowels. Two guys she knew, Donny and Eric, dropped by, wanting us to go with them to get hamburgers. They stood in the doorway with lopsided easy smiles and well-filled jeans. I knew they were hungry for more than food.

I wanted to finish the project, turn it in the next day, and get an easy A. I said that Luke wouldn't like my going.

Alyssa urged me, saying it was all right, Luke wouldn't mind. Still, I refused, and she'd gone off with both of them, saying she'd come back by midnight. I was to let her in the back door.

She wasn't late, and I managed to let her in without waking my parents, who didn't have a clue what she'd done. She came in giggling. "We can work on the project now."

"I've finished it," I said.

"Don't be mad," she told me, waving a paper at me. "I've got the questions Donny gave me for the algebra test tomorrow." His mother was the teacher. I was shocked but not surprised.

"Why do you need them?" I challenged her. "You're no dummy."

She raised a shoulder. "I don't have time to study," she said. "I'll share."

"No thanks." I might be a goof-off, but I couldn't go that far.

"Well, after what I had to do to get them, you might show a little appreciation."

Now I was interested. "What did you do?"

"Actually it was kind of fun," she said. "Like a popsicle." She elaborated.

"That's gross," I said.

"Daisy, you're as uptight as your brother," she said.

At that moment I had a twinge of suspicion that she was not really my friend. But I sloughed it off.

No, I had not seen Luke's body. I had felt the slenderness of his rib cage, the hair on his belly, the heat and slickness that defined his manhood, as we fumbled around in the dark, leaving evidence on the car seats. Then, and only then, I wished I could be as adventurous as Alyssa.

There was that sensation of a bowling ball in my stomach again. Alyssa had known him in ways that I had not.

And now?

I was wet and naked, and he was on the other side of a thin wall. I rose from the tub, pulled the plug, and let the water sluice down the drain. Turned on the cold shower and let the water blast me for just long enough to straighten out my thinking. I recited some of that poem we'd had to learn in fifth grade. *Let the dead past bury its dead . . .*

Footprints on the sands of time. A lot different from footprints on the beach. When I saw Luke freshly showered and changed, looking fabulous in a blue polo shirt, I needed Henry Wadsworth Longfellow's poem more than ever.

Twenty-five

We had a wary dinner in the small café in the next block, chock-full of hip people and delicious aromas. Raj, despite his earlier squeamishness, decided to try all the unfamiliar Cajun dishes we'd ordered, with lemonade for him and beer for us. We explained all the dishes, even down to the life cycles of crustaceans, so Luke and I didn't have to talk to one another. Finally the subject of food had been talked out.

Luke and I looked at each other. I knew that look. He must have been thinking of me on the other side of that wall too. He colored a bit and turned his gaze on Raj. "How do you like New Orleans?"

"It's okay," Raj said. "I liked your house better."

Luke grinned and teased, "Come on. Why?"

Raj grew serious. "It was so big, with so many things, and so pretty, so many rooms. At home I didn't have my own room. I had to sleep on the foldout in the front room."

"Um," I said. "But you were with your mama. Don't you miss her?"

Raj nodded and turned to Luke, his eyes bright. "I've got an idea," he said. "Let's take her back to live in your house."

I looked down, inspecting my crawfish étouffée. "Well, that's an idea, fella," Luke said. "But you know, she might have other plans."

Raj glowered at us. "She used to talk about Vinny. When he was coming back. She said she didn't like him anymore. Wanted to go to Mexico where he couldn't find us. To her cousin. Maybe if she lived in your house I wouldn't have to go to Mexico."

Luke and I looked at each other. He laid a comforting hand on Raj's arm and lowered his voice. "You know, your mom's pretty sick, son. She's in the hospital here. We'll go to see her tomorrow."

Raj shook his head. "She's been sick before," he said. "She gets well and says she's never gon' mix booze and pills again."

I bit my lip. Should we let him go on thinking it's the same old, same old, protecting him from anxiety, or do we tell him? I took a sip of beer, considering.

"Vinny wasn't that bad, Mr. Luke," Raj was saying. "But I'd rather have you for a papa."

I nearly spewed beer on the table and covered my cough with a napkin. Luke, durn him, was grinning. Raj didn't notice but took another forkful of jambalaya. Then he picked up a red crawfish carapace and sucked thoughtfully on it. He laid it down.

He looked up. "Can we have ice cream?"

After dinner was over, it was clear from his eyes at half-mast that he was ready for bed. When we got back to Le Perroquet Bleu, Luke picked Raj up and carried him upstairs on his shoulder. Together we got him into the Scooby-Doo pajamas Moo had bought him and tucked him into bed.

Standing together in the hazy light, we gazed down at the sleeping child. Luke's hand crept into mine.

"Luke, I . . ."

"Tell you what," he said. "Why don't we slip down to the bar?"

I caught my breath and tugged my hand back. "What? Leave the B&B?"

He smiled, that lazy smile I loved and hated. "There's a small bar here on the main floor. I'll show you."

"What if he needs us?"

"I'll see who's at the desk, and I'll have my cell phone. They can listen out for him."

I bit my lip. "Only for an hour, then."

We made our way back down the stairs following a couple, a balding man who wore a bristly mustache and a loud tweed jacket and his wife, elegantly dressed in pink crepe.

Luke showed me to the former library, which had been fitted out with soft chairs and small tables. Scott Joplin was playing in the background, and the room smelled of old books and whiskey. A man and two women were already there, the man with what looked like bourbon and the women with a drink I couldn't place.

Luke took me over to meet a third person, who turned out to be Frédéric, one of the owners, and he laid a book aside and got up to make our drinks.

"Two Sazeracs," Luke said.

"What?" I frowned at him.

"Wait and see." He guided me to a loveseat with a table in front.

The others in the bar glanced our way. What did they see? The boho and the banker. I felt guilty, as though we might be illicit lovers, leaving our unsuspecting spouses at home with their TV sports and steamy novels, or perhaps TV novels and steamy sports.

Frédéric brought our Sazeracs in lovely faceted glasses. I smiled despite myself.

We clinked our glasses. "Am I going to like this?" I asked.

"I think so," Luke said.

I took a sip. "Mmmm." It slid down nicely, warming my insides, leaving a trail of herbal essence that Moo would have loved.

"Remember when we sneaked that beer back when I was fourteen?" I asked. "You told me I wouldn't like it. And I didn't."

"It made you sick, as I recall."

"My mom guessed. And she thought that was punishment enough. What if your daughters sneak beer when they're fourteen?"

"I'll ground them for weeks."

I smiled. "Luke . . . you've changed."

He shrugged. "Not so much. A little more sophisticated, maybe. My brother's leaving made me grow up in a hurry."

"Your brother *what*?"

"You didn't notice Carter wasn't at the bank?"

"I had my mind on other things."

"I'm surprised nobody told you."

My cheeks burned and a slug of guilt hit me. Of course. I'd forbidden anyone in my family to speak of Luke, and they'd respected my wishes. And involved as I was in my own shmuck-ups, it just hadn't shown up on my radar screen.

"Tell me, Luke. I can't believe it. Convince me that handsome, smart guy, your brother, would just up and leave. It's like the king abdicating."

Now it was Luke's turn to blush, and I didn't know why. I took a big sip of my cocktail.

"Well, he and I had fallen out. We still weren't speaking at the time I was about to graduate. He'd already been working at the bank for two years and he and Dad weren't getting along. He was all stressed out and went on a retreat to a monastery. Monastic retreats were all the rage that year. He came back a changed man."

The room chatter, the Scott Joplin faded, and I was aware that I was sitting in a bubble, waiting for Luke to continue. He met my eyes.

"He went back to join the monastery."

The bubble burst and I hit Earth with a jolt. "But your family is Episcopal," I said stupidly.

"There are Episcopal monasteries, Daisy. Not many, I admit." His lips compressed in bitterness. "Dad was after me to come back and help him at the bank, and Alyssa begged me to take the job."

She would. Peace Corps and helping the poor weren't in her plans, I felt quite certain. "And you went along with it, just like that. What happened to the old Luke I knew? We were going to change the world together."

"We were two against the current," he said and sipped at his drink. "We belonged to an earlier time. Most of our generation was into making money. I just got with the program."

Frédéric brought over a dish of spicy potato chips and I reached for one. "It's Carter, isn't it? Do you feel you have to be his replacement, his clone?"

He took another sip of his cocktail. "My father was hit hard when Carter left, staring at the wall and pounding a fist into his other hand. I've never seen him like that. He was all right with me leaving to save the world, but his oldest son was the best and the brightest. I think he felt I wasn't good enough to take Carter's place. I've worked ever since trying to prove that I was."

I couldn't help it. I put my hand over his, aching for him. "We aren't put here to fulfill our parents' dreams, Luke. Your brother picked a particularly spectacular way to tell him that."

His lips compressed. "We can't disregard them either."

"How different our paths have verged, Luke." The pain in his eyes cut me deeply, but I went on. "You've been living someone else's life."

He shrugged. "And now I can't do anything else. I can't be like your father, just go away and start a new career. Look what trouble he caused. It's too late for me." He gave a rueful, hollow laugh. "And I've never been able to sing."

I softened, remembering Luke playing his guitar. He *could* sing, and he had sung to me. He had played and sung at the church retreat we'd attended as teens. I clamped down on those memories before I got all choked up.

"My father's a lot older than you." I took on a brisk manner. "It's just a midlife bump for him. But you? You could join organizations. Run a nonprofit. Run for office."

He smiled at me crookedly. "No, I can't. Who would run the bank?"

"Didn't you have a younger sister? Caroline?"

"Constance. Connie."

"I remember her as a whiz of a student, Luke."

"I'll say. She worked in the bank right out of college and then left when she married a homeboy and had a baby. Dad didn't want her working. He said she belonged at home."

"What did she have to say about that?"

"She didn't like it a bit. Said she could juggle things. Said she was very organized. Dad didn't agree. There was a lot of tension for a while. She's planning to go back to school and study to become a CPA."

I sat and thought a minute. "Have you thought about bringing her back?"

Luke looked at me with surprise. "Actually, I hadn't."

"Maybe you should. From what I remember of her, I think she'd love the job. And Luke, it's a small town. She could even go home for lunch."

He looked hopeful for a minute but then shook his head. "There's no way. I've got to stay there and do my duty, and that's that." He took one of my hands, the way he had done back at the roadhouse, and played with the fingers. "I like the way you challenge me. What happened back then, Daisy? Why aren't you in my life? Why'd you just go away and cut me out?"

I turned my head away. "Excuse me? Are you one of those men who have complete amnesia about the hurt you caused? We'd better go back."

My glass was empty, anyhow.

But now Luke's face had crimsoned. "Dammit, Daisy. I tried to explain. You wouldn't listen."

"Please sign for the drinks. We need to get back to that boy." I pushed with my shaky legs, trying to rise from the soft loveseat, trying to keep my dignity. I flopped back.

Luke rose and offered an arm to pull myself up. I accepted, trying to keep my dignity. "How can I ever repay you for all this? I don't like to be beholden."

"Cook me dinner sometime," he said.

"You'll have to come to the beach." We trudged up the long, curving stairway, its Persian carpet snugged down by brass rods. "All I know how to do is boil shrimp."

"Last I heard, they had shrimp in the Sawyer Piggly Wiggly."

"Frozen," I said.

The mood froze then, and we walked back to rooms in silence. At the door to my room, he leaned over and kissed me on the cheek. "See you in the morning."

My heart gave a treacherous flutter as the door closed. I went straight to the bedside table and called Lorelei's number. Still no answer.

I hoped the snake was all right next door, but I was too tired to go ask. I kicked off my black shoes, shucked off my black pants. I wriggled out of my cotton rib-knit top. *Don't do this*, I told myself. *Don't let down your guard because he told you a sob story.* I glanced at myself in the mirror. I was wearing my brand new lacy bra and bikini set. Why had I brought it?

I rummaged in my suitcase for the tank top and pajama pants I'd brought from Daytona. But I'd left them under the pillow back at Moo's house. I searched for one of my big old T-shirts, but I hadn't packed one of those, either. My cotton kimono was damp from my shower, and the room was chilly. I could ask Luke for a T-shirt. No.

I found the controls of the A/C and switched from HIGH to LOW. I unfastened my lace bra, dropped it into the suitcase pocket, and did the same with my lace bikini. I told myself that I'd bought them for myself, to feel pretty. I climbed into bed in my birthday suit.

Tired, aching in every limb from the long trip, my body sank into the comfortable bed, but my mind wouldn't let me drift off. I blamed the low rumble of the air conditioner, the cars passing on the street below, some far-off thump of music, the dripping of the faucet in the bathroom. I slipped out of bed to tighten it, and then I heard someone walking down the hall. I fixed the faucet and slipped under the covers; I sighed and settled into the pillow. Then my eyes snapped open again. Someone was trying the doorknob.

Twenty-six

Grabbing my damp robe, I unlatched the door and barreled into Luke's room. In the dimness I could make out his well-muscled arms outside the covers and his bare chest with its dark hair. I hoped to God he had something on underneath.

I shrugged into the robe before I walked over. My hand trembled as I touched his shoulder. "Luke, I need you!"

His eyes blinked open. He smiled lazily and reached out a hand. "Come here."

Aghast, I took a step back. "Not that kind of need, Luke. Someone's tried my doorknob." Raj stirred uneasily a couple of feet away. "Don't wake him," I whispered.

"Calm down, Daisy," Luke said. "It's probably somebody who's had too many Sazeracs." He slipped out of bed, fortunately wearing blue-and-gray striped pajama bottoms.

I tightened my kimono sash while we soft-footed to my room. We stared at the doorknob to the hall. It wasn't moving. Luke put his ear to the door and shook his head. He crossed to his own door and opened it. "No one there." Then he did the same with my door.

He opened it wide and stepped out into the hall. He shook his head.

"He could be hiding around the corner," I said.

"How do you know it's a he?" Luke closed both doors and made sure the deadbolts were tight. "I still say it was a mistake. Maybe that guy we followed downstairs."

Maybe I was just jumpy. Here I was in the most mysterious of cities with a little boy, a snake, and an old boyfriend, looking for a snake dancer who got in trouble for breaking cemetery urns.

And looking for this snake dancer was her jailbird jewel thief boyfriend. And did she know he was after her? What was I, Daisy Harrison, doing here, whose only problem up until now was not falling for a good-looking beach bum?

"Stay with me a little while, Luke." I hated myself for saying it.

He gazed at me for a moment too long, then took one of my shaking hands and raised it to his lips. "I can't promise what will happen if I do."

I stared into his cool gray eyes, now the grayness of fresh volcanic ash. I turned away and caught a glimpse of myself in the mirror over the dresser. My short kimono, with nothing on underneath, didn't hide much. My hair was loose and tangled, tumbling over my shoulders. My cheeks were flushed and I had been biting my moist lips. I wore that pained expression of Victoria's Secret models. I looked, in short, as though I was ready to be taken.

And Luke, bare-chested. I found myself looking up at him, lips parted, and before I knew it, his lips had closed on mine. We were clinging to each other, breathlessly, kissing, kissing me into a warm sunrise daybreak feeling, one I hadn't felt in far too long.

He drew me closer, wrapping strong arms around me. I pressed my teary cheek to his chest, and his body told me he was very glad to hold me, and his breath felt warm and tickly against the top of my head. His lips brushed my hair. He tilted my face up and kissed me again. A slip of breath escaped my lips and, in a dreamlike state, one or the other of us, or maybe both of us together, for I do not remember separating, closed the door connecting the two rooms and slid the latch closed.

Still touching, we sank down onto the disheveled bed. He tugged on the kimono sash and the wrapper fell away, and he moved his hands over my breasts and my belly, looking, marveling in the dim half-light. I lay stunned, on one level protesting that this shouldn't be happening, on another urging it onward and upward.

When his mouth touched my breast, seeking, finding, an electric charge short-circuited my protesting mind. My fingers found and stroked the hardness pressing against my belly, and he rolled me on my back and covered me. My legs reached upward to enfold him. "Now, Luke, now."

So long, so long, to wait for our first time, so long, so long, to be complete.

It was over too quickly, and he lay there panting, "Sorry, I'm sorry, Daisy, it's been so long..."

So long.

I was content to stay there with him, in limbo, not having to face anything not having to think what this meant or where it might lead, but he began to stroke me, the part of me that was moist and hot, and it did not take long until I melted, soared, big and little explosions like fireworks over a glassy black lake. And Luke was once again ready, with a desire that had waited nineteen years.

This time, we took it slow and warm, journeying deep into thrilling darkness.

We clung together then and slipped off to sleep holding each other. Sometime during the night I was awakened by whimpering coming from the next room.

I pulled my wrapper around me and opened the connecting door and walked to the boy's bedside. Still asleep, he'd apparently been having a bad dream. In a moment Luke was beside me, one hand on my shoulder. "What's happening?"

"Luke, you'd better get back in your own bed," I said, but in a moment the boy settled back into sleep as we watched him, like any parents who had been awakened by a child. Except this child was not ours and never would be. Our children were potentials that never had happened. Those children that we had talked about as dreamy-eyed students, the children that were going to be so beautiful. One might have been heading off to college this very year.

All the might-have-beens crowded me, and I swallowed.

Luke, misunderstanding, gave my hand a quick squeeze. "He seems to be okay now."

"All right," I said, smiling weakly. "You stay here. I'll see you in the morning."

"It is morning," he said and pointed to the window. The first pale light of dawn lightened the sky, silhouetting St. Louis Cathedral in the distance.

"It doesn't feel like morning." I leaned back against his damp chest, and he rested his chin on the top of my head. "I want to go back to bed."

"You do? I'm ready."

"I'm sleepy, I mean."

Just then another voice broke in. "I'm hungry." I turned to see Raj, sitting up in bed watching us. I sprang away from Luke guiltily.

"Let's get some breakfast, then," said Luke.

Raj sprang out of bed and hurried over to the backpack. He lifted out the laundry bag, untied it, and curled the python around his shoulders. "Bogart needs some exercise."

"Um," I said. "Be sure to put him back before we leave the room," I said. "We don't want to freak out the maids and get thrown out of Le Perroquet Bleu."

"I think we'd better take him with us," said Luke. "Then we can enjoy our beignets without worry."

"Granola and fruit," I said primly.

"Hey, earth mother," said Luke. "Live a little."

"I never eat fried things."

"It won't kill you," Luke laughed. "Come on, we'll have coffee with chicory."

"Without my herbal tea I'll probably fall apart."

"You look pretty well put together to me."

He was so expansive, so happy. But, still. I'd given in to weakness, to wanting. I had to make Luke see how impossible it was. That spaceship cobbled of him and me would never leave Earth.

We closed our respective doors.

I walked out onto the balcony that spanned both our rooms, taking a deep breath of the warming air, shivering at the beauty of the pink glow that foretold a bright and fragrant day. The pink glow of love.

Suppose, just suppose . . . *naah.*

I hurried back in and showered, reminding myself that we were taking Raj to the hospital today to see his mother.

I wondered if she'd be alert enough to talk about the letter from Raj's father.

I was toweling the water out of my hair when my cell phone rang. I dropped the towel and grabbed the phone with one hand and the kimono with the other. "Moo?"

"Nope, it's me, babe," Hoagie said. "Where are you?"

Hoagie! I thought of Lorelei, Hoagie, and me at the Paradise Bar just a few days ago with not a care in the world. "In New Orleans," I said. "With a gentleman." I struggled into the kimono while I was talking.

"Whatever," he said. "Did you find our friend?"

"Hoagie, she's in the hospital. Arrested for breaking cemetery urns. Did you ever get in touch with her about your car?"

I was greeted by a spitstorm of profanity. I held the phone away from my ear.

"Sorry," I said. "Maybe you'd better check with the New Orleans Police. It's probably impounded. They'll give you the details." I just wanted to get him off the phone.

More swearing. "Hoagie, I've got to go."

He made me promise to call him after I'd seen her. I closed my phone and wondered what had passed between those two. No, I knew. She'd learned all the angles, how to get a guy to lend her his car.

A hopeless romantic, that's what I was. I had to believe I was in love with any man in order to sleep with him, and I'd spun myself into love with more than one man at the beach, like Rapunzel spinning straw into gold, until I found it was just straw after all. Maybe that was why I hadn't let myself fall for Hoagie.

Had I thought I was in love last night? I guess I could cut myself some slack for auld lang syne. It wouldn't happen again.

The phone rang in Luke's room, cutting into my thoughts. I heard him pick it up. Most likely his daughters or the nanny calling. That man had tons of responsibility. Good for him. I wanted to travel light.

Well, it was time to put Guy Lombardo back in his grave. I retrieved the towel off the carpet and hung it in the bathroom just as Luke came through door looking for me. "Your mother. On *my* room phone," he said. "She says Raj's father has turned up."

Twenty-seven

I raced to the phone so fast I collided with the bed and fell onto it. I picked up the phone, huffing.

"Well, Daisy," she said, with amusement in her voice, "your line was busy, so I'm glad this good man was so close by."

"It was because of Raj," I blathered. "We got interconnecting rooms so he could go back and forth. He seems to have taken a shine to Luke."

"A boy needs a father. Which is what I called to tell you. There is a Dr. R. K. Patel here looking for his son. Imagine that! So many people looking for this boy."

"Urk," I said.

"Is something wrong?"

"Something is wrong now," I said, my voice escalating a few octaves. "What do you mean *so many people*?"

"I'll get to that in a minute, Daisy. Let me finish telling you about Dr. Patel, a most charming man. He's been giving me some information about Ayurvedic medicine. We've also been having the most enlightening theological discussions."

"Moo, you mean he's there now?"

"That's what I've been trying to tell you."

"How on earth did he trace us to Sawyer?"

"He found those apartments, dear, where you seem to live, and ran into some woman who told him, and I quote her, 'that she didn't know where the hell Lorelei was, but that the boy had gone with you.' And then she had our phone number here, and so . . ."

The apartment manager. The emergency contact number. "Oh my God."

"He's such a nice man, Daisy."

"Moo," I said.

"He wants to talk to Raj," she said.

Not a good idea. "It might get Raj upset. You didn't tell this Dr. Patel where we were, did you?"

"Certainly not. But he seems very kind, and his aura is good."

"Moo, people can be deceptive." I did not know this eastern man. After all, he had abandoned Lorelei and his son.

"Auras don't lie. Why don't you talk to him yourself? He's waiting in the parlor."

"Oh, all right." I glanced apprehensively into the next room, where Raj was watching TV.

Moo came on the line a few minutes later. "Why, I wonder where he went?"

I had a premonition. "Moo, did you make him some tea?"

"I certainly did."

"And was he there with you in the kitchen?"

"Well, of course. He was very interested in my compounds. He pointed out several Indian preparations he uses from time to time."

I knew my mother's habits well. "Moo, look by your telephone. What do you see there?"

"A stack of scrap paper and a cup of pencils and some grocery store recipes, oh, and a teacup."

"Is the B&B and phone number I gave you written down there?"

"Yes, but . . ."

"And what else?"

"Now, Daisy. I might have told him your friend was in the hospital . . ."

"There you go. Off like a rocket. Would you say a smart doctor could memorize what was on your pad?"

"Why . . ."

"And do you think he could figure out where it came from? He's probably got his laptop with him."

"Well, he didn't bring any computer in," she said huffily.

"Poor Moo," I said. "Living with my daddy for all those many years, who never noticed anything short of fire, flood, or plague of locusts, and then only if they landed on the piano keys and whirred their little wings. I'll bet the good doctor is on his way here as we speak."

"I'm sorry, Daisy, but I liked the man. Not like that other person."

"Moo! What other person?"

"I'm getting *around* to that. The other person looking for the boy. I called and left a message. You didn't get it?"

"No! You left it where?"

"Oh, silly me. I might have called your number in Florida instead of your cell phone. Yesterday afternoon some ghastly man, pale as death, came to the door. Said he was Raj's stepfather! Well, I certainly didn't believe him. Then he wanted to know if I had the snake! I told him certainly *not*. Although," she said wistfully, "people are still talking about it...."

I felt all the blood rush from my face. "Did you tell him where we were?"

"I told him I thought you were going back to Florida, which you are, at some point in time, much to my sorrow. But I believe, dear, deep in your heart, you want to come home."

"Moo, please!" Exasperation fought with relief that she'd thrown Vinny Corvo off the track. But for how long?

"Who *was* that man?"

"Was he driving a Cadillac?"

"How should I know? Today cars all look alike, hunchbacked beasts. Oh, there goes the doorbell. Goodness! It's time for my client. I'll try to call you later."

Feeling shell-shocked, I rang off and looked at Luke. "Raj's father is on his way here. He's just left Sawyer."

Luke grimaced. "Let me just make a quick calculation." After a few moments he said, "If he's rented any kind of decent car, or if he can get a plane right out, he should be here somewhere between three and six o'clock."

"Luke, quit being so casual about this. What are we going to do?"

"Do we have to do anything?"

"It's an ethical question," I explained. "He's getting here between three and six and we have to decide what to do about it. And we haven't told Raj's mother yet." I looked to the sky. "God, if you're up there, *do something.*"

Luke followed my gaze into the sky. "Look out," he said. "I see a lightning bolt."

"Be serious." I twisted a lock of hair around my fingers in frustration. "What are we going to tell her? Do you know that Vinny showed up at my house a few days before Dr. Patel?"

"What?" A small voice.

We turned our heads in unison. Raj was looking at us. I'd forgotten he was right there getting into his clothes. "I heard that," he said, his dark eyes staring straight into mine. "Is my father on the way here?" Luke and I looked at each other, and Luke laid his hand on the boy's head. "We think so, fella."

He shook his head, squirmed out from under Luke's touch. "I don't want to see him."

I said gently, "Why not, Raj? He's come all this way."

He looked at us sadly, his face full of love and hate and confusion. "I just don't, that's all. He didn't want me."

Luke shrugged. "Well, there's time to talk about that. Right now we need to go over to the hospital to see your mama."

"Not before we eat. I'm *hungry*," Raj insisted. "I've been hungry for *hours*."

"OK," said Luke. "Beignets, here we come."

"Granola."

"I think we've been through this before."

"Coffee with chicory."

"Chocolate with rum."

"*Luke* . . . I'm not dressed."

He grinned, and I didn't like the way he was grinning. I ducked back into my room. In fifteen minutes I'd put on jeans, pink tie-dyed T-shirt, and the ever-present Birks. Luke was neat and clean-shaven in his business casual gear, and Raj wore a fresh white polo shirt and khaki shorts and sandals. Bogart reposed in his backpack.

Luke hoisted the snake bag and we carried it down with us. As we walked into the breakfast room, a big woman wearing a blond wig, a dusty green pantsuit, and artistic dangling earrings stopped us and laid a hand on my arm.

"How brave you two are, my dear." She looked up at Luke, mascaraed eyes big and liquid. "How very brave."

He looked totally confused. "Well, I . . ."

"You're lucky you got a boy," she said. "However did you manage it?"

"A friend arranged it," I said, deadpan. "It's confidential."

"Bless you," she said and blew us a kiss before she joined her companions at another table.

"What the heck is she talking about?" said Luke. "And why are we lucky to have Raj along?"

"She thinks we've adopted him."

A sheepish smile broke out on Luke's face as we walked into the coffee shop. "Well, we have, in a way." He turned to the boy. "Raj, would you like Daisy and me to be your parents?"

"Yeah, man! Sure, if I can live in your house!" he said and then got thoughtful. "Could Mama come too?"

I had to make Raj see that Luke was teasing him. "What about Vinny?"

"Not him."

"Hoagie?"

"Not him."

"Rasmussen?"

"No!" he shouted but then said, "He'd miss the bar." A young red-haired woman with a full set of body art turned out to be Daphne, Frédéric's niece. She told us to pick any table, and we found one near a window. She came back to take our orders for chicory coffee and hot chocolate.

When she'd gone, Raj said, "I've got it all figured out. Your house is big enough to hold us all, even Rasmussen."

I looked at Luke, smiling. "Filthy capitalist pig, we're going to take your house like the Bolsheviks took Dr. Zhivago's and divide it into apartments. Hello, commune."

Luke raised his eyebrows. "Do I get Julie Christie for a roommate?"

I folded my arms. "Sure. She's a senior citizen now, and I'll even throw in Geraldine Chaplin."

The coffee and chocolate came. Luke took a sip of the steaming brew and looked up. "I'd rather have you."

Raj blew on his chocolate. "What are you guys talking about?"

"Poor kid. We need to show him a few classic movies."

Raj shook his head. "I've seen them. *Snow White*, all that stuff." He started telling us about all the Disney classics he liked, and I thanked the good Lord he was off the subject of being adopted by Luke and me. Kids can take such jokes to heart if you're not careful.

He was a lot happier after we'd tucked into a huge plate of beignets and croissants, accompanied by a trio of decadent sauces—chocolate, caramel, and raspberry—as well as a caddy of jams and butter. And a bowl of cut-up bananas, pineapple, and strawberries.

Between bites of fruit, I explained to Luke about Lorelei's sister's attitude toward the snake. "If I have to take Raj to stay with her, she'd refuse to take Bogart."

"I don't want to stay with Aunt Luz," Raj announced. "Not without Bogart."

I parted my lips, ready to proclaim about things in this world we have to accept. Luke, reading my mind, frowned and shook his head ever so slightly. "Have a beignet, Daisy."

I took one of the sinful things from a plate and gingerly cut it. I put a chunk in my mouth. It was really good.

Curious glances came our way, people trying to figure out this ill-assorted "family." I ate the whole beignet and reached for another, as though a full stomach could solve all our problems, especially what to do about Doctor Patel. If he'd decided to fly, he might be greeting us by lunchtime. But the likelihood was that he'd be here by late afternoon.

Too soon, it was time to go to the hospital. To distract Raj, I suggested that afterward we could visit the zoo, and then the park. "They've got a great carousel," I said.

Raj looked at me disdainfully. "Girls like carousels. I'd rather ride a *real* horse."

I explained no real horses were available. We got up and left, and he skipped up the stairs ahead of us. We followed sedately, or maybe sedated. Those were a lot of beignets.

"How'd you like to see some night life?" Luke asked, squeezing my shoulder. "It'd be fun."

"Please, Luke," I said and wiggled out of the squeeze. "What about Raj?"

"Maybe we can ask Paul or Frédéric if they know a sitter."

He went in search of one of the innkeepers while I climbed the stairs. Raj was waiting for me at the top, uncommonly still. I couldn't tell if he was afraid of seeing his mother.

I stuck the old-fashioned key in the slot of my room. It didn't turn. Maybe I had the wrong key. I tapped my foot and waited for Luke.

It didn't take long for him to come up the stairs.

"Fred's working on the sitter," he said. "He keeps a list for the guests. Let me take you to Arnaud's for dinner."

Then he noticed me with the key in my hand. "Is something wrong?"

I wrinkled my nose. "The key won't work, and all you can think of is having fun. We don't know what kind of a situation we're going to find with Lorelei."

He looked abashed. "Sorry. It's just that my plane ticket's for tomorrow. Maybe I should change it. I ought to stay and help you look for your father. He may still be in Biloxi."

"I can look for my father by myself."

"I have an interest there. Remember?"

All these problems were staring me in the face—how to tell Luke it was no good, what to do about Raj's father, what to do if Lorelei didn't make it, what to do if she did, what to do about Bogart. And then there was Teddy Harrison, nightclub singer and stray father. Luke took the key from my hand. "Let me try."

Suddenly I noticed that none of us had the bag. "Oh my God! We forgot the snake!"

I raced for the stairs, nearly colliding with a tall bronze man wearing several earrings. He looked down his gorgeous nose at me. "Don't worry, dear. I always forget mine."

Daphne was clearing our table when I arrived. I found the satchel still underneath. "Thought you'd come back for it," Daphne said. Thank goodness she didn't look in it. When I arrived back at the room, the door was open. I walked in, peeved at Luke for being better with keys than me. Then it hit me.

A stranger had been in my room.

Twenty-eight

The room carried some kind of lingering odor I couldn't identify, like rancid butter. I stood just inside the door for a moment, scanning the room, while Luke and Raj went to inspect the other room.

Everything looked in order, but hotel guest rooms are kind of hard to disorder. I checked my paltry supply of jewelry. My silver necklace and my silver earrings were in my well-worn red silk Chinese pouch, the one I'd received as a graduation gift, Today I was wearing my gold hoops and gold chain with the little sand dollar pendant I'd bought to celebrate my new life when I'd left Harvey and gone to Daytona. My Timex ticked off the minutes on my wrist and my moonstone ring glowed on my right hand.

"Luke," I called out, "are you missing anything?"

"Missing?" he appeared in the doorway. He patted himself down. "Nope, still got it all. Except my heart, maybe."

"Oh, Luke. Will you be serious? Why do I think somebody's been here?"

His face grew solemn. "Now that you mention it, I did notice something was wrong."

"How so?"

"My bed. I hadn't slept in it, you know. I noticed those tight smooth covers this morning, and felt pleased at the reason why they were unrumpled. But now, it looks like someone's been sitting on it. Using the phone?"

"There's a smell . . . can't you smell it?"

Luke sniffed the air. "Yeah, kind of eau de Fruit of the Loom, air of sweaty Converse. Let's check the closets."

"Let's *you* check the closets."

"Where's Raj?"

"He's outside on my balcony."

A numb feeling crept slowly up my spine. "That's it! I might have left my balcony door unlocked after I came in this morning."

We both gazed at my balcony door. It wasn't locked.

While Raj was out of earshot, I filled Luke in on what Moo had told me about the other man who'd come to her house. I sketched in the little I knew about Vinny Corvo. "In short, he's just gotten out of jail. And looking for Lorelei."

"Do you think he escaped?"

"Could be, but I'm guessing he got some time shaved off his sentence and decided not to tell Lor about it."

"So what was he in for? Nothing violent, I hope."

"He was a burglar. Where else did he get all that stuff he gave her?" Luke walked out to the balcony and I followed him. "Look here." There, on the railing, were smudges in the layer of city grime.

We locked up well and decided we'd have to take Bogart with us. He would surely be all right in the car, if we parked in the shade and left the window open a crack.

"Come on," said Luke. "Let's get going."

Why was Luke rushing us out? Did he think danger still lurked here? I chose not to comment but made sure the backpack was secure. Luke slung a camera bag over his shoulder. My heart was thumping as I closed the door behind me. "Just a minute," Luke said, taking my elbow. "I'm going to tell Paul and Frédéric about the break-in, if that's what it was."

All that hurry-up, and now we waited while Luke talked with the two proprietors. He came back with a map of the city and the Audubon Zoo.

I hoped we'd get to the zoo.

"Now for the plan." He handed me a sheet of paper. "This way we'll get the most out of every minute we have."

My eyes traveled down the page. On it was written a schedule—what we would be doing today. Thirty minutes hither and yon was allotted for transportation.

10:00 – hospital
12:00 – lunch
2:00 – zoo and park

5:00 – come back to hotel
8:00 – dinner out
10:00 – dessert, coffee, jazz
11:30 – bed

Was this supposed to be a schedule of bed with me?

I crumpled the paper into a ball and threw it at him. "Luke McDuffie, this is not some *bank* meeting," I huffed.

He looked genuinely puzzled. "What? Why did you throw away the schedule?"

"We don't know what we're going to find at the hospital," I said. "And we need to know more about what kind of trouble she's in."

"Well, we have to have some plan," said Luke. "And I'm waiting for a callback from my law school friend."

"I am generically opposed to *plans*," I said. "That's why I live on the beach. I have had it up to here with plans."

"What do you mean?"

"Our plans, Luke. All those plans we made all those years ago. They didn't turn out so well, did they? Anyhow, plans are a straitjacket. Life has surprises, and you need to be flexible."

"That's ridiculous, Daisy," said Luke. "You can't just flop around like a fish out of water."

"Ridiculous, is it?" I was building up a good head of steam, but Raj had picked up the balled-up schedule and was unfolding it.

He said, "It says here we're going to the zoo." He grinned at me. "I want to see the alligators and the boa constrictors and the Komodo dragon."

I took the schedule from the boy, not wanting to upset him. "I'll keep it for now," I said, smoothing it out and tucking it in my handbag. No sense in fighting in front of Raj. Luke gave me a tight smile, and I could tell he was gritting his teeth. Then he gave the boy a real smile. "Sure thing, fella."

Since we weren't sure about what parking situation we'd find, Jean-Claude found us a taxi for the first leg of the trip. There was a policeman in the ER waiting room at Charity Hospital, but he told us that he was only staying until the doctors determined Lorelei's prognosis. Then they'd let her go and arrest her later if circumstances changed.

I think that was a fancy way of saying they were waiting to see if she was going to die.

The nurse told us family only was allowed, and she offered to take Raj in to see his mother, despite my pleas that I was her best friend. I knew I couldn't get away with posing as her sister, despite my Florida tan.

After they'd gone, the policeman filled us in on what happened. Around 3 a.m., a cemetery custodian had called 911 and reported someone breaking cemetery property. They crept up and caught her red-handed with a shattered Grecian-style urn, a broken angel, and stuffed pockets.

She broke and run, kicking aside waxed linen bags. She tripped over a stone and ran smack into one of those above-ground crypts, hitting her head. She fell like a rock.

They called EMS to take her to the hospital and found that her pockets were full of jewelry. They were currently investigating to see if it was stolen. The waxed linen bags were taken as evidence.

I caught my breath, putting together the puzzle pieces. Those pots she'd been casting for Vinny Corvo. Stashing the jewelry in the concrete mix. Wanting to split from Vinny Corvo. She'd been intending to make a run for it, taking Raj with her. To Mexico, where she had a cousin. She needed funds, and she knew where to find them.

We sat quietly until the nurse brought a teary-eyed Raj out. "You're Daisy, right? She's asking to see you. I guess it's all right."

Luke got up and led Raj back to the chairs, hand on his shoulder.

Lorelei didn't ask me why her son wasn't with her sister. She didn't ask me anything about Vinny Corvo, the jewelry, or Bogart. She appeared to be out of it, on the verge of slipping back into unconsciousness. Then her eyelids fluttered open and she focused on me. "Take care of him, Daisy," she murmured, and closed her eyes.

Twenty-nine

We walked to the trolley stop from there, Raj holding my hand, trying to be brave. Nobody said anything, because Raj wasn't ready to talk about it. Lorelei was still alive, but it didn't look good.

Pedestrians were out and about, the shopkeepers arranging tables and chairs on the sidewalks for the lunch crowd, for the brunchers coming out for Bloody Marys, mimosas, and whatever potions the house concocted for hangovers.

A man wearing sunglasses and what appeared to be a curly black wig passed us and rounded the corner ahead of us. Something about him caught my eye, but I figured he just might be a vampire in training and dismissed it. My mind couldn't let go of what Daisy had asked me to do. Look after Raj? What about his father? It seemed as if I owed it to the boy to allow him to meet his father, even if Raj said he didn't want to.

Luke must have been thinking the same thing, but I couldn't ask him in front of the boy. Then it occurred to me . . . the vampire man had looked very pale, like vampires ought to. But surely, *that* man couldn't have been Vinny. Didn't Moo direct him back to Florida? With a shudder I recalled his menacing face at the wheel of the maroon Cadillac.

I looked back, but the pale man had disappeared.

We finally arrived at the stop where we boarded the St. Charles streetcar, and luckily we didn't have too long to wait. I climbed the steps with mixed emotions. I wanted to give Raj a day of fun to take his mind off his mother.

As we rattled along, I picked up one of Raj's brochures and read aloud. "It says here that the zoo used to be a sugar plantation." Luke nodded distractedly, and I wondered what he was thinking. At the next stop, a man in an ill-fitting tan suit and a string tie, with wavy blond hair and a malnourished look, got aboard and sat near us paring his fingernails. Not Vinny. I turned around and scrutinized the other passengers, then told myself I was being silly. Many of the other passengers looked like tourists. Like us.

When we arrived at the zoo, several other passengers got off with us, most with children. The thin man got off too, and now he spoke to us. "Your son looks excited," he said. "Had him long?"

These comments from perfect strangers were beginning to annoy me. I wondered if this guy was a pedophile. "Look," I said. "If it's any of your business, we're just looking after him."

He held up his hands in mock self-defense. "Sorry. Was just trying to be friendly."

"My mama is sick," said Raj.

The man smiled and let us go ahead of him to buy our tickets. I looked back at him doubtfully, but he was still smiling.

Of course, we visited the reptile house first. More snakes than I'd ever seen in my life lived there, and it was hard to persuade Raj, awed by the Komodo dragon, that there were actually other things in the zoo he might want to see.

I was happy to see that it was the kind of zoo where the animals are presented in natural habitats. Clouds of flamingos waded in a lake, jaguars prowled mock Mayan ruins, elephants waved their trunks among jungle trees.

Raj, entranced by the sight of zebras and hyenas, lions and leopards, crocodiles and marmosets, lost interest in the two adults at his side. Luke carried the backpack on his shoulders, and if anyone asked he'd say it was camera equipment. We stopped to look into the Louisiana swamp exhibit, teeming with alligators giving us that J. Edgar Hoover look. I laid a hand on Luke's arm, my pique having thawed at last. "What did Paul and Frédéric say at the B&B about the possible break-in?"

He patted my hand. "They'll look into it. Of course, they swore it was impossible for anyone to climb up to the balconies. They were relieved that nothing was missing."

We gazed at the mock Cajun hut in the swamp. An alligator trumpeted, exposing rows and rows of teeth. I touched the backpack and glanced behind us once again. Did I see the vampire man buying peanuts? I told myself that New Orleans attracted all sorts of vampire fans. Raj skipped on ahead of us and then came running back, grinning hugely, the happiest I'd seen him since he'd come to stay with me. "Could we ride the elephants?"

"Sure." I smiled.

"I'll be like Mowgli in *The Jungle Book*."

Luke handed me the backpack, ripped open the Velcro of his camera bag, and extracted a beautiful digital Minolta. "Photo op." He looked at Raj. "Have you ever read the actual book?"

"Is it really a book?"

"Is it a book!" said Luke. "I'll buy one for you."

Raj agreed that would be a fine thing. But Luke's eyes met mine. How long was the boy going to be with us? Me, that is.

I took the backpack so Luke could take pictures. We reached the elephant plaza and waited in line for an elephant to become free. Raj was safely perched in the saddle of his elephant and Luke was snapping away when I caught sight of the vampire man again. I poked Luke on the shoulder. "Look there."

Luke turned and gave me an exasperated look. "Hey, you spoiled a great shot."

"That vampire man. He reminds me of Vinny Corvo."

Luke looked in the direction I'd indicated. The vampire man had disappeared.

"Maybe he was following us," I insisted.

"It's a public park, Daisy."

But then the elephant ride was over, and Raj ran up to join us, smelling like elephants. A boy should be grubby, Moo had said. O-kay. Luke hoisted the camera. "You two stand right over there." We found a spot with an elephant just behind us, waving his trunk over my shoulder, and Luke took shot after shot.

Just then I became aware that the thin blond man was in the crowd, looking on. He gave me a big grin. "Hey, there. Want me to get the three of you?"

"No!" I said, about the same time Luke said, "Sure!"

"Don't do it," I said, tugging Luke's shirtsleeve.

"Don't be paranoid," Luke said. He handed the camera over.

Did I dare make a scene? That was Luke, upright honest Luke, believing everybody was a straight arrow. How on earth had he ever become a banker without going broke?

The guy's teeth looked even worse in the bright sunlight, and his hair looked on bad terms with shampoo. He looked like a man obsessed with something such as iguanas. Or small boys. We posed, arms around each other, each with a hand on Raj's shoulder, and he aimed the camera.

"Smile now, like you love each other," he said. "I was a hospital photographer once, snapped babies. Stand right over there. Say *money*." The guy snapped a few shots and then handed the camera back to Luke.

Luke thanked him. "Glad to oblige," said the man, refusing a tip, and sauntered off in the direction of the reptile house.

Luke gave me a look. "I know you didn't want me to hand it over," he said. "But I had a feeling he was just down on his luck."

"You could have lost that camera."

"Yeah, well, now I've got a picture of the three of us."

There seemed to be nothing else to say. Still I was uneasy. The food pavilions were full, so we bought hamburgers and Coca-Colas from a concession stand and sat on benches to eat our lunches.

I wondered how we were doing vis-à-vis the schedule. "Is it time to go over to the park?" I thought longingly of the art museum I'd seen in the brochure.

"I want to go back to the reptile house," said Raj.

Just then, the vampire man materialized at the corner of the sea lion exhibit. "Look!" I said, nudging Luke. "There he is, the man in the wig." For a moment the vampire was lost in the glare of the midday sun. Not a real vampire, obviously.

Luke brought his hand up to shade his eyes. I felt, rather than saw, a shadow at my side. And then something tugged at my shoulder, throwing me off balance. I landed on the ground. "Hey! What—"

"Bogart!" cried Raj. "He's got Bogart!" The vampire man was running away from us, carrying the backpack.

Camera bag swinging, Luke took off running after the man, who was heading back toward the swamp exhibit. Raj and I followed, sprinting past a startled park security officer, who took up the chase. Luke had just about caught up to the man when he opened the pack and pitched Bogart's laundry bag out—straight at the alligators!

Raj gave a yell and leapt in after him. I didn't stop to think. I leapt in, too, nasty water splashing up my nose. The water wasn't deep, and Luke jumped in after us. He grabbed Raj, kicking and screaming. A woman security guard was yelling at us, and zoo personnel swarmed in. They helped us out, we somehow explained that there was a snake in that bag, and then we had to stand by, wet and dripping, while a Crocodile Dundee waded in and hooked Bogart, pulling him out of the path of a big bull gator.

A crowd had gathered to watch.

"Lucky for this old boy the gators have just been fed," said the Crocodile Dundee man, looking at us as though we were candidates for the Too Much LSD Award. "How did you say you got this python?"

"We weren't stealing him," Raj piped, but the man didn't hear him. Raj tugged on the man's sleeve. "That's my snake," he said.

The man glanced down at Raj and smiled. "Sure, cher." He turned to me. "Funny how kids decide a certain animal is their favorite."

"But it really is his snake," I said. "Or actually, his mother's snake."

The man looked at me.

"We'd like to talk to you," the zoo security chief said.

It was another hour before we got it all sorted out and then I'm not sure if they quite believed us and, in any case, Lorelei's flowered backpack had gone with the snake-napper. We searched as best we could and left word with the zoo official about the pack. They were concerned the man was going to use it to steal a more valuable animal and tightened security on all small species, especially those that could be turned into aphrodisiacs for the Asian market.

They insisted that Bogart needed to stay and get checked out by the zoo vet. It was traumatic for snakes to be trundled around like so much laundry. We were almost guilty of animal cruelty. They told us that we knew very little about snake care, and we needed to learn how to care for one properly. After our lecture they let us leave and told us we could pick him up the next day. With a suitable carrier.

And they asked us if we were the owners of a black wig they'd fished out of the lagoon.

We were not.

Our wet clothes were steaming in the overhead sun. They'd soon be dry, and we decided not to go back to the B&B and change. We wanted to take Raj to the park to keep with our plan to take his mind off his mother. He'd just mope back at the hotel, missing his snake.

With heavy hearts we took the trolley back to the French Quarter and boarded a city bus that ran down Esplanade straight to the park. "Why did he make off with the backpack?" mused Luke.

"That's what I want to know."

Raj looked from Luke to me, as though deciding whether he could trust us. He stuck his hand in his pocket and pulled out a gold chain with sparkly green things dangling from it. "Maybe he was looking for this," he said.

"Where did you get that?" Luke and I exclaimed at once.

He shrugged. "When I was cleaning out the backpack. When I was washing off the poop, I found some secret pockets, and this was in one."

"So Lorelei hid jewelry in the backpack," I mused. "Maybe Vinny knew about it. He found us and found out we had the snake. So he followed us here, knowing we had Raj, after he didn't succeed in breaking in and getting the backpack. Maybe she took it to have it fenced that way."

"Pretty good guess, I'd say."

I could hear Luke's skepticism. "Vinny makes a living by good guessing," I countered.

"So the question is, now he's got the carrier minus the necklace, is he going to cut and run, or is he going to come back after the necklace?"

"There may be more loot hidden out there," I said. "But that's not our concern. What do we do with the necklace?"

"Turn it in, of course."

"Hey," said Raj. "I wanted to give that to Mama, but she told me to save it for later."

I turned the necklace over in my hands. It was gold, finely wrought, with emeralds of various sizes. It looked like something that might have been found in a treasure ship, or a museum. I was sure it was worth many thousands of dollars. Where did Vinny think he could sell such a thing?

"Let me keep this, Raj," Luke said. "In case that man comes back. Tell me, did he look like Vinny Corvo to you?"

Raj shrugged. "He was weird, so I didn't want to look at him."

To think that Vinny Corvo was all that Raj had experienced as a father figure. Should he meet his real father? Why did the man leave his son behind? Maybe he'd been married. Of course. I'd talk to Luke about it later, when Raj was out of earshot.

I handed Luke the necklace. We walked out of the zoo, and Raj took a long, backward look in the general direction of the reptile house.

The City Park, near Metairie Cemetery, the cemetery where Lorelei had been arrested, was crowded with people, all out enjoying the sunshine and fresh spring breezes. The Botanical Gardens were supposed to be wonderful; but we had to cheer Raj up. We wandered over to the playground and carousel first. "Want to ride now?" I asked.

Raj folded his arms in defiance. "That's for little kids."

I loved carousels. "Look! There's a big black horse, looks like a war horse. See his red bridle and saddle? See his teeth? What a stallion! I wish I could ride that horse, but it's just for big kids. Won't you ride it for me?"

"I'd rather ride the train." He looked off in the distance toward the steam engine puffing along the track that circled the park.

"Well, maybe," I said doubtfully. "I don't know if there's time."

He eyed the horse again, and then something seemed to change in his expression and he agreed to the carousel. I should have taken the clue when he agreed so quickly.

Luke bought him a ticket. The carousel came to a stop, the operator waved them on, and Raj took off ahead of the pack of waiting children to claim the black war horse.

We stood there, Luke and I, watching the carousel turn. An ice cream vendor trundled his cart nearby, and in the distance the train circled, hooting.

I watched the ice cream vendor pass a couple on a park bench deep in a clinch. Luke saw them too and nudged me. "Who do you think they are?"

We fell into the game we'd played so long ago, making up stories about people we saw. "You first," I said.

"Okay," he said. "The guy looks like that guy who always loses the girl in the movies. Bill Pullman?"

"Yeah," I said. "And she looks like the star's best friend. Janeane Garofalo? Okay, they work in an office, and one day in the break room . . ."

"They look at each other and bingo. He asks her to lunch in the park."

"He's on the make and she's engaged."

"She's a little bit scared of getting married, and this is her way of testing her feelings."

"He's a regular Casanova, been through all the girls in the office and he wants to score this last one."

The lovers were now eating the sandwiches they'd brought, gazing at each other with raw hunger as they tore into their muffalettas.

"And he's persuading her that their next lunch date is going to be private."

"Maybe it doesn't have to be."

"What do you mean?"

I smiled. "You mean you've never made love in a public park?"

Luke narrowed his eyes in disapproval. "Of course not. And if you have, Daisy, I don't want to know about it."

I was surprised at the anger in his voice. I shrugged. "It was just a wild and crazy idea." He didn't have to know one thing about what I'd done among the sand dunes. Just as well. Beach music is not what it's cracked up to be.

To my relief, the music came to a halt and the carousel stopped. The happy children filtered our way, straight into the arms of their waiting parents. No Raj.

"Where is he?" My stomach sank.

"He must be on the other side." Luke and I walked around twice and looked between the carved horses, but we didn't see any boy. We asked the carousel operator, an ample woman tucked into a snug gray uniform, if she had seen him.

"I've seen so many, cher, one little boy looks like another."

"He's Indian," I explained. "Indian and Hispanic."

She chuckled and pointed at the line of children, children of every shade.

"And this is New Orleans," she said.

Had he slid off the carousel on the opposite side and taken off for . . . where? We saw the train chugging around the park and hastened toward the shiny green depot. Luke turned to me angrily. "Damn it, Daisy, why didn't you watch out for him?"

"And why didn't you?"

"We were caught up in that dumb game."

"Oh? You started it." I glared at Luke, but there was no time to waste fighting. We stopped passersby and asked if they had seen a small boy, Indian-looking, and one person told us we should say Native American, and we explained east Indian, and then they said we should say Asian, and in that case, I said, how are you to distinguish him from Japanese, and they said south Asian, of course. My head was spinning with confusion.

And fright for Raj.

Finally a young man with a Walkman and long slouchy shorts looked us over as though to ascertain that we were not the police and informed us that he'd seen that li'l cat over to the pavilion and he wasn't saying no more.

We thanked him and headed in the direction of the pavilion. "What do you think he meant by that?" I asked.

"I don't want to know."

"Do you suppose child molesters hang out here?"

"It's possible."

"Damn." We searched among the buildings. The museum staff had not seen any small boy. We came out and headed along the broad paths, heading toward park security, something we should have done in the first place. But we were so sure he would be right around the corner.

"You don't suppose . . ." I said. "You don't suppose his father took a flight directly here, and followed us to the park, and snatched him right out from under our noses,"

"Daisy, you have lost your hippie mind."

"What? You provincial tightbutt."

Glaring at each other, we almost missed the security officer walking by. We were just about to hail him when suddenly, out of thin air it seemed, Raj came sauntering up, eating a huge, dripping, chocolate ice cream cone. I didn't know whether to hug him or yell at him. Luke looked at him sternly. "Where have you been, Raj? Daisy and I have been looking all over for you."

"I got bored on that carousel. It was too slow. I saw the train and wanted to ride."

"And you've been on the train?"

He nodded yes and took a swooping lick of the ice cream.

I got alarmed, thinking of the child molesters. "Wait a minute, Raj. You didn't have any money. Nobody bought that ticket for you, did they? Or that ice cream? Did they ask you to go anywhere with them?"

"I know about child molesters," said Raj. "Vinny told me they are the lowest form of scum. I know to run from them."

"So where did the ice cream come from?"

Raj held up a wallet. "It was easy. Now we ditch this somewhere."

All the blood drained out of my face. I looked at Luke and he looked at me. "Where's the money, Raj?"

He patted his pocket.

"Raj. This will not do. We have to return the money."

"But why? No one saw me."

"Hand it over, Raj," said Luke. "We do not pick pockets."

Raj sighed loudly and handed over the wallet. Luke looked in it. "The money, too. All of it," he said.

Raj sheepishly pulled the folding cash out of his other pocket and handed it over. "Kid needs a father," muttered Luke, taking money out of his own wallet to replace what Raj had spent.

He put one hand on Raj's shoulder. "You and I are now going to make a trip to the security office. We're going to tell a little white lie because I don't know the police down here, whether they'd bust a nine-year-old. And besides, your snake is at the zoo, and we're not sure we're going to get him back. Suppose they think you stole him? These are times when kids get arrested for kissing one another. We're going to say we found this wallet on the grass."

"Shall I go, too?" I wanted to know.

"Wait here, Daisy," said Luke. "This is a guy thing."

I watched them walk across the park, wondering what would become of Raj without someone like Luke on his side. I looked at my watch. It was time to head back to the hotel and wait to see if Raj's father would show up.

Thirty

I had no clue what to say to one errant father, seeing that I also had an errant father to deal with. Was Dr. Patel at the B&B even now? It was getting on towards five o'clock, and Luke had estimated he'd arrive between three and six.

The letter he'd written sounded respectful, and Moo seemed to like him. Could he be a truly bad guy? What would make him go off to India and never contact his son?

The sun beat down as I huddled under a tree, sweat pouring off me, further adding to the smelly complexity of swamp-drenched and sun-dried garments. Finally I saw Luke and Raj heading my way, both looking content for some reason.

When we finally got back to the hotel we were met by raised eyebrows and wrinkled noses from the guests having tea in the front parlor, and even Paul and Frédéric frowned at us as if they couldn't believe these dirty, sweaty, rumpled people with squishy sandals belonged in a place like Le Perroquet Bleu.

No Indian doctor was waiting for us.

Once in my room, I stripped off my clothes and left them in a heap on the bathroom floor and jumped in the shower, letting the gunk of the crocodile pond wash away from me and slither down the drain. I shampooed my hair until it squealed for mercy. When I got out, towel-haired, kimono-wrapped, I saw the telephone's blinking message light.

There were two messages. The first was from the desk. An envelope had been left for Miss Daisy Harrison to pick up. The second message was from Doctor R.K. Patel.

He had been delayed by having to stop and assist a victim of a traffic accident. He would arrive at Le Perroquet Bleu around eight p.m. and was hoping to see us then. He had booked a room nearby.

I needed to talk to Luke. I walked over to the connecting door, unlocked it, and edged it open. Raj lay curled on the bed in deep sleep, hair falling over his forehead, while the Discovery Channel dealt out a program about the Hubble space telescope. I heard water running in the bathroom.

It then hit me how tired I was and how much I could use some mothering.

I propped myself on my bed with all the pillows behind me, picked up the phone, and had just punched in "9" for an outside line to call Moo when Luke, freshly showered, dressed in khakis and polo shirt, walked in with two glasses of what looked like bourbon and water. He held one out to me, and I hung up the phone.

"What's happening? Have you heard from anyone?" he said.

"There was a message from Raj's father. He'll be here by eight o'clock. He's booked a room nearby."

Luke looked squarely at me. "We have to let Raj meet him, you know."

"Even though he didn't keep in touch with his son?"

"Remember, he's a doctor, and if he's with the WHO, he's probably busy. Probably married, and probably reasonable," Luke said.

All I could do is stare at him. Sure, people were reasonable if they were the ones that had the power. But most unreasonableness is caused by those that haven't got any power, or want some, or want more of it than anybody else.

"Making this decision about Raj is too much responsibility. Too much to deal with. But I couldn't ask Lorelei." I sipped my drink, smooth and with just the right bite. The warmth in my tummy was more than welcome.

Luke regarded me silently, took a slug of bourbon. "Life is too much to deal with. That's what I thought when my brother left and I had to give up my political ambitions.

That's what I thought when you sent back your pin. That's what I thought when I almost backed out of marrying Alyssa, and what I thought when she wanted out of our marriage."

I almost choked, but recovered. "You almost backed out?"

"You didn't let me tell the rest of the story. Just like you didn't let me explain." He passed me a paper napkin for the dribble on my chin.

"I couldn't Luke, I couldn't. You'd betrayed me, and so had my best friend. I had to shut you both completely out. I felt that if I let down my walls one instant, the whole façade that was holding me up would crumble away and nothing would be left of me but dust."

"I sent you letters."

"I never read them. I thought you would tell me it wasn't me, it was you, or some such *merde*, like I deserved better."

Luke squeezed my hand. "It wasn't like that. Let's go over what happened. Step by step."

"I don't want to." I slipped my hand out of his and took another few sips of my drink, and it was good. He reached for me again, and this time I let my hand stay. He stroked it.

He looked me square in the eye. "Remember you told me today I was too trusting? I couldn't believe how naive I was back then about what Alyssa was doing. Making you and I each lose faith in the other. The evidence was there, telling me things I didn't want to believe of her."

"Luke, what on earth did she do to you? I know what she did to me."

He shook his head. "She played both of us for fools. She convinced you that I had fallen for her, and convinced me that you had been unfaithful . . ."

"Me?" My voice rose an octave. "Unfaithful? Who with?"

"I'll get to that. Needless to say, when you sent back my pin, she was there, willing and able to soothe my broken heart."

"And you fell for it."

He nodded. "She wasted no time in spreading the word she and I were seeing each other. My folks were happy about it. Carter had left, for one thing, and they were begging me to come home and work at the bank. They knew that Alyssa would love to go back to Sawyer to live."

"And you knew I never would. You could have asked me if what she said was true. Why didn't you at least ask? Why couldn't you trust me that much?"

He shook his head. "She messed with my mind. Told me you'd lie about it. Said she had proof."

"Proof of *what*?" I had this huge sinking feeling and my guts turned to ice.

"That you had been with my brother, and that's why he left."

I sloshed bourbon on my knee. "With your *brother*? Carter? How could you, Luke? Did you ask him?"

Luke nodded. "Of course he denied it. But I'd half believed he had a guilty conscience, leaving like that, and I decided to search his room. I found a picture of you in his top drawer."

I blinked, confused. "I never gave him a picture."

"A wet T-shirt picture. And a note, supposedly from you, that left nothing to the imagination. I was appalled."

"A picture? A note?" It hit me then. At one of those church retreats, all the girls were snapping pictures of each other doing stupid things, like pushing each other into the lake before the chaperones found out. "Alyssa had a picture of me like that," I said. "And as for the note, she was pretty good at forging her mom's signature on notes to skip school."

And I thought of the night she had gone out with Donny and Eric. Suppose she had written on that note the things she'd done with them . . . .

The implications hit both of us at the same time. When had Alyssa been in Carter's room to sneak in the note and picture?

Oh.

That was the year that Luke and I had juggled a long-distance relationship. Alyssa, away at school, told me that she was seeing some guy who was older, in the business school. She didn't want to be specific, and I wondered if he was married or engaged or if her folks didn't want her dating him.

I had pinpointed it. Carter had been engaged to a girl he'd met at school before Alyssa came along. That's why Alyssa was so secretive about it. Maybe he'd gone on that monastic retreat to get his mind straight about this muddle as well as working for his dad, and then he'd decided to let it go, let it all go. So Alyssa decided she wanted the next best thing. And I was in the way.

She could have snuck into his room at home, gone over while Miss Lally was out, and told the housekeeper some story about leaving her sweater or something. She would have been let in, no questions asked.

"I was never with Carter, Luke. You don't have to forgive me for anything."

Luke looked stunned. I shook my head slowly. Tears puddled in my eyes. "What's done is done. We can't relive the past."

"Can you forgive me? Can we make a new start?"

"Luke . . ." I dug for a Kleenex. Oh damn, my eyes were going to be red.

"Okay. I won't press you. But tell me more about what happened to you, Daisy. You aren't out there changing the world. Where did the art, the decorating come from? That wasn't the Daisy I knew."

"Political activism wasn't the same without you, Luke. I couldn't think. I couldn't think about all the things we had planned to do together. The children we had planned, the children we were going to adopt. Remember that? Hard-to-place children, with disabilities? Two of our own, and all the rest..."

I wiped my eyes with the now-sodden Kleenex. "I could only immerse myself in art and beauty, thinking somehow all that beauty could drive away the pain." I looked up horror-stricken at what I'd been saying. I'd thought those words so many times, buried them, and here they were coming out to bite me. Like a snake.

"That's all over and done," I hurried on, snuffling. "Somehow what we were together made us more than what we were by ourselves. More than two. Am I making any sense? Oh, what's the use?"

I looked at the lump of sodden tissue and placed it in the ashtray. Luke reached into his pocket and gave me his perfectly folded fresh handkerchief. I had a sudden silly thought of Hoagie wiping his nose with bar napkins.

Luke took another sip of bourbon. "Look, Daisy, you can opt out, ignore all your problems, bury your head in beach sand, or you can do what needs to be done. You might make a mistake. We all make mistakes. But don't hide from life."

Was that what I was doing?

Luke was saying, "So what comes next, Daisy? Go back and hang out on the beach? Hasn't this experience taught you anything?"

I blotted my nose with the handkerchief. "What experience?"

"Right now. All this. Are you going to forget all about the kid and hand him over to a man he doesn't remember?"

I licked my dry lips and, stalling for time, dug in my handbag for some lipstick. I applied "Crazy Mad Love" and inspected my red eyes in my pocket mirror. I shoved it back in my bag and looked up, straight into his eyes. "Of course not, Luke. But what if his father wants him when he finds out what happened to Lorelei?"

"And what if she recovers? Does she deserve him after what she did?"

What? "Luke, I'm not freakin' Judge Judy. All she did was smash a few cemetery urns to get something somebody else stole."

"Doesn't sound like a good role model."

At last I got it. "Are you judging Lorelei or are you judging Alyssa, Luke? Leaving those girls with you? Where is she, anyhow?

"California. On a high hill with a great view of the beach, Daisy. Do I have to spell it out for you? And for the record, I'm very glad I have the girls. They're a great joy to me."

I felt embarrassed, miserable for him, sorry the direction the conversation had turned. And the beach? That hurt. And just because he hadn't talked much about the girls didn't mean he didn't want them.

He tilted my chin up and kissed me very gently. "I was so broken up over you, Daisy. To think you were with my brother . . . that was too much. But I never forgot you."

I shook my head slowly. "We can't hit rewind, Luke. There's no do-over."

"But we can live in the present." His right hand had slipped over to my thigh, and now it was unknotting the tie of my robe. The robe fell open, and I was naked.

"Beautiful Daisy," he said. He bent and kissed my navel, and his tongue traced a curving line down, down, down the inside of each thigh and then up again.

I caught my breath, trembling.

"I'm taking my time, this time," he said. He made love to me then, as gently as he could, at first and then, as passion built and we fell into each other fiercely, it was like my heart had been a ship tied tight to its moorings and had at last burst free, sails billowed, racing over a deep blue ocean behind a sky of sun and clouds, and this sailboat picture by Winslow Homer shattered to fragments and dissolved into a rainbow. We ended shuddering and crying and clinging to each other, tears on both our faces, and I looked into his eyes and I knew I loved him and could never leave him.

But I had to. I had to. I could never live in Sawyer. And he could never leave.

"Luke, Luke."

"Hush." He traced the outline of my lips with his finger.

We lay there for a moment in the afterglow, the late-afternoon sun slanting through the blinds. I was wrapped up in this warmth I had never felt in either of my marriages, never felt with anyone with whom I'd thought I was in love. This wasn't lust. It wasn't adventure. It wasn't escape. It was plunging into something sticky, something deep, some quality of what might be called soul. It was what we had felt as teenagers, taken to a new level. Was it real love? If I didn't know what it was, how could I trust it?

We lay there, just holding each other, from time to time looking at each other, as though we were afraid the other would disappear, that it had all been an illusion.

A distinctive click made us bolt upright. I slowly turned, afraid of what I'd see. The interconnecting door to our room, which we had not bothered to lock, stood open. Raj was standing there, his arms folded.

"This was a LOT better than Nova," he said.

Thirty-one

I blushed red from my head to my toes, and Luke leapt up from the bed, slipping into his khakis as if he'd once been a fireman.

"Well, young fella," he said. "You got an education, there."

"I've seen that before," Raj said, blasé. "What I'd really like to see is snakes. They have two penises, you know."

"Please go watch TV, Raj, while I get dressed," I said, a flush creeping up my neck. "Maybe not Animal Planet."

"OK," he said, with a smile I could only describe as snarky.

"He knows too much about that side of life." Luke tucked in his shirt. "He needs security and stability. He needs wholesome values. To play Little League ball. To go fishing on the weekends."

I rummaged in the closet for a clean outfit. "Lorelei is his mother. She may not be perfect, but she loves him, and we have no right to make any kind of decisions for her."

"She may not make it," Luke reminded me. "We have to consider that."

"Oh." I wanted her to get well; she had to get well. I couldn't let myself believe she wouldn't. After all, people survived brain injuries all the time. Didn't they?

A small voice broke in. "What did you mean about Mama?"

Raj was standing in the doorway. Luke, now fully dressed, walked over to him.

"She's very sick, son." He patted the boy's back.

"She's going to die, isn't she?"

"Nobody knows that," I said. "She's strong. She'll do what the doctors say. She wants very much to be with you again."

Raj shook his head. "When I asked her if she wanted the necklace, she told me to keep it. For my education."

Luke and I met each other's gaze.

"It wouldn't be safe in the hospital," I said lamely. "Too many people coming and going."

"Daisy's right," Luke said, laying a hand on Raj's shoulder. "The truth is, Vinny stole the necklace. Your mom is already in trouble with the police, and this would be even more serious. I saw a police station in the French Quarter, just a couple of blocks. We need to turn this necklace in. Do you both want to come? We'll stop somewhere and grab a bite to eat."

"Do you think we ought to turn it in, Luke?" I asked.

"Why not?"

"Maybe it isn't stolen, after all. Maybe it belongs to her. Maybe she just hid it away."

"Do you really think that, Daisy?"

"No." Why was my inside twisting up? Why was there a pain right below my ribs? I didn't want to see Raj hurt, and if turning in this necklace would put his mother in bigger trouble, he would be hurt. But I knew what Luke would say. It was the right thing to do.

"Okay," I said and squeezed the boy's hand. At least we had saved his snake. If not his education.

I remembered that there was an envelope for me at the desk. I'd been meaning to go claim it and then Luke had come in with the drinks, and then . . .

I finished dressing, and we walked down to the lobby. I stopped at the desk and picked up the envelope and tore the sealed flap. Inside were two free drink tickets from a place called George's Bar, with the address.

"Who left these?" I asked Frédéric, who was manning the desk.

He shrugged. "No clue. Louis was here earlier, and he's off for the afternoon."

Maybe the tickets were an advertising ploy. But my name, Daisy Harrison, was on the envelope. "Did anybody else get these?" I asked.

"Nope. Just that envelope. Somebody who knows you, cher." He smiled, and I showed the tickets to Luke.

He read them and grinned. "Let's go tonight."

Would he never stop trying to distract me? "Hey, we have things to do tonight. And aren't you going back tomorrow?"

He shook his head. "I changed the ticket. I've talked to the girls, and Vanessa won't mind spending another night with them."

When did he do that? How did he get so organized? I guess running a bank will do that to you.

We walked to the police station carrying a paper bag with the beautiful necklace found in the snake poop. A desk sergeant took down all the details, and his red, rough, seen-it-all face changed ever so slightly when we pulled out the necklace. He whistled softly.

We mentioned the name of Vinny Corvo.

"I know that s.o.b.," the officer said. "Second-story man. Wonder where he got something like this. It looks like it belongs in a museum. Where'd you say you came by it?"

I told him the truth, more or less, that a friend had asked me to keep her snake for her, and this was found in the snake carrier.

"Some friend," he said, eyeing us suspiciously. "Where is she?"

I had not prepared for that. I cleared my throat, trying to think of a reply, when Luke took control of the situation.

"She's been arrested and has been hospitalized. But she didn't steal this necklace. Vinny Corvo was her boyfriend. He gave it to her."

"For Christmas when I was real little," Raj piped up. "I saw her unwrap it. She got so excited."

"This is her son," I explained.

He raised an eyebrow and took down all the other details, and I finally said goodbye to the necklace. It winked its green emeralds, its finely filigreed gold hinting of ancient lands, of sumptuous fabrics belonging to a Castilian queen. Maybe I'd see it again in a museum somewhere.

As we'd promised Raj, we stopped at a sidewalk café and had a supper of gumbo and rice. He still had a small-boy appetite but answered any questions we put to him with a noncommittal shrug. I knew he was thinking about his mother.

By the time we walked into the lamplit lobby of the B&B, the sun was going down, and I was tensing up. Maybe there would be a message waiting.

A man sitting in one of the comfortable upholstered chairs in the side parlor closed his *Times-Picayune*, laid it on the table beside him, and rose. He approached us. "Miss Harrison?" His voice was gentle, and I found myself facing a handsome, bespectacled man with a neat head of wavy black hair and skin the color of my young companion's.

Luke stepped forward and held out his hand. "Dr. Patel? I'm Luke McDuffie."

"I'm very glad to meet you." The man shook hands with Luke, then offered his hand to me. I took it, noting his charming smile. I could see why Lorelei had been attracted to him.

Then, and only then, he betrayed a little nervousness. He looked behind me, where Raj was hiding. "And this is . . .?"

Raj slid out from behind me. I rested my hands on his shoulders protectively, feeling their tenseness. His breathing came shallowly. I felt him begin to tremble beneath my hands.

Doctor Patel stooped and held out a hand to him, as you would to a nervous animal. Raj took a slow step forward. I looked over at Luke, he looked back at me. I think we were both as tense as Raj. The boy lifted one hand slowly. My cell phone rang.

We all froze. I fumbled in my bag.

"You are a fine boy." Dr. Patel, his voice husky, shook his son's hand.

The phone kept up its blithering while I dug it out. Dr. Patel asked Raj a few questions in his very British English, and the boy answered shyly, his eyes downcast.

I recognized the number and answered.

Thirty-two

"Just a minute," I said. I'm not sure how my voice sounded, but Luke cut his eyes at me. *Not here*, I mouthed, and gestured we should all go into the parlor, as Paul was at the desk, maybe expecting late guests.

Dr. Patel looked disconcerted for a minute and then his features relaxed. I suggested that he and Raj might like to relax on the sofa and get better acquainted while I talked on the phone, and both agreed. This was going better than I had imagined.

"What is it?" I asked, edging out of earshot to a far corner. "You're here in New Orleans? Did you get your car?"

Hoagie gave a long, long sigh, and something about that sigh made a chill run down my back. I stood stock-still. "The car's all right, but I have bad news. She's gone, Daisy."

His voice shook, as near to breaking as I'd ever heard. "I've been here looking for her, leaving messages on her phone, and now this. She finally woke up enough to ask the nurse to call me, and of course I went right over. I was five minutes too late."

"Oh, Hoagie," I said. "You really cared about her, didn't you?"

"I guess so," he said. "Now's a funny time to find out. I knew she wanted to get away from Vinny. I just didn't want to get mixed up in all that. I wanted to be sure she wasn't playing me for a fool."

So there was more to Hoagie than I'd given him credit for.

"I think Vinny is around here," I said. "Somebody broke into my hotel room but didn't take anything. I think it was Vinny, looking for a certain necklace he'd given her."

"Geez," Hoagie said. "I thought I'd given him the runaround when he came to the bar looking for her."

"He found her anyhow," I said. "He's probably got connections here. He's been trailing me too. I have Raj, and the snake."

"Are you okay, Daisy?" he said with concern. "What happened to Lor's sister?

"Her sister is a long story, but I'm okay. My mom made sure my friend Luke McDuffie came with me."

"I'm right here," Luke said.

I waved my hands at him to shut up and glanced over to the sofa where father and son were talking earnestly.

Luke gazed back at me with a concerned expression. He'd figured from the conversation that something bad had happened.

I talked awhile longer with Hoagie. He was going to get in touch with Lorelei's sister, Luz, and together they'd decide what would be done about the funeral. He told me that he'd pay for it, if they couldn't. He would sell his pieces of eight.

"I can't let you do that!" I exclaimed.

"I'll go on another dive," he said. "You have no say in this."

I had to agree. And felt low as a snake.

I glanced over at father and son, who seemed to be getting along at least amiably, though Raj was sitting back a bit, a serious look on his face. And now I had to tell both of them Raj's mother was gone.

I was absolutely no good at this kind of thing. I was the youngest, I was the screw-up, I'd never even wanted a baby doll to practice mothering. I liked to sculpt things with Moo and make monsters from clay. Cute monsters. Cute snakes. The kind that didn't move.

Luke was good at this. He had kids. He could deliver bad news. He was used to doing it at the bank. "Let me," he said.

I liked to deliver happiness, but I said, "Lorelei gave me a job. I'd better do it."

I walked over to the two of them and pulled over a footstool and sat on it so that my face was even with Raj's. I took his hand. "Raj, I have something to tell you about your mother."

"Is she getting well?" He shrank back and I felt he knew exactly what I was going to say.

"She wanted me to look after you," I said. I glanced at the doctor and he nodded slightly, but remained very still. He knew I was delivering bad news too.

"When can I see her again?"

"Maybe tomorrow. We'll see." I couldn't do it.

Raj sat and swung his legs back and forth, back and forth. "Tell me the truth, Daisy."

"She's gone to be with Jesus," I said, not knowing what else to say. "Did your mom tell you about Jesus?"

"No!" he shouted and jumped up from the sofa, almost knocking me off my stool. "No, No! Aunt Luz is always talking about Papito Diego going to Jesus! And crying!" He pointed his finger at his father. "And I'm not going with you to India!"

He raced out the door, edging between two late guests who were coming in, and I had no doubt he was heading toward the French Quarter and try to find his way to the hospital.

Luke, Dr. Patel, and I burst out of the hotel and raced after the boy, but he was too quick for us, dodging and feinting until he'd lost us in the milling crowds on the sidewalk. There was no way to tell which way he'd gone. Luke and Dr. Patel put their heads together for an instant.

Luke turned to me. "Daisy, you wait here in case he doubles back. The doctor will go that way, I'll go this way."

We exchanged mobile numbers. Dr. Patel decided to go in the direction of the hospital, saying that Raj may have headed there as he was an observant boy and would know it was the tallest object on the skyline.

I didn't want to stand there and wait. "I'm going to search too, Luke."

Luke, seeing my set jaw, my blazing eyes, decided not to argue. "Daisy, we need a plan, then. You take the streets on this side of Bourbon Street and I'll take those on the other."

I took off at once, worrying that Raj would lose his way and be frightened and go off with any stranger who promised to take him to his mother. I passed a cop on the corner and wondered if I should tell him. But I didn't want any more complications or delays, and I dodged my way through the crowd hurrying, looking down and looking up, while the smells of creole cooking wafted from the cafés, and the music wafted from the bars, and the mood percolated jubilation, and people had such smiles. Color was all around me, and in that riot of color and revelers was one frightened, confused little boy.

I passed a clutch of people listening to a singer on the corner, looked into open shops, and stopped in front of a bar. If he'd gone into one of those would they throw him out? I had the feeling he'd keep going as long as he could run, running off all his grief and pain at the thought he'd never see his mother again.

I hurried up and down the streets, peering down sidewalks, finally asking people if they'd seen a boy alone. No one would say, until one of the sidewalk sitters, homeless or drunk, pointed a thumb at the corner. "Dere," he said.

I dropped some bills in his hat and ran around the corner he'd indicated. Sure enough, a boy was standing at the end of the street looking right and left. I sprinted toward him, but before I could reach him, something whapped me in the back and I fell sprawling to the ground.

When I looked up, Vinny Corvo was running past me.

Thirty-three

I saw it all, trying to pick myself up. Vinny tried to grab Raj, but the boy kicked Vinny in the shins, head-butted him, and then dropped to the ground, escaping the older man's grasp. He rolled around, got behind Vinny, and planted a foot kick to the back of Vinny's knee.

When Vinny stumbled, Raj took off again.

Now Vinny saw me. He crouched and came at me like a charging bull. My knee was killing me, but adrenaline had long since kicked in and I scrambled into the middle of a partying crowd, praying that another cop would be on the corner.

I didn't see one. Vinny was gaining on me, but even with my bum knee I was in shape from running on the beach. I didn't stop until I got to the front of the French Quarter precinct and burst through the front door. But dammit, Raj was out there and so was Vinny! I was shaking and the world had turned upside down.

"Help you?" a voice said.

After what seemed like light years, Luke joined me at the station and we outlined the situation to the police, including Lorelei's involvement. We contacted Dr. Patel and filled him in. He had reached Charity Hospital, introduced himself, and asked the receptionist to watch out for Raj. He'd start back to meet us, taking a different route.

The cops said they'd find Vinny Corvo's mug shot and put out a bulletin for both him and the boy.

"Somebody made off with two more of the cemetery urns last night," we were informed. "Think it might have been Corvo?"

"I'm almost sure of it," I said, "but right now the boy might be in danger. Corvo doesn't know Lorelei's dead, and he thinks the boy's got a necklace he wants."

"Look in the bars," one cop suggested. "He might have ducked in one to hide."

"Won't they throw kids out?" I asked.

"Not here," the cop said. "Who knows who the kids belong to? And if it's crowded and dark, who notices? We don't bother them unless somebody complains."

We'd told Dr. Patel where the police station was, if he wanted to check with them or had any information to give them, and that we were going to check some bars along routes Raj might have taken from the side street where he'd left.

We reasoned that Raj would be focused on avoiding Vinny Corvo and not on getting to the hospital right now. He'd come out when he thought the coast was clear.

The big bars were too loud and noisy and bright with lights. Not a place he'd hide, maybe. We passed sandwich shops, smaller bars, game rooms, knick-knack shops, and galleries. Jazz notes followed us from sandwich shop to art gallery to bar as we searched.

My back was beginning to hurt where Vinny had shoved me, and my knee was throbbing. I couldn't let it slow me down. We saw some cops cruising. We hoped they were looking for our boy.

We hurried on, wondering how Dr. Patel was faring. Just when he'd found his son, he'd lost him. I felt a trickle of despair as we approached the entrance to yet another bar. From inside came the tinkling of a piano and a hauntingly familiar sound. I edged closer and peered in the door. Somebody was singing "Feelings."

I grabbed Luke's arm. "Holy spit!"

"What?"

"That voice. Don't you hear that voice?"

"A past-his-prime crooner with a better-than-average voice. So?"

I sniffed. "That's my father."

"What the hell, Daisy. You can't be serious."

I ducked into the small, dark, smoky piano bar where light glinted off metal signs: PURE gasoline, LIFEBUOY soap, and DUTCH cleanser, with that Dutch-capped woman about to beat the devil out of somebody with a stick. As my eyes adjusted to the dimness, I saw movie posters of Myrna Loy, Edward G. Robinson, Tyrone Power. I saw that the bar wrapped itself around the piano man, white-haired with a jovial face. The face of Teddy Harrison. My father.

Thirty-four

Luke right behind me, I elbowed my way through the crowd to the piano. My father glanced our way and smiled, unsurprised, as though he had been expecting us.

I hadn't seen Pop in over a year, but he hadn't changed. His sparkly pinky ring still floated over the keys, his wavy hair still drew the eye of every widow and grass widow in the room, his China blue eyes still twinkled with a hint of mischief. He finished the song, leaned into the mike, and told the audience, confidentially, that he was taking a short break because his daughter had just turned up. Hands clapped, and thirty pairs of eyes turned toward a red-faced disheveled Daisy.

Luke spoke first. "Mr. Harrison. I'm floored."

Pop rose and shook his hand. "Young Lucas. It's a pleasure to see you."

Now, my father was the kind of father every kid wants and no kid needs. Bluff and hearty, just the kind of man who'd sell you a house, sing at your wedding, and put a whoopee cushion under your chair, all on the same day. He and Moo made a weird pair. She was always the grown-up until he left.

How many times had I heard him sing "Ave Maria" or "One Hand, One Heart" at weddings? He'd steadfastly refused to perform anything recorded in the last fifty years, despite pouts and tears from brides. I think he drew the line when one requested "I Don't Know How to Love Him."

And now here he was, singing "Feelings."

"Pop!" Tears stung my eyes.

"Daisy, my little Daisy." He came out from behind the piano, made his way around the bar, and enveloped me in a huge bear hug. He looked from Luke to me. "So you finally claimed her, did you? A little late, isn't it?"

"Pop, it's not that," I said, trying to keep my voice from ratcheting up a few hundred decibels. "There's no time to explain. We want to talk with you later, but we're looking for a boy."

"A boy, you say?"

"Yes!"

"Not your own boy, I assume? You haven't been keeping anything from your old dad?"

"No, of course not, Pop." I pushed my hand through my hair and looked at Luke. "We'd better go."

"Not so fast." Pop held his hand a Raj-height off the floor. "Is the boy about so high? Toasty complexion? Knows about séances and dressing up in a turban?"

"Turban?" My eyes grew wide.

Pop raised his eyebrows and looked downward. We followed his gaze and saw, sticking out from under the piano, two small sandals with two brown feet in them.

"Come on out, boy," said Pop. Raj unfolded himself from the piano and crawled out. Pop turned to me. "I got a call from your mother saying you were headed to the city. George, the owner here, is a friend of mine, and I finagled a few days off from that other gig to play for him. He doesn't have anybody regular. Thought I'd look for you while I was here."

"Moo called you?"

Pop nodded and smiled. "You could have knocked me over with a feather. First time she's called me since I've been gone. I've called and left messages. She always knew where to reach me."

I cried out with exasperation. "She said she didn't know where you were. Did she tell you about the stock? The house?"

"What stock? What house? No, she was just concerned about you. Said she got some kind of . . . what did she call it? 'Emanations of danger.' I tried to call you today but didn't catch you in. Figured I'd try again in the morning if you didn't take those free drink tickets I left at the B&B." He looked toward the bartender, nodded, and the bartender slid him a big glass of water. Pop chugged it down. He drew a large handkerchief from his pocket and mopped his rosy brow.

I took a quick glance at Luke before I turned back to Pop. "You left us those tickets! Why didn't you leave a message? Why didn't you tell us you were here?"

He grinned. "I wanted you to come in here and let me surprise you. And look, here you are. But I can't quite figure out how the boy knew where to come."

Raj piped up, "I heard the music, so I came in. I heard you singing back at Miss Essie's. I figured it might be safe here."

Pop's face, if it was possible, beamed even more. "So Muriel was listening to my CD, was she? Maybe she misses me a little after all."

"She told me I'd like it," Raj said.

So Moo had been playing Pop's CDs. I remembered a stack of CDs on her dresser, the one of Pop mixed in with the Michael Crawfords and the Three Tenors and the Yo-Yo Mas, but I hadn't thought about it at the time.

Pop's bushy brows had drawn together. "Say, young fella, what did you mean by safe?"

Raj was about to tell him when I interrupted. "It's a long story," I said. "We'll save it for later. How about tomorrow?"

Pop gestured at the piano. "I'll call you. My fans await."

I glanced at my watch and my heart gave a thump. "Oh my gosh, we've got to tell Raj's father we've got him. It's really complicated, Pop."

"Oh? What's all this about?"

"I'll explain it when we see you, Pop, about the stocks, about the house, about Raj, about everything. You'll call us tomorrow?"

"Daughter," he said, "it was damn good to hear your mother's voice. And to find she was listening to my CDs? That makes me feel like I might be welcome after all. I think it's time to go home."

"I need to talk to you, Pop, before you leave." It was hard to tear myself away. I gave him a hug, and he shook Luke's and Raj's hands. A pleasure to meet you, young sir," he said.

I took Raj's hand in my own. "Come on. We've got to get you to your father."

He pulled back. "I don't want to go away with him. I don't want to leave Bogart behind. My father . . . I just met him."

"We'll work it out." I tried to sound hopeful, but I was having a sinking feeling.

Pop wiggled his eyebrows at Raj, trying to crack him up. "Go see your daddy."

I blew Pop a quick kiss and we hurried back through the crowded bar and out into the streets. I heard the beginning notes of "Memory."

Thirty-five

Dr. Patel rang me on my cell phone just as we were climbing the steps of the B&B. "Great news," I said. "We've found him."

"Thanks be," said the doctor. "I am several blocks away."

"Come have dinner with us," I said.

Raj was exhausted, too tired to eat, and that was saying something. We thought he ought to at least have a snack available. We made sure the doors were securely locked and then cadged some praline cookies and milk from our innkeepers. We left Raj munching cookies and watching TV while we took the doctor to dinner at Luke's favorite little Cajun restaurant nearby. We made sure the balcony doors were locked and the curtains drawn. Paul said he'd ask Daphne to run up and check on him.

Dr. Patel wasn't strictly vegetarian and dug into a bowl of seafood gumbo while we explained what had happened.

"Vinny stashed his loot from the heists at Lorelei's, and she wrapped it in waxed linen bags and cast it in the urns. This was when she was living in New Orleans. She figured they were safe there in the cemetery next to graves nobody visited. You can tell the ones that look shabby. She cleaned the graves up a bit and pretended she was a relative.

"I think she was falling for Hoagie and thought Vinny would be in prison a while longer. She'd liberate the loot, maybe hide out in Mexico for a while. At some point she'd get back in touch with Hoagie. From there, who knows?"

"Could be right, Daisy, but there's a lot you don't know."

"Guilty."

Dr. Patel wanted to change the subject and quiz us about Raj's upbringing. I decided to tell it like it was. Lorelei was no longer with us, and she couldn't be hurt by what I said.

He listened well and nodded.

"Yes. I know I should have come sooner. Dolores sent a letter to me at my work address when he was about a year old, but I am embarrassed to say I kept prolonging my reply. With her beauty and her performing, I was naturally suspicious that the boy might be someone else's child. She eventually stopped writing.

"Before you ask, yes, I was married. In my position I travel a great deal, and I met her here in New Orleans when I came for a medical conference. One night I was on my own and saw an advertisement for her act." He smiled.

"I'd always liked snakes, ever since I was a boy, and so I went to see. After her act, I bought her a drink, and we talked about snakes. One thing led to another, as sometimes happens. I made a mistake. This boy should not suffer any longer for my mistake. I have no doubt now that he is my son. I want to claim him."

"But what would your wife say?" I asked.

"My wife died last year, and I have no wish to remarry. My two daughters are now almost finished with school and living with my sister. I expect them to go on to university, perhaps in London."

For some reason the thought of Raj having to uproot himself once again and follow this stranger around the world was unsettling. "Why don't we ask Raj how he feels about having a father?" I asked. "I don't want him running away again."

"I'd like to stay another day or so here," the doctor said. "Get to know my son. Tell him about what I do, the work. And perhaps attend Dolores's funeral with him."

We left him after dinner, promising to call him with the funeral plans.

Walking back to the B&B, I told Luke that Hoagie was going to foot the bill for the funeral, but I didn't know anything else. I wondered if Hoagie had managed to get in touch with her family, or if the hospital had been able to reach anyone. I didn't have long to wait.

No sooner did I open the door to my room than the message light hit me like a lighthouse beacon. One message. From Luz, asking me to call her. I dreaded it, but I picked up the phone.

"Dai-see," she wailed when I got her on the line. "She is gone."

"I'm so very sorry," I said. "I got to see her in the hospital before . . . that is, have you talked to Hoagie? Have you decided where, um, to lay her to rest? Can you come?"

Another shriek of pain. I felt helpless.

"My baby," she sobbed. "My baby is still in the hospital. I cannot leave."

Luz kept sniffling and hiccupping while I gathered my thoughts. Her sister Dolores, with her parents gone, wouldn't have anyone to attend her funeral except me, Hoagie, Luke, and Dr. Patel. And, of course, Raj. Would the paper mention her obituary at all? Did she have friends still here in New Orleans?

"Daisy," Luz spoke at last. "What did she say to you?"

I swallowed. First, the easy part. "She told me she wanted to stay away from Vinny Corvo." I wasn't going to tell this sweet, grieving woman that her sister had planned to smuggle herself and some stolen jewelry into Mexico and had gotten arrested trying to get the goods away from Corvo.

"That is good. What else did she say?"

I guess I had to tell her. I took a deep breath.

"She asked me to look after Raj."

A fresh round of crying ensued. Just when I had opened my mouth to assure her I would bring him to her as soon as we were able, she said, "*Gracias a Dios*. Daisy, you are the answer to our prayers, with our *bebito* needing so much care."

She was sobbing and laughing at the same time. She called out the news to Ricky. I hung up the phone.

Luke had joined me, since Raj was sound asleep. I told him I needed a drink. We went down to the house bar and had a Pernod each while I told him of my plan to tell Dr. Patel about the situation. Maybe he would have an answer. Maybe he would take Raj with him. I wasn't so sure about the snake.

A tiny demon of negativity flitted across Luke's face before it was exorcised with a smile. "Come on, Daisy," he said. "There'll be time enough to think about that in the morning. In the meantime, let's go to bed."

That sounded wonderful to me.

Thirty-six

The first mistake I made the next day was taking my phone to the breakfast table. The second mistake I made was answering it. The zoo vet's office was on the line, telling me I could pick up my snake anytime, fine and rested from her ordeal.

"Her?" I asked.

"Your snake is female. Didn't you know?"

Well, I didn't. And if I wanted to leave the critter longer than today, they would have to charge me a boarding fee. "I don't suppose you'd like to keep him, er, her, permanently?" I ventured. After all, what's a snake without a snake dancer?

"I'm afraid not," the woman said. "You're trying to sell sand to Arizona. We've got more reptiles than we need, actually. Especially pythons. Amazing how people think a pet snake will stay little forever."

Raj was taking it all in. "You're trying to give Bogart away!" As I closed the phone, he waved his beignet at me, scattering strawberry jam across the table. I lowered his arm and was about to whisk the glop away with one of the lovely white napkins when Daphne dashed in with a wet cloth and made short work of the mess.

I promised Raj that we'd go for Bogart today, though I didn't say exactly when. And I wasn't sure whether to tell him about the sex change. Should we start calling her Bacall? Raj didn't say anything about his father, and his father hadn't called. Had I given him my phone number? I couldn't remember.

While Daphne cleared the breakfast remains and poured more coffee, Paul came in and told me I had a message to call someone named Hoagie. I went up to my room so I wouldn't disturb the other folks who'd come to breakfast.

Hoagie told me that cryptside services would be held at Metairie Cemetery this afternoon at three o'clock, and Lorelei would be interred in the new section. He told me that afterwards he'd be heading back to Daytona. "Need a ride?" he asked.

"I've got the bus," I said.

"That's why I asked if you needed a ride."

"Ha." I hung up and then called him back and thanked him for all he had done for Lorelei.

"Sounds to me like you're doing a lot more," he said.

"Maybe not. I'll see you soon," I said. I wondered if Vinny Corvo might show up at the funeral and if I should tell the cops.

Back at the table, I sipped my chicory coffee and told Luke about the plans for the funeral and thought Dr. Patel ought to know, but I didn't know where he was staying.

"I do," Luke said. "I'll call him."

"I guess you'll miss the funeral," I said. "Aren't you flying out today?" Somehow, I wanted him there with me, maybe to pass me his handkerchief.

"Actually," Luke said, "I canceled the ticket. I've rented a car to drive us all back."

"Yay! Bogart too!" Raj said.

"Luke!" I huffed in exasperation. "I haven't agreed to go back to Sawyer, and what will I do with my purple bus?" *And what about my plan of asking Dr. Patel about taking Raj . . . .*

"Listen, Daisy, be reasonable." Luke reached for my hand. "There's nobody waiting for Raj in Daytona. The sister'll be gone as soon as her baby's out of the hospital. Don't you want to go see your mom and dad back together?"

"Well, yes, but . . ."

"I'll call my law school friend Will to sell or donate the van somewhere for you, or have it hauled off to the car cemetery. You can send Will the papers when he finds a buyer. Why keep something that reminds you of pain?"

I hadn't thought about it like that. I had thought of it as scoring one off Harvey, but maybe the joke was on me.

"I want to go to Mr. Luke's house," Raj said. "He told me that you and him were going to get married and me and Bogart could stay with you."

"He said *what*?"

Luke grinned at me like he was saying Cheese.

I was not saying Cheese. Somebody had moved my cheese. Without my permission.

"I don't recall being asked," I said. "I was not consulted. And Raj has a father who needs to weigh in on that."

Luke was attempting to run my life. I was almost free of responsibility, and he was going to strap my getaway horse to my back!

I raised a finger. "You're already raising two daughters. Not only do I not recall a proposal of marriage, I don't recall anybody asking me if I was willing to be a stepmother. Have you ever considered how hard that would be?"

"Don't fight, Daisy," Raj wailed.

Oh, yikes. My face became hot, hot, hot. This boy didn't need to hear all that, with his mother just gone, and he probably hadn't really taken it in that she was gone for good. In the past, she'd gone out and left him at home, but she'd always come back before.

Raj would think I didn't want him, when the truth was he tugged at my heartstrings in a way I hadn't felt before. But he came with a snake. And now, it seemed, with a man

I couldn't trust. And the room was full of people looking at us, all poised with coffee cups halfway to their lips.

I threw down my napkin. "I've got to get some air!"

I ran upstairs and grabbed my bag, flung it over my shoulder, and charged out of the B&B. I walked over to the side street where I'd parked my van. I'd go . . . somewhere else. But where else? I had a map in my bag. Maybe I could drive to the zoo and get Bogart. It had to be done anyhow.

I racewalked the two blocks to the parking place and tried to forget my two days of bliss. Just when I'd found it in me to forgive him, he showed me I was right in moving on.

Then why did I feel so wretched?

And where the heck was the bus?

Maybe I had the wrong street. Maybe it was the next block. But I walked and walked as though I had a bee in my britches and did not find a purple bus. I was getting tired. I wasn't going back into the B&B and cry on Luke's shoulder.

I found my way to the French Quarter and the police station and reported the bus stolen. When I told them what kind of vehicle it was, they looked at each other and told me I'd be lucky to ever see it again. But they would keep a lookout.

When I finally returned to the B&B, Luke, of course, was overjoyed. I wouldn't have put it past him to have stolen it himself. But hey, he said, those old vehicles are easy to hot-wire. Not so easy with the new ones.

The worst was yet to come. Luke had heard from Dr. Patel while I was out working off my steam. Something had come up with work, some kind of new virus, and he wouldn't be able to meet us until the funeral, if then.

Surely he'd come, if only to see his son again. He'd said he wanted a relationship with him, and I felt Raj was open to having a real father at last, even one who couldn't teach him how to pick locks.

Which reminded me that Vinny Corvo was still out there somewhere, and I had never gone to the zoo to pick up Bogart. Vinny had stolen the carrier, the plastic box was in the bus, and I'd have to buy a new snake habitat for a long car trip.

When I put the question to Luke, he just smiled. "Don't worry," he said. "I have a plan."

"May I get in on the plan?"

"Nope. It's a surprise."

I couldn't budge him. I didn't like the way he kept smirking.

The funeral brought even more surprises. I'd been surprised that Lorelei was welcome at Metairie Cemetery, where she'd stashed her loot in urns she placed by graves nobody visited. She'd even planted the urns with flowers.

Hoagie had explained the whole thing to the cemetery people, and they were forgiving as long as the money was good, i.e., it came from Hoagie. They were used to having scandalous people to bury but hesitated when the scandal was directly associated with themselves. But Hoagie was a natural salesman and I guess he'd honed his persuasive tactics behind the bar.

Dr. Patel showed up, to my relief. Afterwards, he asked Luke and Raj and me to join him for a cup of coffee or tea. I had a moment of happy anticipation until he told us we'd have to meet him at the airport. He was headed straight there as soon as he could catch a taxi. And Luke, the fiend, offered him a ride in his newly rented car.

My phone rang in the car, but I ignored it. I had to think.

Thirty-seven

At the coffee shop, Dr. Patel couldn't have been nicer. He explained that he was with the World Health Organization and traveled constantly and could not provide a home for an active nine-year-old. His own sister was older than he and didn't have the energy. She'd insist on a nanny. His daughters were busy at school. He didn't want to tear his son away from familiar surroundings.

My phone rang again. I knew the doctor was going to say more, and I didn't want to interrupt him. I ignored it.

"I now must make a full confession," he said. "I asked a New Orleans colleague to find Dolores for me and make sure I could see her. Before I came to meet you, I went to the hospital. She had a rare moment of consciousness and seemed glad to see me. I told her I now knew her boy was my son. I would claim him."

She lay back and closed her eyes, he told us. "She had a peaceful look. And then she said something else. You know what it was."

His dark eyes were compassionate and hopeful. They were telling me he hoped I would do what she asked of me.

He wanted me to say it.

"She asked me to look after Raj," I said.

I knew why she had asked this of me. She was afraid her sister and unwell mother would treat him as an unwanted child, a child of sin, and she knew I liked him. Heck. I loved him.

She had seen through my act.

"Okay, Daisy?" Raj asked, with a side glance at his father.

"I can come to visit," Dr. Patel said. "And he can come to India to meet his people when he is ready."

"I'm right here," Raj piped up.

"You can come for visits," Dr. Patel corrected himself. "I would like for you to meet your sisters and to show you some of your heritage."

"Does this mean I can stay here now? With Bogart?"

"Yes, it does," I said softly.

"Do we have to live at the Sea Spray?"

I froze then. What was I going to tell him? "Well . . ."

He interrupted. "Can we live in Mr. Luke's house?"

"Wait," I said. Wait."

The phone rang again, and I had no excuse not to answer it.

"Ms. Harrison?" An official-sounding voice.

"Yes?"

"This is Detective Gonzalez calling with information about your stolen vehicle."

"You found it?" My stomach turned a flip. Somehow I didn't want it back now. Somehow I didn't want to deal with yet another decision.

"Well, it's not good news, I'm afraid. It was involved in an accident and we'll have to keep it a while for evidence. As soon as we pull it out of the bayou."

I couldn't believe what I was hearing. "Why do you have to keep it?"

"The driver is deceased. I think you may know of him. His name is Vincent Corvo."

I thanked the detective and told him I'd be in touch soon, but right now I had very pressing business.

Thirty-eight

The whole world waited. The three other people at my table hovering over the cups of tea and coffee and Orangina and the people rushing to be the first ones in line, the people sitting behind their newspapers and magazines, the people murmuring sweet nothings into their phones, my father in his car going back home and my mother getting the house ready for him because she knew he was coming back, and Gordon in his school and Luz and Ricky with their baby and Hoagie who'd said goodbye forever to the woman he loved.

They were all waiting for me.

Waiting.

Even though living in Luke's house would mean I would have to marry him and then I'd have to move away from the beach and the life of freedom and no responsibility and I'd have to deal with Moo and Pops and Gordon and Lally McDuffie and spirits and ghosts and the spirited ghostly past. And the magnolia tree and what did not happen under it but which had happened since.

I considered my future with Luke and knew it would be a long and challenging road, not without its turns and twists, but not without its flights to the stars. My life had been a Lewis and Clark expedition into my soul since I'd left Daytona in a purple bus smelling of plastic and weed and fried potatoes.

Luke was on his knees before me. Right there in the airport coffee shop before God and everybody. And a sunbeam lit him from the back, haloing his head.

I couldn't argue with God.

"Yes," I said.

"I don't want my son to be a burden to you," Dr. Patel said. "He is now my responsibility."

A burden? This amazing boy? I knew then that what we may call burdens are truly gifts, that carrying the cargo makes us strong enough to be our best selves.

Lorelei had taught me this: you had to crack the concrete to get the good stuff you've buried inside. "Yes, Luke," I said, my heart freed at last. "Yes, yes, yes."

He rose and picked me up and hugged me and kissed me and Raj and Dr. Patel clapped, and then the whole coffee shop clapped.

Three new people said goodbye to Raj's father.

And then we went to pick up our snake, the three of us, holding hands.

Author's Note

My thanks to the snake dancer I met many years ago, whose experiences lodged in my mind, and thanks, too, to Snakey Sue, the contemporary snake dancer in the UK, who operates a reptile rescue center and graciously answered my questions.

I had to cast a smaller snake than she recommended, because I didn't want one of those nine-foot ones with a nine-year-old. (I started to say, around a nine-year old. My point exactly.)

Thanks to Joe, for accompanying me to New Orleans and being patient while I walked around cemeteries and parks in the hot sun, and thanks to all the great people of New Orleans who made the trip so much fun.

The story is set in 2005 because that's when I first began it. I had almost completed a first draft when Katrina struck. Shocked and saddened, I consigned the chapters to the files and forgot about them. No one would want to read a humorous story set in New Orleans then. After my second book, *Saving Miss Lillian*, came out, my daughter called me. "Where's that snake book you were working on?" She'd read part of it as a teenager and given me a beanbag snake for Christmas.

My thanks as always to my family, my friends, my cheering section back home in Dublin, to Georgia Romance Writers and the Atlanta Chapter of Sisters in Crime, for Sally's class (you know who you are), the Midtown Writer's Group, and, as always, Nanette and Peter from Words of Passion for their editorial and design skills. Couldn't have done it without you!

Read On

www.annelovett.com

Saving Miss Lillian

Nurse Sunny Iles thinks she's found the perfect job looking after a wealthy and eccentric grande dame. But a murder plot is afoot and an island is at risk, an island where an unexpected romance awaits. Can Sunny overcome her aquaphobia to foil the plot and fall in love in this quirky romantic caper?

Rubies from Burma

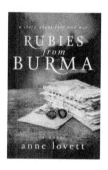

1941. Mae Lee Willis is only eight, but she has her heart set on her older sister's boyfriend, a dashing paratrooper. Years later, a sudden tragedy commits her to her sister's care on the farm where she lives with the Burma veteran. The heartsick teen must make a decision that will change her life forever in this enthralling page-turner.

The River Nymph

Georgia, 1924. Young Tenny Chance, a runaway from bleak prospects on a sharecropping farm, must battle for survival in a world of dangerous men. Student Pete Godwin sees her bathing in the river and falls in love at first sight. When they finally meet again, they face emotional turmoil and the demands of duty in this captivating historical saga.